THE PRESERVATION PLAN

THE VEXTON SERIES
FINAL BOOK

ALSO IN THE VEXTON SERIES

Manufractured [Book One]

Moon Shade Bluff [Book Two]

THE PRESERVATION PLAN

THE VEXTON SERIES
FINAL BOOK

Paul A. Trinetti

IGUANA

Copyright © 2017 Paul A. Trinetti

Published by Iguana Books
720 Bathurst Street, Suite 303
Toronto, Ontario, Canada
M5V 2R4

This is a work of fiction. All of the characters, organizations, and events portrayed in this novel are either products of the author's imagination or are used fictitiously.

All rights reserved. No part of this publication may be reproduced, stored in a retrieval system or transmitted, in any form or by any means, electronic, mechanical, recording or otherwise (except brief passages for purposes of review) without the prior permission of the author or a licence from The Canadian Copyright Licensing Agency (Access Copyright). For an Access Copyright licence, visit www.accesscopyright.ca or call toll free to 1-800-893-5777.

Publisher: Kathryn Willms
Cover design: Meghan Behse
Interior design: Meghan Behse

Library and Archive Canada Cataloguing in Publication

Trinetti, Paul A., 1968-, author
    The preservation plan / Paul A. Trinetti.

Issued in print and electronic formats.
ISBN 978-1-77180-207-9 (softcover).--ISBN 978-1-77180-208-6 (EPUB).--ISBN 978-1-77180-209-3 (Kindle)

    I. Title.

PS8639.R573P74 2017	C813'.6	C2017-900714-9
		C2017-900715-7

This is the original print edition of *The Preservation Plan.*

CHAPTER 1

"Open the damn door! Open the damn door! This is an emergency! We need help—somebody please open the door! My wife's about to give birth!" Dr. Jack Ahar shouted as he pounded the front door of what was supposed to be a hospital. It was a bitter cold morning. The pavement was a giant ice rink, and the streets were strangely silent.

He stepped back in defeat when his wife gripped his arm tightly. "Come on, Maria, let's head back to the car."

Jack fought panic. Her struggle was apparent with every heavy footstep. By the time they got back to their vehicle, Maria was shivering uncontrollably. The doctor tried to open the sedan's passenger-side doors, but they wouldn't budge. He scurried around the car and tried the passenger door there, then the driver door. "Damn it! They're all frozen!" he cried, his voice rising in fear.

Maria sagged against the car; Jack eased her to the icy pavement. "Just hold on, honey, I'm here for you."

* * *

While speaking at Summit University as President Westgale's executive director, I once referred to America's War Within as "the perfect dinner gone wrong." In this incredible country, there is no reason why all of our appetites can't be satisfied. The problem is, there are so many disagreements over what dishes to make and what *ingredients* to use. Too much of this. Too little of that. Too tender. Too tough. And of course the hungry become impatient, as the politicians—or "the chefs of life"—fail to find a way to satisfy the varying appetites of those they've been summoned to serve. Maybe there are too many chefs. Maybe the dinner guests should focus on what they *need*, as opposed to what they *want*.

How much government is too much government? Can civility and absolute liberty coexist?

* * *

A lady came running from a nearby building. "Sir, my name's Anya. Here, take these blankets. There's a hospital right over there. I'll get you some help." She thrust a bundle of blankets into Jack's arms.

"It's no longer functioning as a hospital," Dr. Ahar sobbed as he tucked one of the blankets under Maria and draped another over her contraction-wracked body. "This war will be our final undoing," he murmured under his breath, his anger growing by the second as he bent over his laboring wife.

Minutes later, he delivered a newborn girl and swaddled the crying baby in the last blanket. He sagged with relief when a passing car stopped to help. Handing off the baby to the driver, who quickly placed her in their car, the doctor turned back to frantically tend to his wife. She lay so still. Stifling a sob, he checked Maria's vital signs.

"Nooooo!" he wailed. He checked again, and again, his movements urgent, frantic. "This can't be—no!" he sobbed. "My beautiful Maria." He wept, wild with shock. His hysteria abated to violent trembling, and he lifted the edge of the blanket covering her body and lowered it gently, slowly, over her face before collapsing to the pavement beside her.

* * *

As I continue preparing for my presidential campaign, the extreme challenges I'll be facing have become very clear to me. Sure, the discovery of the VX drug has greatly aided the cause of the PBA. The recent energy deal President Westgale has made with Pinia will enable us to eliminate the debt owed to the Outer Commission, thus restoring our complete independence. However, uncertainty and tension are high throughout the land. I truly believe a *new war* is on the horizon.

My campaign manager rushes into my office. "Nicole, I think you should tune into UCIT," Beth says.

I comply. The screen displays Gerald Levin standing outside the Militant Alliance headquarters, part of which was recently destroyed by extremists believed to be part of AXE.

"How dare these extremist punks think they can create such mayhem in this country and get away with it?" a furious Levin almost sputters. *"And moreover, how dare the Westgale Administration stand by passively and let it happen? These pathetic excuses for life hide under disguises. They set buildings ablaze and run away like the cowards they are."* His scowl deepens with each breath. *"They claim they want a voice. They want to be heard. Well, if that's the case, then take off those masks and face the world like real men and women. I guarantee you that under my leadership, you will be dealt with in the most..."*

"This isn't good. This isn't good," I say to Beth as I listen to Levin's rant. "He's throwing fuel on the fire."

As the Peace-Bringers and the Militants prepare to clash in this current political arena, it has become obvious that America's rebellious youth, with Anya Ahar as their symbol for the rebirth of a new age, have emerged as a third major player.

CHAPTER 2

With Shadow Pix out of the hospital, President Westgale has decided to show him his appreciation for saving his life with a dinner gala at the Freedom Home.

"Nicole Kratz, please meet Shadow Pix," Jessica Westgale says, quickly suppressing a smirk of—pride? Infatuation?

"Pleased to meet you," I reply, gazing up at the imposing figure before me. I quickly label him a gentle giant in my mind. Understandably, he's noticeably nervous, surrounded by America's leading politicians and military chiefs. Prior to recent events, just getting into America was next to impossible for him, let alone being the president's guest of honor.

Westgale approaches us. "Well, well, my two *lifesavers* in the same room," he says with a chuckle, acknowledging Shadow and me with nods. "I'm so grateful to the both of you. Sadly for me, there are a lot of people out there who wish you weren't so brave," he says wryly.

"I don't buy that," my husband, Lowell, chimes in.

The president laughs. "That's easy for you to say when you're the country's premiere golfer, loved and praised by millions." His jocularity fades to sincerity. "In all seriousness, this dinner does not come close to repaying the debt I owe to this man," he says as he places his right hand on Shadow's shoulder.

My gaze drifts as the small talk continues, and I notice Dr. Ahar waving me over from across the ballroom. I excuse myself and move toward him.

"Did you wish to see me, Doctor?" I ask as I join him.

"I hate to steal you away from the party, but it's urgent that I speak with you," he replies, his expression serious. "Would you mind coming to my office?"

"Not at all," I reply, and he turns and leads the way.

"I've been meaning to speak to you since the council's decision was made regarding Anya, but as usual, I've barely had a minute to breathe," Ahar says as he directs me to a chair in front of his large desk. My eyes are immediately drawn to several photos of Anya and his late wife, Maria, on the credenza behind the desk.

"How are things going with the VX drug?" I ask.

"Honestly, I never thought I'd be part of something so astonishing," Ahar replies, leaning back in his chair. "The process of turning that mineral into the drug is simple and completely foolproof. And the great thing is that once it's converted into the drug, its composition can't be altered in any manner whatsoever." He leans forward again and says earnestly, "When I think that this miracle was withheld from our society for thirty years, it really crushes my heart."

"I know what you mean, Doctor. Sometimes it becomes so difficult to trust in humanity, knowing such evil prevails," I reply. "So, what is it you've been wanting to speak to me about?"

He regards me for a moment. "I want to thank you for continuing to support Anya. I realize my daughter will never be free again, but the thought of her being executed... she doesn't deserve that, Nicole," he replies. He turns his chair enough that he can gaze back at the photos, and shakes his head. Tears slowly begin to stream down his cheeks. "She's such a lost soul. Of the five times I've asked to see her, only once did she agree to see me, and even then I couldn't get more than a few words out of her," he says, his voice thick with emotion. "Her eyes... they've become deep, black holes. I'm really terrified there's no hope for her."

"And I understand Dr. Durant hasn't had much success reaching her either," I say gently.

The doctor sighs and nods. "He told me he's lucky if he can get a few words out of her, too."

"I'm so sorry, Doctor."

Ahar stands up and steps over to the credenza to pour us both a glass of water. "If anyone's to blame, it's me, Nicole," he says as he hands one of the glasses to me, then sits down. "I've never been there for her the way I needed to be. Sure, I funded and aided her with her schooling, but obviously that wasn't enough, and sadly, I was so caught up in my own world that I failed to see that. I'm convinced the way I handled my success set the stage for Anya's descent into her world of misery." He stares blankly into his glass as if conjuring a memory from the past.

* * *

"Do you remember Cassandra, Anya?" Jack asked her. It was a week after Anya's fifteenth birthday. "She sang that amazing song I played for you. The one called 'Dreamscape.'"

"Yes, I remember," Anya answered quietly as she studied the glamorous Cassandra Dennison, dressed in a tight-fitting turquoise leather outfit. Jack's much younger girlfriend also happened to be a celebrity singer.

"Your father told me you really enjoy playing the flute," Cassandra said.

Anya didn't respond; she continued to stare at her. Trying to break the awkward moment, Jack quickly changed the subject. "I also told Cassandra that you just won first prize in the New York State High School Science Competition," he said, beaming. He pulled Cassandra close to him. "I just feel so terrible that I'll be out of town and have to miss the presentation gala. Now, I told Shannon to make sure she records the event and sends me the view-file," Jack added, referring to Anya's nanny.

When Anya eventually learned that the only reason her father missed the gala was because Cassandra was performing in Boston that evening, she was devastated.

* * *

"I hope you don't mind me saying, Doctor, but I don't think you're being fair to yourself," I answer. "As the country's premiere scientist and doctor, you've contributed so much to America."

"Yeah, but at the expense of my daughter's well-being," Ahar responds. As he takes a drink of water, I find myself pondering what he just said. "Since the day I revealed the truth to Anya about how her mother died, it's obvious she's kept her true feelings shrouded," he says solemnly. "And regrettably, the animosity she feels toward me is justifiable. I guess, in a way, living extravagantly helped me camouflage my own sadness and guilt over my wife's death."

"Guilt? Why should *you* feel guilty?"

"I'm a doctor, Nicole. I should have saved her."

"Come *on*, Doctor, you can't do this to yourself. No one could have saved your wife that day. And it surely wasn't your fault that that hospital was closed."

Dr. Ahar reflects for a moment before saying, "I only wish, somehow, I could reach her. It's been so long since I've seen her smile. In her current state, I don't know how any court will see a reason to overturn her death sentence."

"Well, this just might help her case," I say as I take out my flashpad. "So far, besides myself, only the president and Director Perry have been privy to this, but I think it's important you see it as well." I show him the list of substantial charitable donations Anya anonymously made before turning herself in.

The doctor looks at me in disbelief. "Anya made these donations?" he says, his voice cracking.

Once again, he stares into the middle distance as his mind travels back to some memory only he can see.

* * *

"Whoa, if you keep collecting these awards, soon you'll be flying around in a bigger plane than mine," the doctor quipped after she'd been presented with a $200,000 award for academic excellence at Summit University. He spread his arms, mimicking the wings of a plane.

"Yeah, and when you're in need of your own luxurious condo, I know someone you can call," said Meredith, another of the doctor's much younger girlfriends, who happened to be an aspiring real estate agent. The couple roared with laughter. Anya was far from amused.

* * *

"How did you find out?" he asks, nodding at the information displayed on my flash-pad.

"After I handed in my resignation, I continued learning as much as I could about your daughter, and through some sheer hard work, I was able to trace these donations back to her," I answer. "I see them as a sign of hope."

"Will this be made public? Doesn't it have to be submitted to the court beforehand?" Ahar asks, still looking at the screen.

"No, and I advise holding off until the hearing. It'll be far more impactful," I reply.

Turning, the doctor lifts one of the photos of Anya and smiles. He draws a deep breath and exhales. "Will you do it, Nicole?" he asks.

"Do what?" I reply with a raised brow.

"Represent her again."

"What about Arthur? He's one of the best there is," I respond, referring to the doctor's long-time attorney, Arthur Fine, whom I'd studied under at Summit University.

"That's true. Arthur's a fantastic attorney and a good, decent man, but I know Anya sees him as an extension of my life. I highly doubt she'll respond to him as positively as she might to you."

I think for a moment, and softly reply, "I don't know, Doctor. With the election around the corner, and the fact that Anya's story now has America's youth questioning everything about this country, this is something I'll have to really think about."

Dr. Ahar sighs and nods. "Well, I guess that's all I can ask. I realize it would put you in an uncomfortable position during the election, but other than those creeps from AXE, you've been the only person she's willing to speak with in quite some time. I sincerely believe that you're our only hope when it comes to bringing my daughter out of her malaise."

"I promise you I'll give it some real thought."

When I return to the gala, Shadow Pix is speaking from the front of the ballroom. "I'm extremely excited and honored to be welcomed into your Freedom Home. Thank you so much for having me," he says sincerely. The audience cheers with enthusiasm. "I'm also thrilled that the Westgale Administration has accepted the proposal to allow Pinia to supply America with our treasured natural resources. Just as your country's VX drug is changing the face of medicine, experts around the world believe the Pinian fera-bean will forever change the face of natural energy. And we are elated to share this with America." The cheering grows louder.

CHAPTER 3

Before heading back to Pinia, Shadow and Jessica decide to visit his mother, Luanda, at her Manhattan apartment. As Jessica's chauffeur drives the grand-electro through the crowded streets, Jessica senses the anxiety radiating from Shadow, seated beside her in the back of the car. "Are you okay?" she asks him.

Shadow doesn't look at her. He continues staring out the window at the pedestrians and buildings they're passing. "I feel really guilty, Jessica," he replies after a moment.

"Guilty of what?" Jessica asks. She leans forward to look at him.

Shadow turns his head to look at her. Anger hardens his face. "All this time has gone by, and now I find out it was my father who forced my mother to leave her homeland and avoid having contact with me. I should have known… I should have known!" Shadow looks away again, staring out the front windshield.

"How were you to know your father would wield his power in such a corrupt manner?" Jessica asks, resting a hand on his arm.

"I was very naïve. I should have investigated the matter and rectified the situation," Shadow responds with feeling.

"Let's move forward. Now that we've found your mother and she appears willing to reestablish a connection with you, you must embrace the opportunity," Jessica says gently.

The grand-electro slows and stops, and Jessica looks around. They're in a seedy area of Manhattan, and the driver is parked in front of an old, run-down apartment complex.

"Thank you, Douglas. I'll contact you when we're done," Jessica says to the driver, and she and Shadow exit the vehicle.

"Are you certain you want me to join you?" she asks Shadow as they cross the sidewalk to the entrance.

"Of course," Shadow replies. Smiling, he takes her by the hand.

Just outside the front entrance, a panhandler sits cross-legged against the building. He's wearing a tattered, bright red bandana and a t-shirt reading *Stalin Lives!* "Hell knows no end—and that's a good thing, my friends, because it's where we're all going," the man hollers as Jessica and Shadow walk past. Jessica turns and backtracks to give him a couple of dollars. "Thank you, sister," he says, "I'll be sure to put in a good word for you."

She turns back to Shadow, and they step inside. The lobby they enter is cold and damp, the walls grimy and the floor tiles cracked, their grout blackened with tracked-in filth. There are several empty liquor bottles lying beside two empty syringes on the dirty floor to one side of the door. There is no elevator; Shadow leads Jessica to the stairwell, then hesitates and turns to her. She can see the tears welling in his eyes. "To think my mother is living in such an appalling place really tears at my heart," he says, fighting for composure. Jessica squeezes his hand.

There is a young lady picking up a bunch of clothes in the hallway when they reach the second floor. "You bastard!" she shouts, pounding on the door of unit 206. "If you think I'm going to keep paying for that habit of yours, you're badly mistaken, jackass!" They sidle past her; she ignores them, intent on hurling invective at whoever's inside 206.

A few doors down, Luanda is standing in her doorway, arms crossed, listening to the ruckus. She grins when she notices Jessica and Shadow approaching. "Wow, what a surprise!" she says. "Come on in."

"Does this kind of thing happen often around here?" Jessica asks in reference to the angry woman in the hallway. Shadow glances back, shaking his head in disgust.

"I'm used to it," Luanda replies, shrugging it off with a sigh. "I just mind my own business and nobody bothers me."

"I won't have you living in a place like this, Mother," Shadow says firmly.

"With Kolton in and out of rehab and my job paying so little," she says, referring to her husband, "well, this is affordable." She smiles, but Jessica can tell it's forced, and her eyes are sad.

"How long will he be in rehab?" Jessica asks.

"I'm hoping he'll be back home in the coming days," Luanda answers solemnly. She looks at Shadow. "I think you'll like Kolton, son. He may be troubled, but he's a good man. Unlike your father, he actually has a compassionate side." She smiles. "Please, sit down. I'd offer you a drink, but we can't keep alcohol in the apartment. How about a coffee?"

"That'd be fine, Luanda," Jessica replies. She sits on the couch, looking around the tiny apartment. She's astounded by the number of music books she sees, all neatly arranged on side tables and a bookcase.

"So, what exactly led to Kolton's downward spiral?" Shadow asks when Luanda returns with a tray holding three mugs of coffee, a sugar bowl, and a small creamer.

Luanda sets the tray down on the coffee table, not looking at them. "Like many Americans after the War Within, he's had to battle his own personal demons. We're both trying to look forward, and embrace the future. So I really don't like speaking about it," she replies as she hands each of them a mug.

"And how are *you* doing, Mother? I still can't believe what my father did to you all those years ago," Shadow says, frowning.

Luanda straightens. "Please, Shadow, forget what I told you the other day. It's all in the past and there's no point in creating tension between you and your father," she pleads.

Shadow sets down his mug and rises to walk over and embrace his mother. "You need not worry. I will deal with this. My father will not treat me as if I'm one of his pathetic minions. And in turn, I assure you, you will always have a loving place in my heart," he says, his face lighting up with joy.

* * *

As she and Shadow prepare to return to Pinia, Jessica takes a moment to call her dad. "We'll be off tomorrow, Dad," she says when her father's face replaces the presidential seal on her flash-pad screen.

"You just make sure you remain safe over there, honey," Westgale replies. "I must ask you, Jessie: what are your plans, once your mission in Pinia has been completed?"

"To be honest with you, that's not something Shadow and I have even discussed," Jessica answers.

"Next to his father, Shadow's the most important man in the country. Would you be willing to leave everything behind and make Pinia your home?" Westgale asks.

Jessica hesitates for a moment. "I'm sorry, Dad, but I'm hoping for a future with Shadow, and if that means living in Pinia, then yes, I'd be more than willing to make the change," she replies with conviction.

"Well, if you do, you'll have to promise me that Washington will be your favorite vacation spot." Westgale chuckles, but his eyes belie his lighthearted tone.

CHAPTER 4

With the election coming up, I've attempted to learn everything possible about being president of the greatest country in the world. Over the last several months I've also tried to learn everything I possibly can about Anya Ahar. As difficult as it is to believe, how our government deals with this brilliant, yet highly troubled young lady will turn out to be of paramount importance to America's future. First seen as evil, she's become a sympathetic figure: a victim of a failed system. Adding fuel to an already raging fire is the disclosure that General Sims and Barry Kent, a.k.a. Johnny T, lied to the nation regarding AXE's intentions.

I recall the UCIT coverage of the reaction when the disclosure was made:

"Who's in charge of those in charge?" protesters chanted.

"What brings you out here?" Cryptic asked one of the protesters.

"This is a joke. A complete joke," the young lady said, shaking her head in disgust. "To make us think AXE was planning to kill innocent people when they were actually planning to do society a favor."

"So let me get this straight. You're saying that by bombing government animal research labs, this group was doing society a favor?" said Cryptic.

"That's correct, my friend. The people working in those labs don't deserve to live on this amazing planet!"

Strangely, it now appears as if most young adults have become affiliated with this generic brand of rebellion. They're angry, and demanding change. It doesn't matter if they are a down-and-out street thug willing to set buildings on fire, or a law-abiding, aspiring doctor or engineer. It doesn't matter if they view the AXE doctrine as a guide to life, or see it as useless drivel. The youth of America want a voice. They want to be heard.

Westgale and I meet for lunch at my campaign headquarters.

"I truly believe representing Anya will be a huge mistake, Nicole," Westgale says, regarding me across the table.

"I've given it a lot of thought over the last few days, and it's something I have to do, Mr. President," I reply.

"Will she even speak to you?" Westgale asks. "From what her father has told me, Anya won't even speak to him."

"There's a reason for that, sir."

He looks up from his vegetable soup. "Oh?"

"According to the doctor, Anya's deep feelings of anger stem from Jack's flamboyant lifestyle and the fact he was rarely there for her, growing up. He believes that's what sparked her rebellious attitude and led her to join AXE."

Westgale leans back with a sigh and runs his hands over his face. "Are you not concerned this is going to be seen as a weakness? Pandering to our disenfranchised youth?" he asks bluntly.

"I'm sure many will see it that way. But believe me when I tell you, I don't plan to lose that hearing. Nor do I plan to lose the election."

* * *

This morning I'm picked up by my driver and brought to the airport. I've yet to pay a visit to Vexton, but today that'll all change. Like most Americans, I've become fascinated with this idyllic farming town, which I only knew as the home of Vexton-Tech prior to recent events.

Wyatt Murphy from Vexton Land Protection meets me and my security team when we land in Vexton. He escorts us into his robo-copter and we lift off for Moon Shade Bluff. I'm excited to be visiting what is now being referred to as the eighth wonder of the world.

We fly over lush forest as we approach the mountain, and I lift a hand to shield my eyes from the brilliant sunlight and gaze down at the trees below, gently swaying in unison. I feel a deep sense of serenity. I look up and all of a sudden, there it is: Moon Shade Bluff. Its majesty takes my breath away, and my heart pounds. I immediately think of my dear friend Rosie, who recently lost her life to illness at way too young an age, while fellow human beings kept this medical miracle a secret for three decades.

When we land at the base of the mountain, I step out into the middle of an argument. "I don't care who you are, you are not permitted within this fenced area," says the military man in charge.

As I approach, the man he's speaking to turns around to look at me. "Well, I'm sure *she'll* be given access," he sneers, and snickers. Gerald Levin is spewing out his usual sarcasm. He and his MAA associate, Earl Pemberton, are both agitated; I gather that they are being asked to leave the area.

"Don't fret, Gerald. Soon we'll be in control of this entire thing," Pemberton says as he looks directly into my eyes. Throwing their arms up in disgust, Levin and Pemberton turn away and head down the path to be whisked away in their own copter.

When I turn to my right I see Heath Claremont a few feet away. "Heath, it's wonderful to see you again," I say.

"Hello, Nicole. Welcome to Vexton," he replies in his usual friendly manner. "What brings you to our town?"

"I figured, since I'm hoping to become president of this great land, it'd be wise to visit its new pride and joy in person," I reply, gazing up at the mountain.

"Come on, I'll bring you up," Heath says, leading me to his robo-copter.

Minutes later, we're touching down.

"Wow, it's so awe-inspiring up here," I say in a hushed voice as I stand atop Moon Shade Bluff with a cool breeze teasing my hair and a green vista stretching away at my feet.

About twenty yards away from us, several men are performing

some type of analysis on the mountain's surface. "It's nonstop activity up here," Heath says, seeing me watching them.

"Unbelievable," I say, continuing to watch them. "Do you think we'll ever figure out how this all came to be?" I ask.

With a subtle smile, Heath shakes his head. "Oh, there's an awful lot of theories being thrown about, but I highly doubt we'll ever know the true answer," he says as he waves to a couple of the workers.

"Yeah, it sure is fascinating. Before coming out here I checked what we refer to as the government's 'unsolved mysteries file' and let me tell you, that database is full of theories," I reply. "The latest is that this is one of those massive government cover-ups, and this mountain is maintained by some benevolent extraterrestrial power."

"I think most of the people here in Vexton are looking to the town's ancient history for the answers," Heath responds.

"Oh yeah, I see that the *Book of ZeZ* is gaining quite a bit of interest across the country," I say as I look at the view in wonder. "How tiny we actually are. And how little we actually know," I murmur. Then I look back to Heath. "I'd be remiss not to ask you how your father is."

Heath's eyes open wide and his smile broadens. "Now that he has everything cleared up with the authorities, I'm elated that we'll finally reconnect," he says with excitement.

"I can only imagine how surreal it must be for your entire family," I say sincerely.

He nods. "Yeah, it's definitely been a whirlwind of emotions. The last time I saw my father, I was ten years old. And now thirty years later, he appears out of the blue. Surreal, but amazing at the same time, to say the least."

The next stop on my Vexton journey is Talbot Farms. As I exit the grand-electro at the front gate, I notice a burly man approaching. I can barely see his face through the smoke emanating from his old-fashioned pipe.

"Hello, I'm Rusty Talbot," he says in a gruff voice.

"I'm Nicole Kratz. It's a pleasure to meet you, sir," I reply as I wave the smoke away.

"Likewise," he replies. "Hunter's waiting for you," he adds as he takes another puff. He opens the gate for me, then makes his way toward a waiting electro.

The farm is orderly and bucolic, yet modern, with several pieces of high-tech farming equipment visible as I move closer to the main house.

Hunter greets me at the front door. "Nicole, come on in," he says enthusiastically. "Let me take your coat." Then he guides me to the living room. "Have a seat."

"Thanks for seeing me," I say as I sink into a sofa. "Both your farm and your home have such a rustic, yet modern feel," I add.

"Well, Dad brings the rustic and I guess I bring the modern." Hunter chuckles. "I was surprised when your office requested this meeting. Knowing how busy you are, I'm sure this must be important."

"I saw the recent interview you did with UCIT," I say, leaning forward.

"I hope the PBA folks aren't *too* angry with me, but I just expressed my true feelings."

"Judging by how most of the youth across this country have been acting out lately, it appears you're not alone."

"Yeah, and unfortunately some have taken things way too far. Setting those buildings on fire was complete stupidity, regardless of how marginalized they feel. That's not the answer to the country's problems." Hunter's tone is disapproving.

"Do you have the answers, Hunter?"

He grins before replying. "I don't know if they're answers, but I certainly have plenty of ideas."

"Well, that's what I want to hear," I say as I rise from the sofa.

"I don't understand."

"Would you be willing to share those ideas?"

"In another interview with Cryptic?"

"No, in my office." Hunter looks at me, perplexed. "As my executive director… if I'm named president, of course."

"Executive director?"

I nod. "Correct."

"But I don't have a single ounce of political experience," Hunter protests.

"No, but you do have what the PBA needs: a fresh, young, innovative mind."

"Wow... you can't be serious."

"Like you said, I'm an extremely busy person who doesn't have time to play games. I'm asking you to join my team. I've done my homework on you, and your work at Forever Green is out of this world, not to mention the fact that you saved close to half a million young American lives by discovering those teal-berries," I say firmly.

"What about Dave Perry?" Hunter asks.

"David has an astute political mind, and I'm hoping he'll assist me in other capacities, but new blood is needed within the PBA, and I'm trusting you'll bring us that much-needed shot of youthful energy," I reply with conviction. "I'm aware you've promised to manage your father's farm, but I'm sincerely hoping you'll aid me in managing our country."

Hunter thinks for a moment and then walks toward a picture of him and his father that sits atop the mantel. "Well... I've already been able to make some major changes around here, and with the trustworthy farmhands I've brought on board, this place is pretty much running itself nowadays," he says, staring intently at the picture.

"Besides, with Washington being so close to Vexton, it won't be very difficult for you to address matters when the need arises," I add.

He turns to look at me. "I don't know, Nicole. My support for the PBA has been really waning of late," he says, rubbing his chin. "As far as I'm concerned, making that deal with Cobra Pix was extremely hypocritical. I mean, the guy goes against everything the PBA has supposedly stood for. And there's the whole Anya Ahar thing."

"I'm not going to tell you that anything Anya has done is justified, but then again, neither of us have walked in her shoes."

"What about Pix? I'm still shocked Westgale decided to make a deal with him."

"I understand your concern, Hunter, but after performing due diligence on Pix and his militia, Westgale and his people weren't able to find any damning proof against him. What they did find was that Pix was opposing a very corrupt Pinian government. I'll send you the report for your review."

"What about the threats he made against America and Westgale himself? Are they not of concern to the PBA?"

"Of course they are. But one needs to remember that American forces, under Westgale, justified or not, killed six of his seven sons, so I guess we can cut him some slack on that one. Besides, the generosity of his recent energy deal is a good indication that he's changing for the better," I reply.

"I don't want to offend you, but before I make a decision, I'll need to review that report and I'll also need clarification on your intentions," Hunter says.

"My intentions?"

"If you're hoping I'll simply act as some kind of figurehead appealing to America's youth, I'm not interested. I'd want to be able to make a real tangible difference."

"I came here asking you to join me in my quest to turn around not only the PBA, but this entire messed-up country. And I'm not asking you to do this because of your newfound hero status. I'm asking you, because I believe in you," I say emphatically.

"The last time I checked, the PBA's fifty-three-member Strategic Council didn't have a single person under the age of fifty on it. I highly doubt they'll be very eager to work alongside someone my age."

"Yeah, you're correct. And under my leadership, that will change. My plan is to create a council that will always be partly represented by young adults, much like you. I'll also be creating several youth advisory panels, which I will have *you* overseeing."

Hunter looks at me with wide eyes. "Well, it sounds like you're actually serious about giving a voice to the youth of America. This is exactly what this country needs," he says with a smile. "I'll give you my answer tomorrow morning."

CHAPTER 5

The following morning, much to my delight, Hunter formally accepts the offer to be my running mate. I immediately notify the PBA chairman of my selection and also address the matter with Dave Perry in the presidential lounge.

"Though I was looking forward to continuing on as executive director, I think you made a wise choice," Perry replies after I explain.

Phew, I'm relieved.

"Hunter's a very impressive young man. I think he'll fit in great with your agenda. And if you ever require my assistance, I'll be there for you in a heartbeat," he adds sincerely.

I smile. "I'm thrilled to hear that, because I'm hoping you'll consider another position within my administration."

Perry's eyebrows rise. "I'm all ears."

"I'd really appreciate you overseeing the VX drug program. If I'm fortunate enough to become president, that program is going to be important to my administration and will require someone with your experience and political acumen."

"You can count on me, Nicole." Perry sounds and looks excited. I'm elated.

After my meeting with Perry, I am unsurprised to be summoned by the PBA's newly appointed chairman, Justice Thor Hardy, for a meeting in his office.

"Please have a seat, Nicole," he says in his usual serious tone, indicating the chair in front of his desk. "How's Lawrence?" he asks in reference to my father.

"He's doing well, sir. Thank you for asking."

"Larry's one of the good ones," he says as he sits down behind his desk. "I just heard about his new foundation, and I've instructed our finance people to provide a very generous donation."

"Thank you, sir. I'm sure he'll be very pleased."

He leans forward and clasps his hands, elbows resting on the desktop. "Now, you must be wondering why I called you to my office."

I smile. "Somehow I think it has to do with my appointment of Hunter Talbot as my running mate."

Hardy sits back with a sigh. "Look, Nicole, I'm not denying Mr. Talbot is a fine young man, and I can't, nor do I want to, tell you whom to choose as your executive director, but heaven forbid, if something unfortunate were to happen to you, we'd be left with a twenty-six-year-old president."

"And I'm confident he'd do one heck of a job," I reply with a confident smile. Then I lean forward and say solemnly, "I understand your concern, sir, but I wouldn't have brought Hunter on board if I didn't have complete faith in him."

Hardy shakes his head and purses his lips before saying, "This whole youth thing... Do you not think you're getting a little caught up in this current wave of hysteria?"

"Not at all," I answer. "The people have spoken, Justice Hardy. We must not just govern; we must also learn through listening."

"Like everyone else, I'm well aware of those mass gatherings young people are holding across the country, and I'm also aware of the fact that they've been calling for the release of Anya Ahar, which leads to my next question. Why are *you* so interested in coming to the aid of such a vile young lady?"

"Because I believe in her," I say simply, then I amend that with, "There's far more to her than any of us know."

"How could you possibly believe in such a person?"

"I realize she's troubled, but I also believe that, with some guidance and understanding, she can easily be rehabilitated and use her extraordinary gifts to contribute to society."

Hardy still appears skeptical. "And just how do you think you're going to reach her when the country's premiere psychologist and her own father have failed so miserably?"

I sigh. "I don't have an answer for you... I just know I can."

"Unless you can prove to me that you actually have a chance to win that hearing, I may have no choice but to file an appeal with council, requesting a revocation of your motion being heard."

I throw pleasantries out the window as my anger spikes. "And if you do such a thing, this association can go searching for another presidential candidate," I say as I rise and stride out of the room.

* * *

The following morning, while preparing to meet with Anya at the Federal Justice Center, I receive a memo from Attorney General Sutton informing me that a date for Anya's Judicial Triangle hearing has been set. The memo states that the Outer Commission has declared the hearing a Code Three, which means three non-American judges will preside over the case. It also means the Militant Alliance of America will be permitted to argue against my motion.

In order to properly prepare for the hearing, I've asked my former law professor Arthur Fine and his staff to assist me. There is still so much more about Anya Ahar I'll need to learn, and I'm aware it won't be easy. Fortunately, the hearing is scheduled to take place prior to the stretch run of the election, so at least it'll give me a little breathing room.

What do I really know about this person I'll soon be placing my reputation on the line for, once again? What does anybody really know about Anya Ahar? Other than the fact that she is a scientific genius trapped in a world of personal despair, not a heck of a lot, it appears. Her teachers and classmates from high school and university describe her as being impossible to get to know and socially inept, someone who always presented a cold, empty stare to the world. One professor from Summit recalled how Anya would always sit in the back corner during his lectures in what was a half empty room. Another said he doubted Anya ever paid attention to his lectures and eventually came to realize that half the time she was aimlessly doodling or sleeping as he spoke. Nonetheless, when her courses were completed, Anya always seemed to achieve a perfect grade.

While I wait for the guards to bring her to the visiting room, I watch a view-file of an interview with Anya's mother, Maria, not long before she died:

"*I'm joined by the incredible Maria Ahar, one of this country's all-time great gymnasts, who today has officially announced her retirement from competition,*" said the excited young sports reporter. "*I understand you have a little one on the way.*"

"*Yes, I'm two months into my pregnancy,*" Maria answered with a pleasant smile.

"*Is this a permanent retirement?*"

"*Most definitely,*" Maria replied mildly. "*I feel I've accomplished everything I can in the sport of gymnastics.*"

"*You're definitely one of the more fascinating athletes this country has ever seen—continuously donating your medals, trophies, and prize money to children's hospitals. What made you choose to do that?*"

"*It was never my wish to receive accolades. But it is my wish to help others.*"

"*Would you want to see your child follow in your footsteps as a gymnast?*"

"*Whatever it is my child chooses to do with their life, I just hope they help make the world a better place.*"

I hear the sound of clanking chains out in the hallway. The door in front of me opens, revealing Anya, with two burly guards on either side of her. She barely reaches their elbows. She appears even more fragile than she did in our prior encounters. The guards slowly escort her into the room and place her before me. Her expression and eyes are empty.

"Hello, Anya," I say calmly. I look at the guards and order, "Gentlemen, please remove the shackles."

"Sorry, ma'am. We can't grant your request. It wouldn't be following proper procedure," one of them replies.

"I'm not asking you to. I'm *telling you to* remove the shackles. Please."

After a moment's hesitation, they oblige.

"That'll be all, gentlemen." I wave them back toward the door. When I turn back to look at Anya, she looks confused, as if she's wondering why I care.

"I'm here to help you, Anya," I say. She remains silent, gazing into her lap. "But there's no way I can, if you're not going to speak with me." I get no response. I'm trying to remain relaxed, but I'm becoming frustrated. "Okay, have it your way. I was planning to fight for you, but if you prefer to have your life come to an end, then—"

"It's a hopeless situation. Look what happened the last time you tried to help me," she mutters, still gazing into her lap.

Well, at least I got her to speak. "You're correct, Anya. I failed you in that hearing. But you see, that experience has made me a stronger person, and I'm even more determined to get it right this time."

She abruptly raises her head and looks me directly in the eyes before speaking. "Did my father put you up to this? Did he ask you to represent me again?"

"Yes, he did, but I wouldn't be doing this if I didn't want to, or didn't believe I could help you. As far as your father is concerned, he loves you with all his heart, Anya. He's even admitted to me that the extravagant life he led was his way of covering up his own sadness and guilt."

"I see. And now he thinks he can just wipe away the past and heal his guilty conscience by saving me from being executed," she says sarcastically. "What I don't understand is, why do *you* care? Am I a pawn in your political game?"

"You see, Anya, I know that despite your thick shroud of doom, there's reason for hope," I reply calmly. "I know the hypocrisy that fills our world tears at your heart. And I also know that the reason you're filled with such anger is because you know the world *can* be and *should* be a better place."

"You don't know a damn thing about me!" she replies angrily.

At least she's finally displaying some form of emotion. "Oh, I know more about you than you think," I reply as I take out my flash-pad.

"What is that supposed to mean?"

"Here." I slide the flash-pad over to her.

She studies it for a moment. "How... how did you find out about this?" Anya asks, reading the list of charitable donations she'd made prior to turning herself in.

"When I care about something... or someone, I never leave a stone unturned," I reply. "What *I* don't understand is why you wanted this to be kept a secret. Disclosing this information could very well have changed the outcome of the last hearing."

"I never wanted to receive accolades," she replies, looking startled. "I applied my life to science and medicine because I wanted to do my part to make the world a better place."

For a moment, I'm taken back to her mother's final interview. Through the lenses of her enormous horn-rimmed glasses, I see tears forming in the corners of her eyes.

"I'd like to go back to my cell, please," she says softly, bowing her head. I press the buzzer to call the guards. When they enter, they gently place the shackles on her wrists and ankles then, as if raising a stack of feathers, effortlessly lift her from her seat.

* * *

"How did it go with Anya?" Dr. Ahar asks me as we settle down for dinner in his opulent penthouse condo.

"Surprisingly, I was able to evoke far more emotion in her than I thought I could," I reply as I gaze at the appetizing seafood platter his butler places on the table.

"I had a feeling she'd respond to you. Do you think she'll cooperate with you for the hearing?" Ahar asks as he begins to fill his plate.

"I have no idea what to expect, Doctor. I think it's best we take it one day at a time. I just need to keep chipping away at her shell."

He looks at me. "In all honesty, do you think you'll be able to keep my daughter alive?"

"I don't mean to be flippant, but I think that'll depend entirely on Anya and whether she shows the court there's a reason to *keep* her alive," I answer while cracking open a lobster tail. "Actually, if she's willing to work with me, I'm confident I'll not only get her a stay of execution, but her complete freedom."

The doctor looks at me, puzzled.

CHAPTER 6

This night, sleep won't come. The thought of that pointless war that led to so much heartache, including the senseless death of Maria Ahar, and the tragic impact it has had on both Anya and her father, continues to fill me with overwhelming sadness. I begin thinking back to the most horrific day of my life, just a little more than twenty-five years ago.

When I completed high school, I decided to follow in my father's footsteps and study law. I studied criminal, constitutional, and environmental law at the country's premiere university, Summit. The Democratic president at the time, Jackson Snyder, had been making incredible inroads in convincing Congress to pass several bills that would help with eco-efficiencies. But like the dilemma faced by President Westgale more than two decades later, in order to facilitate these programs, a large amount of government funding was required. By instituting a number of very strict environmental laws, increasing taxes for the country's leading industrialists, and drastically decreasing military funding, Snyder and his administration believed the American government, after decades of failed attempts and false promises, would finally be able to properly fulfill its role in making America a far more peaceful and eco-friendly place to live.

I'll never forget the sound of that siren while attending class at Summit. It had jarred me right out of my seat. I immediately sensed it wasn't a false alarm or some kind of fire drill. I knew that one was for real.

In the preceding months, the largest military cutbacks and the strictest gun laws this country had ever seen had created mass paranoia among right-wing Americans. The political divide had reached frightening new depths. This led to all kinds of speculation that a political uprising might be in the works.

But how could this happen in America? After all, the country's Constitution provided mechanisms that, if push did come to shove, would prevent such a thing. And then there was the military; it very rarely ever became involved in the dark world of politics. But this had been an unprecedented era, with America feeling increasingly threatened by the HKM, a country of immense wealth and power that was more than capable of destroying it. And the night *the* interview aired on First Source News, that paranoia had become like a giant pitchfork, piercing the heart of the nation.

* * *

"Good evening, America, I'm Carly Taylor and you're watching First Source News. I'd like to welcome from an unknown location Mr. Kenneth Pahl, the former chief military commander of the HKM. Mr. Pahl, welcome to First Source News."

"Thank you, ma'am."

"Wow, this is incredible. I understand you've asked exclusively to be on First Source this evening to deliver a very serious warning to America."

"Yes, that is correct. I'm appearing with you this evening to warn America that the HKM is currently planning to destroy the infrastructure of several major American cities."

"My God... Do you know when and how this is going to happen?"

"I don't know how it'll happen, I just know it will—and soon."

"Is this attack being coordinated by the HKM government?"

"Yes, coordinated and funded."

"Have you contacted American authorities about this?"

"No, that definitely would not be in my best interest."

* * *

After the interview, Kenneth Pahl was never heard from or seen again.

The American government found itself in a state of confusion, not knowing how seriously Mr. Pahl's warning should be taken. Was he telling the truth? Did he have his own motive? Was he coerced or bribed to come forward? President Snyder placed the country on high security alert, but to many, especially members of a new far-right movement called the Militant Alliance of America, this was not enough. Although no such attack ended up taking place, it was never determined whether the information Kenneth Pahl provided was or wasn't accurate. Nonetheless, it became a key factor in events to come.

* * *

Reeling, I grabbed my belongings and made my way out of the building as the terrifying words were repeated over the university's sound system: "Evacuate immediately; evacuate immediately."

I hurried down several flights of stairs with other students, all of us scurrying toward the exits. Some I knew very well, while others were complete strangers. On this day, we were all instantly bonded by what eventually became known as the War Within.

"Nicole, are you okay?" a young man asked, stopping me out on the street. It was Andy Pemberton, who also studied law at Summit. Andy and I had known each other since childhood. His family controlled the American energy giant, ERT Power Corporation. It was no secret they were leaders in the recently formed Militant Alliance of America.

"Andy, what is going on out here?" I said fearfully as a dozen or so military vehicles pulled up around the building.

"Come with me. I'll get you out of harm's way," he replied, leading me to his electro.

"Oh my Lord. Your alliance finally went through with it," I gasped.

The order to "Evacuate immediately" was now being broadcast into the streets, booming out of enormous speakers mounted on top of military vehicles. Pandemonium erupted as soldiers strode toward the university, shouting orders. Some of the school's security personnel resisted following the orders and were immediately taken away.

"Oh my God!" I cried as I watched the mayhem unfold, shivering in the bitter cold.

I noticed several distinguished-looking men in long overcoats handing out booklets to the students. To no surprise, copies of those same booklets were piled in the back of Andy's electro. As we drove away, most of the students were now peacefully exiting the premises, while others stood speaking with the men in the overcoats, skimming through the literature. Then all of a sudden several objects came flying toward the electro, barely missing the passenger side where I was sitting. As I turned to look back, I saw half a dozen students being forcefully apprehended by the soldiers.

Minutes later, we arrived at the Last Frontier, New York City's preeminent steakhouse. When we exited the electro, a soldier greeted us. "Hello, Mr. Pemberton. Hello, ma'am," he said as he led us into the restaurant.

It immediately became obvious that the restaurant was not functioning in its normal manner. The room was filled with a large contingent of soldiers, and several men and women in business suits and overcoats, focusing on their flash-pads. All this confirmed my suspicion that Andy knew exactly what was happening. As the soldier led us to our table, we walked by an area that had been cordoned off with a black curtain. Through a break in the curtain I saw a group of men seemingly celebrating. I immediately recognized Andy's uncle, Earl Pemberton, along with Gerald Levin and Domingo Diaz, Chairman of First Source News, among the group.

"How can this be?" I murmured as Andy and I sat down at our table. I held my hands to my face.

"It had to happen, Nicole," Andy said matter-of-factly.

"Had to happen!" I responded, raising my head.

"This government went too far," Andy replied, his voice hard with conviction. "If we didn't do this, Snyder and the rest of his cronies would have drained the lifeblood from this country and we would have ended up being the HKM's own little experiment."

I stared at him in disbelief, shaking my head. "A civil war? Is that the solution, Andy?" I said as tears welled in the corners of my eyes.

"Regrettably, there's no alternative," he calmly replied. "This government refused to listen to the people who matter in this country, and now, sadly, we'll all have to pay a price in order to clean up the mess."

"The people who matter!" I said, my voice rising. "I guess you're speaking of the wealthy, like your family and all its influential friends."

"Oh, come on, Nicole! You speak as if your family's one step away from the poorhouse." He snickered.

Sirens wailed outside the restaurant. I reached for my flash-pad to contact my parents to make sure they were safe. There was no signal. "This damn thing!" I hissed. I tried again and again. When I looked up, Andy was grinning, as if he knew something I didn't.

"It's not your flash-pad, Nicole," Andy said. "The signal's been disabled. It'll only be temporary," he added.

One of the soldiers stopped at our table with a platter of sandwiches. "Help yourself," Andy said as he chose a roast beef sandwich and pulled it from its wrapper. He took a bite and began chomping away, talking around the food in his mouth. "It's all going to work out. We'll be fine. Besides, I've been telling my Uncle Earl about you, and if you're interested, he'd like to speak with you regarding a future position in ERT's legal department." Smiling confidently, he looked out the window.

"How... how in the world can you be so cold!" I said angrily. I too then looked outside. "Just what in the hell is happening out there?" I exclaimed, watching the chaos. Sirens continued to wail.

"It's very simple, Nicole. The Militant Alliance of America is rising up to take back this country," Andy answered. "I guess you could call it the Preservation Plan."

A loud cheer echoed through the room. I turned to look toward the sound—several soldiers stood before a large flash-screen. "Turn up the sound," Andy called eagerly.

I froze in shock. There was the White House in flames, barely recognizable. I recognized the voice of First Source News anchor Carly Taylor, describing the scene.

"Hold on... I'm now receiving official word that the battle on the White House grounds has already concluded, with President Snyder and his executive committee in full retreat. As shocking and appalling as this may seem to some, with the continuous threats from the HKM, this may go down as the most important day in American history. I think they'll now get the message that America is not to be messed with," she said calmly as images of a burning White House continued to flash across the screen.

"I'm learning that the Militant Alliance of America is also currently seizing other prominent government properties across the land. They realize there'll be resistance, but they are predicting that within a month or two, they will have accomplished their goal. Hopefully, casualties will be minimal. It's amazing to think how the nation's leading industrialists and our military have come together to create this powerful alliance—I guess you could say they've emerged as our liberty fighters. God bless America," she concluded with a glowing smile.

Seconds later, an elated Earl Pemberton appeared at the front of the restaurant. "Let's see Jackson Snyder try to take this from my hands!" he shouted as he held up an antique rifle he'd removed from the wall. Gerald Levin and the others smiled and cheered. Domingo Diaz, the man behind First Source News, was now nowhere to be seen. "Hey, everyone, sweet blue-eyed Carly said it best when she called us America's liberty fighters!" Earl hollered.

I was sickened. How could they be so excited about something so horrendous? I couldn't bear it any longer so I got up, grabbed my coat, and prepared to leave.

"Nicole, why don't you stick around and join the celebration," Andy said, tugging on my coat.

"Our country is being torn apart, and you expect me to celebrate? Are you out of your mind, Andy?"

"Well, at least let me have one of the soldiers take you safely to your apartment."

"I guess I don't have much choice," I replied in a huff.

Instead of heading back to my apartment, I decided to pay my parents a visit. I needed to be with them and ensure they were okay.

On the way, I witnessed street after street lined with military vehicles. Every few blocks I saw angry civilians confronting the soldiers. Some were being apprehended. Sadly, I also witnessed some lying in the streets, badly injured or dead. It was a scene that would forever haunt me.

When I arrived at my parents' house I was relieved when Mom opened the door and gave me a hug. "I'm so glad you're okay, honey," she said as tears streamed down her cheeks. "I can't believe this is happening in our country. It's just so terrible," she cried.

In the living room, Dad sat on a sofa in front of his flash-screen, watching the news and shaking his head in disbelief. "Come here, my dear," he said, waving me over to him. He set his glass of vodka and orange juice on a side table and put his arm around me as we watched the news. I'd never seen him so distraught.

"How... how in the world did this happen, Dad?" I asked.

"It's all been brewing for quite some time, Nicole," Dad said sadly.

"Being Attorney General, you must know how the government is planning to respond?"

He sighed. "It's a battle that can't be won. Some of our local police forces are doing the best they can, but they're going up against the military."

"Are you telling me the entire American military is on board with this uprising?"

"Sources from my office have informed me that we're looking at about eighty-five percent. We're in the midst of establishing a peace coalition to see if we can slow the MAA's momentum."

"Oh my God! What is going to become of this great country?" I cried.

Dad had no response. He simply shook his head, ran his hands over his face, dropped a few more pieces of ice into his glass, and refilled it.

I turned off the flash-screen and closed my weary eyes.

* * *

Upon the War Within's conclusion, and a year after the Militant Alliance's failure to properly reshape the country, a shattered

America was in dire need of rescue. The country's economy and political infrastructure were in peril. Nationwide, morale was at an all-time low. Thankfully, with the exception of the HKM and Pinia, the world's major countries came to the rescue by forming a commission to oversee America's reformation. The Outer Commission immediately began developing the New Order Treaty, under which America would be governed, with the idea of protecting the country from itself and avoiding a repeat of the War Within. Although to most Americans the notion of the Constitution being tampered with was unconscionable, there was no choice.

CHAPTER 7

I enter the living room early in the evening to find my fifteen-year-old daughter, Tiffany, sitting on the sofa, reading a book. "Hey, Tif, what are you reading?" I ask.

"*The Book of ZeZ*," she replies, showing me the cover. Because of her recent interest in the mysteries of the universe, I'd bought her a copy while in Vexton.

"So, what do you think?"

"It's fascinating," she answers, barely able to lift her eyes from the page. "I love the part about when these birdlike demons tried to fly over Moon Shade Bluff and the Moon Lords destroyed them with lightning bolts." She sets the book facedown on the side table and says, "If you ask me, Moon Shade Bluff is definitely a healing temple."

"Well, I didn't ask, but thanks for enlightening me anyway," I respond with a chuckle, then turn as Lowell and Tiffany's thirteen-year-old sister, January, enter the room.

"Hey, Mom, when we live in the Freedom Home, will I be allowed to decorate my room the way I want?" Tiffany asks out of the blue.

"If you are, they'll have to change the name to the Freaky Home," January quips.

Tiffany sneers at her. "At least my walls won't be pink and covered with pictures of cute little bunnies."

"Okay, girls, that's enough," Lowell says with a laugh. "If you keep this up, *I'll* be the one decorating both your rooms—and trust me, you wouldn't want that."

"Now, now, let's not get carried away; the election is—" My flash-pad buzzes. It's Hunter.

"Nicole, I think you'd better tune in to UCIT," he says anxiously.

"What's going on, Nicole?" Lowell asks as I turn on the flash-screen.

"Central Park... Look at them," I say in a hushed voice. What appears to be thousands of people dressed in black, all wearing balaclavas, have gathered peacefully around a flagpole bearing a giant American flag.

"My Lord. It looks like five times the number of the prior gatherings," Lowell says.

Seconds later, in unison, those gathered pump their fists into the air, and for the next minute or so they chant, "Free Anya! Free America!" Then, simultaneously, at the count of three, everyone gathered removes their mask.

"Wow—unbelievable," I exclaim.

The camera pans across the gathering, then closes in. I see young Americans of every ethnicity and color. There appears to be an equal number of males and females. Seconds later, the group separates into smaller groups, once again chanting, "Free Anya! Free America!"

"This should be interesting," Lowell says as Cryptic begins moving through the crowd. The robot's green eyes shift from oriental to occidental. Its chest displays a flashing neon image of the Statue of Liberty.

"Excuse me, ma'am. May I have a moment of your time?" the robot asks a young lady with a shaved head who's wearing an excessive amount of purple eyeliner.

"Ask away," she replies excitedly.

"Who am I speaking with?" Cryptic asks.

"My name is Monica."

"Would you mind divulging your age?"

"I'm twenty-two."

"What brings you here to Central Park on this splendid evening?"

"I'm here to celebrate the coming of a new age."

"A new age?"

"Yeah, America's rebirth."

"Would you kindly enlighten me?"

"We are tired of being dictated to, of being told how to live. To our government and our corporate leaders: you don't speak for us. You're not America! This country belongs to its people!" Monica says with passion, staring into the camera. "We will continue to send out our message until we are heard and America is a country that permits all of its citizens to have a voice."

A large crowd is gathering around her and Cryptic.

"When you say 'we,' are you referring to AXE?" the robot asks her.

Monica looks blankly at Cryptic. "I have no idea what you're talking about."

"After your last two gatherings, AXE's supposed leader, a young man referring to himself as Blackheart, immediately came out and claimed responsibility for setting buildings ablaze."

"Those crimes had nothing to do with our peaceful demonstrations," Monica insists. "For some reason I guess this Blackheart guy and whoever committed those crimes wanted the authorities to believe otherwise."

"So, are you telling me you and the rest of these people are not affiliated with Blackheart and AXE?"

"Obviously I can't speak for this entire group, but I know I'm here of my own accord. I'm here representing the youth of America. I'm not here in the name of anarchy. This is a peaceful movement and we're growing by the day. Soon, our government will have no choice but to give a voice to the youth of this country."

"That's right," a tall, skinny young man chimes in as Monica drifts away into the crowd. "Strength in numbers," he adds.

"And what is your name?" Cryptic asks the young man.

"Lance. My friends call me Lanny," the young man replies.

"Tell me, Lanny, what is it you and your friends expect from your government?"

"A voice. I'm nineteen years old. My peers and I don't feel relevant. Just consider who makes all the decisions in this country."

"So, this all comes down to giving the youth of America a voice?"

"That's the main reason we're here, robot man," Lanny replies. "We're also demanding accountability. We're sick and tired of hearing about corrupt government officials, and powerful corporations that believe they have a right to place business before ethics."

I'm hanging onto every word this young man says, and wishing I could go down to that park and shout out my platform.

"Your request to free Anya Ahar—is there a general feeling among this group that the AXE doctrine should be recognized as a guide for your 'new age'?"

"It's not about AXE or the doctrine," Lanny insists. "In fact, I haven't even read the doctrine, nor do I intend to. That being said, that doctrine has every right to exist—it's called free speech. It's what used to be regarded as the First Amendment."

"And Anya Ahar?"

"Her story is tragic. This government needs to right a wrong and give her back her freedom, which she so rightly deserves."

"Are you not at all concerned by the fact that she manufactured helcin for the purpose of one day possibly using it against the American government?" asks Cryptic.

"Why is that any different from what the world's arms manufacturers are doing as we speak? She never personally used that poison as a weapon." Lanny shifts forward and leans toward Cryptic, shoulders hunched, hands open, palms up, as if pressing his point home. "Look, if I learned my mother had died—or I should say, was killed—by our government in such a horrific way, I'm certain I too would want to be protected. Our society owes it to her to set her free."

"And what if the government doesn't listen to your plea? Will that mean your peaceful demonstrations will turn violent?"

Lanny steps back and says proudly, "This government will have to listen to us. Like I said, our strength is in our numbers. Similar demonstrations are currently taking place right across the country."

"I have one last question for you. Why the dark and threatening appearance, if these gatherings are meant to be peaceful demonstrations?"

"Well, that was all about gaining the attention we deserve. After all, the perception of evil can be a very powerful weapon."

"There you go, Nicole. It sounds like your platform will be garnering quite a bit of support," Lowell says.

"Yeah, but I just can't rely solely on young America for support. I'll have to reach the other side of the spectrum as well, if my campaign is going to be successful," I respond.

* * *

In Champ Sutton's office at the Freedom Home, he and President Westgale are watching the demonstration. "This movement is like an unstoppable force, becoming more powerful by the minute," Westgale says as the flash-screen displays images from other rallies across the country.

"Ah... here we go," Champ says, reading a message from one of his staff. "It looks like UCIT is about to air another view-file from our friend, Blackheart."

"Damn it!" Westgale hollers. "I personally told those idiots that from now on we need to review these view-files before they go to air."

"There's nothing we can do, sir. We have to remember that when the Outer Commission set up UCIT, its goal was to eliminate all forms of censorship," Champ explains.

"You don't need to remind me, Champ," Westgale murmurs. "I'm not a fan of censorship, but thank God the day is soon approaching when we won't have to answer to that damn Commission, and live by that shambolic treaty."

Seconds later, the view-file appears on the flash-screen. In what looks like the same basement he had spoken from before, Blackheart appears, once again dressed in black and sporting a balaclava.

"*Hello,*" he says. "*I'm sure you know me by now. If you don't, my name is Blackheart.*" He snickers. *From within his balaclava, brooding eyes peer into the camera.* "*As you witnessed today at Central Park and across the rest of the country, the revolution is well underway, my friends. In this insurgency, there is no place for injustice! We will stand as one, united by—*"

With a report like that of a gunshot, the window behind him breaks. "What the hell—oh no!" *he shouts, scrambling back, out of range of the pickup.*

A powerful explosion rips through the room, and the screen goes black.

"What in the world was that?" Westgale says, staring stunned at the screen for a moment. He and Champ exchange glances.

Westgale's chief of security, Gil Robichaud, bursts into the room. "Did *we* kill this guy, Gil?" Westgale asks as he rubs his hands over his face.

"I know Bradley Peters and his team have been trying to track the guy down, but to my knowledge they had no idea who he was. And besides, they were under strict orders to inform my office if they did have any leads," Gil replies. He then proceeds to contact Bradley on his flash-pad and put the call up on the room's flash-screen.

"I know nothing about this, sir," Bradley answers when questioned by Gil.

"Is it possible one or a group of your men went rogue and killed him?" Westgale asks Bradley.

"There's no way, sir. When my grandfather placed me in charge of this operation, I made sure to recruit only our top agents. But I'll look into it." Bradley ends the call.

Westgale looks at Champ and Gil with a raised eyebrow. "Hmm… if it wasn't us who took this guy out, then I can't help but wonder if it was the MAA that did."

* * *

Twenty minutes after the Blackheart view-file ended in the likely death of its subject, the UCIT Network returns to Cryptic, now standing in front of the Statue of Liberty, its eyes flashing red and blue, an American flag displayed on its chest.

"On behalf of UCIT, I wish to inform the American people that the airing of today's shocking event was simply the result of uncensored news," the robot announces. "We do not apologize if you were offended, and will continue to present America with the unfettered truth."

"Please note that, at this time, both the PBA and MAA have refused to comment on this matter or claim responsibility," the robot says in its monotone voice. "Other than information obtained in an interview I conducted with him in Los Angeles and the view-files he sent to our network, the only thing we know about this extremist who referred to himself as Blackheart is that whatever's left of his body has been decimated beyond recognition."

CHAPTER 8

Since the day Blackheart made himself known to the public, law enforcement agencies across the country had been attempting to uncover his identity. The person they hoped would provide answers was one of the creators of AXE, Morris Johns. Unfortunately, he'd contracted a serious illness while in prison, so Gil had been unable to interview him until now.

"I'm very glad to hear you're feeling better, Morris," Gil says as he meets with the man at the Federal Justice Center.

"Yeah, somehow I don't think you came here to bring me chocolates and flowers," Morris sneers. "So what is it you want?"

"Information."

Morris snickers. "Wow, I'm going to have my lawyer demand you guys put me on your payroll." He regards Gil for a moment. "I get it. You still don't have a clue who Blackheart is, so you've come running to me."

"You're correct. We don't know a thing about this guy, but we *do* know something about your father. It looks rather certain that his dealings with Edgar Fryman are going to land him in prison for quite some time," Gil says matter-of-factly.

Morris leans across the table to growl, "And do you actually think I care about what happens to my self-serving, ostentatious imbecile of a father? As far as I'm concerned, both he and his company can go to hell."

Gil is undefeated. "I'm well aware of the resentment you feel toward your father," he says calmly. "I'm also well aware of the love you feel for your sister. And regrettably, it appears she'll be taking the fall along with him."

Morris sighs. "Jackie's a good person. She's the only decent executive in that entire greedy corporation. She's not guilty of anything, other than being the daughter of an idiot."

"Yeah, it's unfortunate that she'll have to face the consequences of that 'idiot's' crooked ways. I really feel for your mother—her husband and both her children locked away. That's just plain—"

"Okay. I get the point," Morris interrupts. "I'll tell you what I know, as long as you promise Jackie doesn't go to prison." He sighs and flops back in his chair. "Don't you guys ever get tired of this game?"

Gil offers a tight smile. "It's called leverage, Morris. Now you have a deal—providing, of course, what you tell me turns out to be true. So, after all the questioning we did with you guys pertaining to AXE, please tell me why it is that you and Dwight Wagner felt so obliged to protect Blackheart."

"Blackheart was never a part of AXE. When I met him he was involved with an extremist group out in LA called the SOH."

"The Spirit of Hades?"

"Yeah, those are the guys. Before we began AXE, Dwight and I attended a couple of their meetings."

"In the hopes of joining?"

"That's right. At first we gave it some thought, but after seeing what they were about, we got the hell out of there."

"Why?"

"Well, let's put it this way: with AXE, Dwight and I wanted to *reshape* America. These guys, their goal was to *destroy* it."

Morris describes elaborate view-files created by the Spirit of Hades that he'd seen—files describing the future bombing of the Statue of Liberty, the presidential jet being shot down by laser blasts, President Westgale and the Lady of Honor being electrocuted and beheaded, and the Freedom Home burning to ash as the White House had done all those years ago.

The revelation chills Gil to the bone. "After LA Justice was tipped off about them, they instantly shut the operation down. What else can *you* tell me about them?" he asks.

"From what I witnessed, it appeared to be quite an operation. Highly financed and technologically advanced."

"Do you know if they were domestic or international?"

"That, I couldn't tell you. They were extremely guarded. At the meetings Dwight and I attended, Blackheart was the only person who spoke."

"So, was he the group's leader?"

Morris shakes his head. "No, he was like some kind of spokesman. There was some other guy who was directing Blackheart. I'm certain he was the leader."

"Were you able to see any faces, or were they all wearing those stupid ski masks?"

"Yeah, they all wore masks, but they weren't ski masks," Morris says. "They looked like some kind of fencing mask, very high-tech."

"Now, did you have any further contact with Blackheart or anyone else from the group, once they shut down the operation?" Gil leans slightly forward.

Morris exhales and leans back in his chair. "That's when Blackheart came to us. He'd heard we were starting AXE, and he wanted in. He even went so far as to get the AXE insignia tattooed across his chest." He lifts one eyebrow and snorts with disgust.

"But you didn't let him in?"

"Dwight was all for it, but I sure as hell wasn't. This guy was a complete lunatic. And you have to remember, I already had my hands full with Dwight. Anya wanted nothing to do with Blackheart, either. So we gave Dwight an ultimatum. Either you can accept our funding *without* Blackheart, or you can run off with him and start your own group."

"And how did he feel about being left out?"

"He didn't put up a fight, but he did tell us he was planning to start his own extremist group out on the West Coast. So, after you guys brought us down, I guess that's what he did out in LA, and he called it AXE because of all the attention *we'd* received."

"Do you have any idea who would have wanted this guy dead?"

Morris snorts a laugh. "Probably quite a few people. And after seeing firsthand that group's sheer contempt for this country, I'd think you guys were right at the top of the list."

* * *

Upon returning to Pinia, Shadow and Jessica learn that Cobra has planned an extravagant "welcome home" party in honor of Shadow. Invited are all the high-ranking members of the Iron Lotus and their families, along with many of the country's elite.

"Are you going to go public regarding your mother?" Jessica asks Shadow as they prepare for the gala.

Shadow's fingers slow on the shirt he's been buttoning. "I think it's very important to keep it out of the public domain," he replies solemnly. "This country sure doesn't need any more turmoil." Jessica nods her understanding. "The Iron Lotus is now in power, and I have no intention of bringing my father and his militia down. I refuse to resort to his ways. Let's do our best to enjoy this evening, and then I'll deal with him."

The event is being held at the theater where Cobra first met Luanda. Over the years, Cobra had developed the property into a multifaceted complex, including a beautifully appointed banquet hall.

When Shadow and Jessica arrive, Shadow is greeted with a hero's welcome. It's not every day that a Pinian saves the president of the United States. "Hey, Jessica, I hope your father remembers he owes us one," jokes Theodore, military commander of the Iron Lotus. The small crowd gathered around them laughs.

"Don't worry, Theo, I'll make sure his office sends you an autographed American flag," Jessica quips back.

After dinner, the guests make their way to the theater. The evening begins with a performance by Pinia's sensational eighteen-year-old acrobatic dancer, Isabella. The crowd gasps as she performs her stunts, displaying incredible skill and concentration.

"Smooth as silk," Jessica whispers to Shadow.

"Utter perfection," Shadow agrees.

After a brief intermission, the crowd returns to watch a play titled *The Mighty One*, which pays tribute to Pinia's sacred legend, the Sortar Dragon. When the curtain opens, the first scene begins with a young, wide-eyed child discovering a mysterious-looking fluorescent stone in a dense forest.

"Isn't that Ulu on the stage?" Shadow whispers to Jessica, recognizing the sweet young child who'd endeared herself to Jessica and her fellow aid workers.

"Oh wow, it is," she replies with a smile.

They both turn as Cobra slides into the seat beside Jessica. "I had my staff arrange this entire event the day I learned Shadow was going to be okay," Cobra says proudly. "You've done such wonderful work with the children; they're so smart and adorable," he adds to Jessica.

At the conclusion of the play, the crowd reconvenes in the ballroom for dance, drink, and dessert. Theodore approaches and says to Jessica, "I had the opportunity to spend some time with your fellow aid workers while you were tending to Shadow in America." He offers Jessica a glass of Cobra's homemade white wine. "Very impressive young men and women. The future of America appears to be in very capable hands."

"Thank you, sir. I think a new America is on the horizon," Jessica responds, her voice confident.

"Well now, here's to a new America," Theodore says with a wide grin. He raises his glass, and Jessica and Shadow touch their glasses to his.

The guests are invited back to the theater to end the evening. Cobra takes the stage. "I hope everybody has had a wonderful evening!" he roars. "Let's hear it for my incredible son, Shadow Pix!"

Shadow rises from his seat in the center balcony and waves to the crowd. They respond by giving him a standing ovation.

"I'd like to present our final act of the evening," Cobra announces. "Please welcome to the stage an orchestra that has deservedly garnered praise from across the globe. They call themselves Shades of Night."

Shadow is deeply affected during the performance, which conjures memories of his mother. He remembers how she played the piano for him at bedtime, which had erased his childhood fears of the night and sent him off into a peaceful sleep.

As the orchestra concludes with "Starlight Serenade," Shadow squeezes Jessica's hand as his body starts to shake with silent sobs. She leans over and gently whispers, "It'll be okay, Shadow."

Later in the evening, at Cobra's palace, Shadow realizes the time has come to confront his father. "Father, will you join me for a cup of tea?" he asks, his heart pounding. He leads Cobra into the main den, where he's had one of the servants leave two cups of tea. Cobra looks closely at him and Shadow looks away, trying to conceal his uneasiness.

"I hope it wasn't too much for you this evening, Shadow," Cobra says before taking a sip of his tea, regarding his son carefully.

"No, it was a wonderful evening," Shadow replies, staring into space as he gathers his thoughts.

"If you don't mind me saying, you don't seem to be yourself, son."

"I've just been doing a lot of thinking about my trip to the US," Shadow replies, lifting his cup and staring into it.

"I understand you were honored at the Freedom Home. I'm sure it must have been quite an event. You must have met some very important and interesting people," his father says.

Shadow meets his father's eyes. "Actually, the most interesting person I met in America wasn't even at that event. In fact, they weren't even from America."

"Oh?"

"Yeah, she was from Pinia. Her name is Luanda," Shadow answers, feeling his face heat up.

Cobra abruptly sets his cup down on the side table next to his chair. His face tightens. There is a beat-long pause before he asks, "Your mother?"

Who else? Shadow thinks angrily, and he can no longer feign calm. "How could you be such a heartless man?" he blurts.

Cobra holds up his hands. "Whoa... what are you talking about?"

"You know damn well what I'm talking about," Shadow growls, glaring at his father. "How could you be so cruel!"

"Wait a second."

"Don't deny it. I'm not one of your little puppets, Father."

Cobra sighs and studies Shadow. "She gave me no choice, son."

"Oh, what was she going to do? Bring down your empire with her music?" Shadow sneers.

Cobra leans toward Shadow and says earnestly, "Listen to me, Shadow. I did everything for that woman. I gave her a life she could only once dream of."

Shadow leaps up and whirls to confront his father. "Yeah, and then in a flash, because of your giant ego, you turned that dream into a nightmare by ordering her to leave the very country she was born in—her home."

Cobra's face darkens with anger. "She brought it all upon herself. That clueless bleeding heart thought I'd actually turn my back on my father for her. She didn't deserve to walk on Pinian soil!"

"Well then, I guess I don't deserve to either," Shadow says, his voice taut. "Once I tie up the US energy deal, Jessica and I will be out of here—for good! And don't worry, I won't tell our people how cruel you really are."

"So you're just going to turn your back on your father and your country for a mother who's a mere stranger. A person you don't even know anything about," Cobra replies, punctuating the last sentence by sweeping his arm up.

"That person brought me into this world," Shadow says. He stares at his father as if seeing him for the first time. "The more I think about it, I realize you're the one I truly know nothing about."

"Well, I'm sorry you feel this way, Shadow," Cobra sneers, hands on his hips. "Now that we've attained our goal and gained complete control of this country, it's a real shame you're choosing to abandon ship." Again he flings his hand out.

"That's your problem, Father: your sickening desire to control… to control everything and everybody." Shadow whirls and stalks out of the room.

* * *

After Shadow exits, Cobra heads toward the palace's front hallway. When he comes to the wall photos of his six deceased sons, he stops and gazes at them. Opening his arms, eyes closed and head tilted back, he murmurs, "The day will soon come… the day will soon come."

The following morning, when Cobra and Theodore meet at the Iron Lotus's military headquarters, Cobra is in high spirits. "Everything is running perfectly, Theo. My father was so correct when he used to tell me there's nothing more beneficial in battle than gaining the blind trust of your enemy. The energy deal is in place, and Shadow's become quite a hero in the US—which bodes very well for us. Soon he'll be flying off into the sunset with his American dream girl. It's absolutely perfect," Cobra sneers.

"And what about that imbecile, Blackheart?" Theodore asks.

"He's been dealt with. Our American associate took care of him as planned. Remember, Theo, for this plan to be successful, we must ensure the Peace-Bringers remain in control of that poor excuse for a country," Cobra replies, handing Theodore a data chip. "This contains the details for your final visit to the HKM. President Woi will be notified upon your arrival."

"And the green hearts?" Theo asks.

"Soon the shipments will begin arriving," Cobra replies, sitting back in his chair and swinging his feet up onto his desk.

* * *

When Theodore arrives in the HKM he's immediately brought to President Woi's presidential palace. After being cleared by security, he's escorted into Woi's lavish den.

"Ah, come on in, Mr. Theodore," Woi says from the front of the room. He seems preoccupied by a view-file playing on his flash-screen. "This is my grandson, Oliver, recently winning our national junior fencing championship. My daughter just sent it to me," he says with his eyes glued to the screen.

"You must be very proud," Theo responds, glancing at the screen.

"To tell you the truth, a competition such as this is way too docile for my liking, and certainly isn't something that's ever going to fill me with true pride. With all of that protective gear, this is surely not real dueling," Woi answers, aimlessly twirling a forked scepter. "Now, if you want to learn about real dueling, you need to go back in time to when warriors would engage in combat on horseback, and use their sabers to slash their enemy to pieces."

Theo moves closer to the screen. "Those masks they're wearing; they look like the same masks Cobra supplied to that Spirit of Hades gang out in Los Angeles," he says.

"Well, that's because they are," Woi says, and laughs harshly.

CHAPTER 9

"Are you sure about leaving?" Jessica asks Shadow. "After all, Pinia's always been your home."

"I don't *want* to leave, Jessie; I *have* to," he says sadly as they spend their final evening in Pinia sitting by a crackling fire.

"I'm actually going to miss this place, and of course the children," Jessica says, looking up at the stars.

"By the behavior of the children earlier today, it's obvious how much they're also going to miss *you*," Shadow says as he pulls Jessica close to him.

"I feel really comfortable about leaving Trevor in charge of the team. He's really developed into quite a leader. He certainly understands the children, and they've taken a real liking to him."

The next day, they travel back to the US, and a few days after that, after settling into Jessica's New York City condo, Jessica watches Shadow pulling on his coat, her head cocked to one side in uncertainty.

"Are you sure you don't want to call her first?" she asks.

"I'd much rather surprise her," Shadow answers with a smile.

"Fine," Jessica says, throwing up her hands before reaching for her own coat. "Since the reservation is for seven, we should get moving."

When they arrive at Luanda's apartment building, they hear shouting and pounding from the second-floor hallway as they're climbing the stairs. As they step into the hallway, they see a police officer pounding on the door of unit 215, the apartment across the hall from Luanda's unit.

"This is the police! Open the door!" the officer shouts.

"That's it," Shadow says in disgust as they walk toward Luanda's apartment. "I'm so glad we'll be getting her out of this hellhole." Ignoring the officer, he knocks on his mother's door. There's no answer. He drops his hand and sighs. "You were right, Jessie; we should've called."

"Here, let me call her," Jessica replies as she pulls out her flash-pad.

Before she can make the call, Luanda appears at the end of the hall carrying bags of groceries. Shadow and Jessica head toward her.

"Let me take those from you, Mother," Shadow says, reaching for the bags.

"Wow, this is quite a surprise," Luanda says with a smile as she relinquishes the bags. "I thought you'd already left for Pinia."

"We did, and we're back—back for good," Shadow replies with a smile.

"Back for good?" Luanda says, shocked. She frowns. "But Pinia's your home, son."

"It *was* my home."

Luanda regards him for a moment, then sighs. "Oh, Shadow, I've caused you so much grief."

"You couldn't be more wrong, Mother," he replies softly. "By opening up to me and telling me how my father forced you to leave Pinia, you opened my eyes to reality. My father only cares about the person he sees in the mirror." He turns businesslike. "Now, let's get these groceries put away so we can get to the restaurant on time."

"Restaurant? Oh my, you guys are filled with surprises," Luanda exclaims. "I love you so much," she says as she hugs Shadow.

"That's not our only surprise," Jessica adds.

"Tell her, Jessie," Shadow says.

"Well, Luanda, soon you won't have to worry about all this yelling and police officers banging on doors," Jessica says, glancing back at the ruckus in the hallway before closing Luanda's apartment door. "We were able to secure a unit for you in the building where I live."

Luanda gapes at her for a moment. "Oh my, I could never afford to live in such a place," she says, then she looks at Shadow. He responds with a wide smile. "No, Shadow, I won't let you. I mean, I don't expect you to—"

"Nothing would make me happier than to do this for you, Mother," Shadow insists. "Nothing."

* * *

"Your daughter's arrived from New York, sir," Westgale's secretary informs him.

"Send her in, Susan," he replies, rising and moving around his desk to meet his daughter as she enters his office.

"I can't believe this!" he exclaims as he and Jessica embrace. "Your mother's waiting for us in the lounge." He steps back. "Wow, this is amazing. How in the world did you convince Shadow to come and live in the US?"

"I think you'd better have a seat, Dad," Jessica says, frowning.

"What is it, Jessie, aren't you happy with the decision?" Westgale says as he sits down on the couch. Jessica sits in the armchair across from him.

"Of course I'm thrilled to be home, but I must tell you *why* Shadow decided to leave Pinia," Jessica says, and tells her father the story Luanda told them.

"Whoa... he forced her to leave her own country?" Westgale says when Jessica finishes. "He threatened to kill her family if she didn't comply?" He shakes his head.

"That's correct," Jessica replies.

"How long have you known about this?" Westgale says, rising to his feet, brow puckered in concern.

"We found out when Shadow was fighting for his life."

"So, are you telling me Shadow never knew about this before?"

"Yeah, all these years, he had no idea. And when he found out, he was furious and decided he no longer wanted to live in Pinia."

"Are you certain Luanda Rollins is being honest with you guys about this?"

Jessica nodded. "When Shadow confronted Cobra, he admitted it was true."

"Bah, you know I admire Shadow, but darn it, Jessie, I'm concerned about you being caught up in such a messed-up situation," Westgale says, placing his hand on Jessica's shoulder. "Who else knows about this?"

"According to Luanda, Shadow and I are the only people she's told."

"I just hope that's true. What about her husband?"

"She says she doesn't intend to tell him. In fact, it's something she despises speaking about."

Westgale drops his hand. "Damn. Here we've been telling the American people that Cobra isn't the ruthless tyrant he's been made out to be, and now I learn this," Westgale says, scratching his head. "Every night—every night I question whether making that deal with him was the right thing to do. If the public ever found out about this…"

"It happened many years ago, Dad. From what I witnessed in Pinia, I think Shadow's influence has actually rubbed off on Cobra, in a positive way. I think he's a changed man."

"That's what I so admire about you, Jessie," Westgale says as he sits back down. He smiles at Jessica and laces his hands behind his head.

"What's that, Dad?"

"Your innate ability to bring calmness to any situation, regardless of how turbulent it may seem."

* * *

In the Freedom Home's press room, Champ Sutton sits glaring directly into the UCIT camera. At a nod from the cameraman, he begins his announcement.

"Recently, our nation witnessed a young extremist who referred to himself as Blackheart being murdered by an explosion. This individual claimed responsibility for four recent arsons. We have now learned his identity. His name is Mason Unger, twenty-four years of age, an American citizen who was born in and was still living in Los Angeles at the time of his death. I will now turn the podium over to our Administration's chief of security, Agent Gil Robichaud."

Gil steps up to the podium as Sutton backs away from it. "Thank you, Attorney General Sutton. An investigation into Mr. Unger's murder is currently underway. At this time, we have no suspect or direct motive. What we have been able to determine is that in the past, Mr. Unger belonged to an extremist group in Los Angeles that referred to themselves as the Spirit of Hades, or SOH. This was a well-financed and technologically savvy group determined to see the destruction of America.

"We do not know if they were a domestic or international group. Once Homeland Anti-Terror became aware of SOH, the group was somehow warned, and they shut the entire operation down.

"I must stress that we firmly believe Mr. Unger was never a member of the AXE extremist group and was acting on his own with the assistance of some hired accomplices. By linking their own extremist crimes to AXE, he and his cohorts were attempting to ride on the coattails of AXE's infamy. They were also trying to make it appear as though they were part of the recent mass rallies being held throughout the country. Let me stress: they were not."

* * *

The press conference prompts an urgent meeting of the Militant Alliance of America's executive committee at its headquarters.

"So tell me, Ivan, have I been making an idiot of myself in front of the country, condemning these mass gatherings?" Gerald Levin says, directing his anger toward the MAA's own chief of security.

"We were misled, sir. All the data my team collected, including several tips from the public, seemed to indicate this Blackheart character was leading the charge. Someone really wanted us to believe that was the case," Ivan answers, shaking his head in disgust.

"Damn!" Gerald yells, slamming his fist onto the table. "This is really going to set us back. We'll now be lucky if we get *five* percent of the youth vote," he adds, taking a deep breath and slowly regaining his composure.

"Yeah, but when Nicole Kratz officially announces to the public that she's decided to once again represent Anya Ahar, our Peace-Bringer friends will be lucky to get five percent of the over-thirty vote. I'll take our position over theirs any day," asserts Earl Pemberton.

* * *

The day has come to announce to the public that I'll be representing Anya in the Judicial Triangle. While the UCIT crew makes last-minute preparations to broadcast the announcement in front of the Federal Justice Center, I'm joined by Hunter.

"Are you sure about this, Nicole?" he asks nervously.

"I wouldn't be putting myself in front of the country in a few minutes' time if I wasn't," I reply confidently.

And indeed, a few minutes later, I begin speaking calmly, but firmly. "My representation of Anya Ahar in the Judicial Triangle is about attaining some form of justice for a young lady whose mother, upon giving birth to her, was taken from this world in a most horrendous and unforgiving manner. And who was guilty of this egregious act? We were! A society so driven by madness that we didn't think twice about turning hospitals and other government buildings into makeshift prison camps!

"Since Anya's heartbreaking story was made public, it has touched the hearts of many Americans, both young and old. It has prompted us to both lament the past and fear for the future. Her indiscretions were a product of our ignorance, and for that we must make amends by showing compassion and forgiveness. Young Americans across the country have made it abundantly clear how they feel, demanding that both Anya and America be freed from injustice."

Now it's time to drop the bombshell. "In the upcoming hearing I will not only be requesting that Anya Ahar be granted a permanent stay of execution and life in prison; instead, I will be requesting, under a strict set of guidelines, her release from prison."

With every word, I feel a rush of elation. "It is time for young Americans to matter. If I am fortunate enough to become your next president, I guarantee you: *you will matter!*"

At the conclusion of my speech, I relay the fact that Hunter Talbot has been named as my running mate, and also speak of my plans to incorporate youthful representation throughout my administration.

With its eyes flashing between red and blue, and its chest displaying a neon Eye of Providence, Cryptic makes its way toward the podium. "How do you answer to the fact that you want to set free a young lady who has engaged in some very serious crimes?" the robot asks. "Does this mean you believe we should excuse every criminal who claims their tragic past has led them to commit crimes?"

"No, not at all," I reply.

"Then why are you making an exception for Anya Ahar?"

"I'm not here to speak to the specifics of Anya's case. I will do that in the Judicial Triangle," I say firmly.

"Are you not concerned this coddling of Anya Ahar and America's disenfranchised youth will lead the majority outside of that demographic to turn their backs on you as a presidential candidate, and the PBA as a whole?"

"I give the people of this country far more credit than that. This is about bringing all Americans together, regardless of age. And that means creating a government that is reflective of that concept," I state.

* * *

The response from Gerald Levin follows immediately on UCIT. During a gala hosted by Earl Pemberton and his family, celebrating the fiftieth anniversary of ERT Power Corporation, Levin unleashes a vicious verbal tirade.

"As I listened to every preposterous word out of Nicole Kratz's mouth this evening, I kept telling myself, 'This is a nightmare and soon I will awake.' How she can stand in front of the American people and tell us she is going to walk into the Judicial Triangle and ask not only for Anya Ahar to be granted a permanent stay of execution, but be set free and permitted to reenter society, it's complete lunacy!

"Anya Ahar has not only admitted to manufacturing helcin, the poison used to kill General Vance Gibson, she also has admitted to being a leader of a domestic terrorist group, the same group that had planned to blow up six government animal research labs. That's not all; she also assisted in creating a doctrine filled with hatred against the American way of life.

"Nicole Kratz has said we must show Anya Ahar compassion and forgiveness. I find it very interesting that in Miss Ahar we have a scientific genius, yet she doesn't appear to know the most basic difference between right and wrong!" Levin says, his voice rising. The veins in his temples are bulging now.

"Don't fret, my friends; the Militant Alliance of America is here for you. We will lead this country properly, and not allow a deranged terrorist to escape her deserved penalty of death."

* * *

Westgale has called me to the Freedom Home. I'm directed to the main conference room, where he is waiting. I've known President Westgale long enough to sense his imminent fury. It doesn't happen very often, but when he gets angry, his very light complexion turns crimson red.

Before I have time to be seated, he attacks. "What in the hell are you thinking? Released from prison?" he shouts, pounding the table. "You told me you wanted a chance for a permanent stay of execution—not complete freedom!"

I study him a moment, allowing him time to settle down. "I understand your concern, sir, but the people of this country have spoken. And if I'm going to be their leader, I'm damn well going to listen to them," I say firmly.

He shakes his head. "I can't believe they got to you. You're pandering to a group of self-entitled greenhorns who are so lost in their own insecurities that they will go to any length for whatever attention they can get. You know as well as I do that wisdom comes with age and experience, and so does importance and privilege, Nicole. They'll have their turn. When their hair starts graying, their bodies start aching, and their skin starts wrinkling, they'll be the ones doing the dictating," Westgale states, his voice heavy with scorn.

"I thought you understood me better than that, sir. I'm not pandering. I'm strictly standing up for what I believe in. Anya Ahar is a victim. A victim of hatred and greed, stemming from the idiocy of a political divide and that damn war." The words soar now. "It's time for change, Mr. President. And yes, it's time we listen to our youth, and give them a voice. I think it's vital. Why, Mr. President, as a society, is it okay for us to dictate to our country's youth how they should live their lives, without their actual input? And then when they rebel, we shake our heads in disbelief!"

I'm glad to see the president's demeanor is slowly growing calmer. His face, so recently flushed red, is now fading to pink. *Thankfully, he's listening.*

"And tell me, Nicole: how do you expect this to all work out when your little 'scientific genius' is being so defiant with everybody?" he says calmly.

"I'm starting to reach her, sir. I know I am," I reply confidently. "All I ask is that you trust me. You've done some wonderful things for this country, and it's my goal to continue where you left off."

"Well, you're now within reach of the torch, my dear. I just hope it doesn't burn you along the way."

I admit Westgale's concerns are warranted, as I'm well aware of the massive political risk I'll be taking by representing Anya in the Judicial Triangle. I also realize that my open-mindedness toward the country's disenfranchised youth could very well serve as a form of political suicide. But I have a plan. A plan to bring this country together again and ensure that no political divide ever brings about the horror we felt all those years ago.

CHAPTER 10

Before most of my time will be occupied with Anya's hearing, I realize it's vital for my presidential campaign to gain as much momentum as possible. I've been traveling so much the last few days that it's been difficult sometimes to remember where exactly I am. While Gerald Levin's been busy getting his message out on the West Coast, my focus has been on the east. This evening is my third in a row speaking at Summit University in New York City.

Before I take the podium, Jessica Westgale approaches me backstage. "Wow, Nicole, you're really packing them in," she says, looking out at the audience from behind the curtain.

"Jessica, I'm glad you're here. This is excellent timing," I tell her. "My father's been wanting to speak with you."

"Oh?"

"Hold on, he's right over there," I say as I wave him over to us.

He finishes up a conversation with the dean of the school and comes over.

"Hey, Jessica, how was your trip home?" Dad asks her.

"For such a long flight, and considering the fact that flying sure isn't one of my favorite pastimes, I'm just glad it went as well as it did," Jessica replies in her usual cheerful manner.

"Congratulations on the incredible work you performed in Pinia. What you and your team have accomplished is very impressive," Dad tells her.

"Thank you, sir. It really means a lot to me to give back."

"I realize that, and that's why I'd love for you to head up my new foundation."

Jessica hesitates a moment. "You'll have to forgive me, but being out of the country for so long, I'm not familiar with your new foundation."

"It's the Lawrence Kratz Foundation. Its purpose is to assist recovering addicts and ex-cons by providing education, guidance, and financial assistance. We've already received substantial backing from many of the country's largest corporations and philanthropists. Nicole was originally going to take the helm, but as you can see by the crowd of people here today, she's become preoccupied with other things," Dad jokes.

"Well, it sounds like a fantastic cause, and another great way to give back," Jessica replies.

"I can't think of anybody better for the job."

"I have to second that," I add.

"So, what do you say, Jessica?" Dad asks. "Will you at least consider it? I could have my secretary send the details over to you tomorrow morning."

"Great. I'll give it some real thought," Jessica says.

"Take a few days to mull it over, if need be."

I leave Jessica and Dad to firm up the details and peek through the curtain. I'm thrilled to see another outstanding turnout. When I take to the podium, the crowd breaks into a roaring chant of "Nicole for prez!"

From the second I take the stage, it feels as though my supporters and I are riding a giant wave of emotion together. When I look into their eyes, I can see their hearts. They're hurting, yearning for change, craving to be heard. They want a new direction. A new age.

I spend the next forty-five minutes telling them how I will deliver that.

Afterward, when I meet with my campaign team in the dressing room, their faces are sullen and the room is disturbingly silent. "I received the recent poll numbers just as you took the stage," says Beth. "It's not good, Nicole." She looks dejected. Though I'm not surprised, considering the PBA's turmoil in recent months, actually hearing the news hits me hard.

"There's no hiding from the truth. Let's hear the numbers, Beth," I say, trying my best not to display my worry.

"The MAA is leading us fifty-seven percent to thirty-two percent, with eleven percent undecided." This draws a collective gasp from the team. I need to take charge.

"People, we must remain positive. Sure, it's important that we heed what these numbers might tell us, but we can't let results such as these dampen our spirits to the point they hinder our efforts moving forward," I say firmly.

Seated to my right, Hunter begins dissecting the numbers. "The age factor really appears to be in play here," he says with a pained expression. "We're getting absolutely killed when it comes to the thirty-five and older demographic. On the other hand, we're completely dominating the other side of the spectrum."

"Look over here," says Beth, directing our attention to a flash-screen. Cryptic is interviewing famed civil attorney and long-time PBA supporter Gloria Lee.

"Are you surprised by the just-released polling numbers?" the robot asks, displaying the numbers on its chest.

"Absolutely not," Lee replies, glowering. *"I'm actually surprised the PBA is as high as thirty-two percent. Nicole Kratz's campaign has been an outright disaster."*

"Since you were one of the potential candidates who backed out once Ms. Kratz entered the picture, do you have any regrets?"

"Definitely," Lee says with a short nod. *"I'm certain both Justice Malone and myself would have fared much better. In fact, I think there are loads of people who would have fared better."*

"Do you think it's all this pandering to the youth of America that has set her back?" Cryptic asks.

"Actually, I think bringing some youthfulness to our government is a very valid and wise idea," says Lee.

"So when you refer to her campaign as being 'an outright disaster,' what is it you're referring to?"

"How she can stand in front of the American people and tell them it's her wish to free Anya Ahar... Well, it's extremely baffling and disturbing to me, as I know it is to most of my esteemed associates and the majority of the public."

"Do you feel she's letting her sympathy toward Anya cloud her judgment?"

"Certainly. I can't think of another reason why she'd feel so compassionate toward a young lady who displays such contempt for our country."

CHAPTER 11

When people in this country speak of past American presidents, the name "Jackson Snyder" usually stirs up mixed feelings. To PBA followers he is considered a true hero, a Democratic president who steadfastly stood up for his beliefs. Referred to as the War Within President, he has remained somewhat reclusive ever since his administration was so ruthlessly taken over by the Militant Alliance of America. Having been his Attorney General, Dad always spoke of President Snyder with great admiration. I was fortunate to have met him on a few occasions in my younger days, and found him to be gracious with his time. I was pleased that he was interested in hearing about my studies, as well as my thoughts on the current state of the country. When I met him for the second time, which was about two years later, I was amazed that he remembered everything about our prior conversation. That is something I'll never forget.

Among the current politicians who revere President Snyder is President Westgale. Westgale not only admires Snyder, he has patterned his own presidency after his. Everything from his political agenda to the design of his office are influenced by Jackson Snyder.

Now seventy-one years old and widowed, he lives on a farm in West Virginia. Since the day his presidency abruptly ended he has refused to comment on both past and present politics. I remember President Westgale attempting to contact him on several occasions, only to be denied. Several other presidents have received the same response, and so has the UCIT Network which, although it has aired features on his time in office, has never been granted an interview.

Thus I was surprised to hear from his son, Warren, that his father is willing to meet with me. I'm elated to have the opportunity to speak with a man I admire so greatly. The timing couldn't be better, since I'm planning to spend the next few days campaigning in the southern part of the country.

When my driver pulls the electro onto the property, Warren is there to greet me. "It's a pleasure to meet you," he says, leading the way to the house.

"Likewise," I reply.

"I'm really pulling for you in the upcoming election. Your political views remind me so much of my father's. It's what this country so badly needs."

"I'm a great admirer of your father. I'm really honored he's agreed to meet with me." As part of my preparation for Anya's hearing, I'm hoping Snyder will shed some light on how hospitals throughout New York State were converted into detention centers during the War Within. My research has told me that there were actually hundreds of people negatively impacted by the closing of those hospitals: some more than others, like Dr. Ahar and Anya. What my research has failed to tell me is how and why those hospitals were converted into PBA detention centers. I thought about asking my father, but I've learned over the years that even the mere mention of the War Within makes him extremely anxious, which does nothing for his heart condition.

"Actually, I was quite surprised that my father agreed to meet with you," Warren says. "Since the War Within, his interest in politics has been nonexistent. He's really found his peace of mind, out here on the farm."

"That's understandable," I say, admiring the picturesque scenery.

"My family lives in this house here," he says, indicating a rambling red brick house with beautifully crafted arched windows. "And this is where Dad resides," he adds as we turn to our left. "Please, go ahead. He's waiting for you."

"Thank you, Warren."

I approach the walk. This house, built with the same red bricks and arched windows, is a smaller version of his son's.

"There she is," Snyder says as he opens the door, greeting me with a wide smile. "Come on in, my dear. Make yourself at home."

"Thank you, sir. As I was telling your son, I'm truly honored by this," I say as I settle onto the living room sofa. I notice several antique radios and telephones placed throughout the house, which seems devoid of flash-screens, flash-pads, and other modern devices. I wonder how he keeps current. Then again, he probably doesn't care to.

"You should be very proud of yourself, young lady. One step away from taking the captain's seat. It looks like those big dreams you told me about years ago are soon going to come to life," he says as he presents a tray of coffee and biscuits before sinking into an easy chair across from me. Time has not been kind to him. His once rugged features are now fleshy. He has bags under his eyes, and with each movement, pain flashes across his face.

"I am very proud, sir. I've worked very hard to get here, but I've also been very fortunate to have support from President Westgale, and of course my amazing father."

"Speaking of your father, how is he enjoying his retirement?"

I blow air through my lips. "Yeah. Technically he's retired, but with the new foundation he recently created, he'll probably be busier than he's ever been." I tell him about the foundation.

"None of that surprises me. The one thing I'll never forget about Lawrence is how focused he was on his work, and how compassionate he was," Snyder says, smiling. "So, how can I be of assistance to you? I must warn you that if you're looking for political advice, you've come to the wrong place. That game has long passed me by." He chuckles. "Now, if you want some advice on how to grow scrumptious fruits and vegetables, well then, I'm your man."

"I'll keep that in mind, sir," I reply, laughing. "Actually, I'm here to learn some specific details about the War Within. Since the Outer Commission placed a ban on the dissemination of information pertaining to the war, learning what really occurred is a challenge."

"As it should be. I've always believed it's best to look ahead. Digging up the details of that dreadful period can only bring heartache for everyone."

"I agree," I reply, "but there is one thing I desperately need to know."

"Well, if I'm able to, I'll gladly help," Snyder replies as he dips a biscuit into his coffee.

"I was hoping you'd enlighten me regarding the hospitals in New York State—why they ended up being converted into detention centers."

"Ah." He nods slowly. "This must relate to the upcoming Anya Ahar hearing."

"Yes. Are you aware of her story?"

"Somewhat. I try to avoid most current affairs, but I must say I find that particular story fascinating."

"Because I'm representing her, it would help me to learn how and why the decision was made regarding those hospitals."

Snyder sighs, looking pained. "I'm not trying to tell you how to go about arguing your case, but like I said, I think it's wise to not revisit that horrid period."

"Believe me when I tell you the last thing I want to do is relive that bloody war, but for me to be successful in that hearing, I have no choice," I answer, studying Snyder, who is definitely on edge. But why? "With all due respect, sir, is there something you're afraid to tell me?"

He takes a deep breath and slowly exhales. "Well, as much as it pains me to do this, I think it's in your best interest to know the truth."

"I need the truth, sir. I really do," I reply, trying to keep my voice even.

"My Administration was well aware the MAA had been formed, and we feared an attack was imminent. We also knew that no matter how hard we tried to fight back, we were going to be taken over, so our key members quickly began putting together a plan to create the Peace Bringers Association," Snyder begins.

"I'm aware of all that," I reply.

"But are you aware that it was your father's idea to convert those hospitals into detention centers? There was even an official document that he signed off on. And I backed his decision."

I'm in shock. My heart begins to pound like a drum. "Oh my Lord," I finally sigh. "I take it that includes Green Light Memorial?" That was the hospital Dr. Jack Ahar and his wife Maria were denied entrance to on that dreadful day.

"I'm sorry, Nicole. I hate laying this on you, but it's the truth."

"I can't believe this," I say. I bury my head in my hands. "Why wouldn't he have told me about this?" My voice comes out muffled.

"It was one of those decisions we all regretted," Snyder says gently.

I drop my hands and look at him. "And what became of that document?"

"When the White House was attacked, more than ninety percent of everything was destroyed," he says somberly, "except for the contents of my office area."

I catch my breath. "Is that where the document was stored?"

"Yes."

"So, do you still have it stashed away somewhere?"

Snyder shakes his head. "I wish I did, but regrettably, it was taken from my office."

"How do you know that?" Disappointment makes my question sound harsher than I'd intended.

"I was there when it was taken. Several men wearing long overcoats and carrying flash-pads and briefcases stormed in and began taking everything they could get their hands on, including that document," Snyder replies. He seems nervous, as if he's reliving the moments in his mind. "I never informed your father that this happened."

"Now I know why whenever I or anyone else brings up the War Within, Dad becomes all worked up and quickly changes the topic."

"It was war, Nicole, and in war, decisions are usually a product of fear and panic... which is why I find being Jackson the farmer far less taxing than being Jackson the president."

While flying to New York to discuss this matter with Dad, I'm lost in thought. It feels like the wind has left my sails. Questions keep racing through my mind. Does the MAA have possession of that document? If so, are they planning to use it during the hearing? How will I be able to stand in the middle of that triangle and fight for Anya, knowing very well my own father was the person who ordered that hospital to be closed?

Damn it! I was so confident I could win this hearing. Now I don't even know if I have a right to take part in it. All this, just when Anya's beginning to open up to me. Just when, little by little, I'd felt as though I was pulling her out of her emotional abyss.

"Your father told me to inform you he'll be by shortly," Mom says as I settle in at my parents' house. "Is everything okay, Nicole? You seem rather stressed."

"I'm sorry, Mom, but I have a lot on my mind," I reply.

She chuckles. "I wonder why that doesn't surprise me. In all seriousness, you be careful, honey. I realize the position you're in, but too much stress can be very unhealthy."

"Thanks, Mom; I'll do my best to take things in stride."

"Hey, before your dad comes home, would you give me your opinion on some paint colors? I've finally decided to make some changes around here."

As I stare blankly at the various sample files on Mom's flash-pad, I try my best to hide my anxiety, but she knows me too well. "All right, Nicole, are you going to tell me what actually has you so uptight? You know you can always confide in me."

I try to compose myself as I take a deep breath. "I'm okay, Mom... I like this group here; I don't think you can go wrong with any of—"

"Nicole, sorry I kept you waiting," Dad says as he enters the living room. "I just finished meeting with Jessica, and I'm glad to tell you she's accepted my offer," he adds happily.

"I'm glad to hear that," I reply solemnly.

Dad instantly notices I'm subdued. "What's going on, Nicole?" he asks, studying me closely. "What is it that's so important?"

"Can we please take this into your office?" I ask.

"Of course," he answers with a raised brow, and leads the way. Mom watches us curiously.

Once inside, he closes the office door behind us. "My Lord, Nicole, I'm afraid to ask... how did it go down south? You seem so preoccupied. Did something happen on the campaign trail to bring you down?"

"Actually, for the most part, it went rather well. But then there was West Virginia."

"What happened in West Virginia?"

"I met with President Snyder."

"Jackson? I'll be darned. What made you go see him? I'm surprised he agreed to meet with you."

"I'm so glad he did. It was very enlightening," I reply.

"How so?"

I pause and take a deep breath. "How come you didn't tell me?" I ask gently.

"What... what didn't I tell you?"

"Green Light Memorial. The hospitals. I know it was you who was responsible for turning them into detention centers. How could you not tell me you signed off on that order? Did you not think that I was going to eventually find out?"

Dad appears startled. He takes a deep breath of his own and then exhales. "I thought about telling you; believe me, I did."

"Were you not concerned I'd learn about it from another source? After all, it's such a key issue in Anya's hearing."

"To my knowledge, President Snyder is the only person who knows I signed off on that document. Besides, it was probably buried in the White House rubble."

"But it wasn't. The MAA confiscated it from Snyder's office."

"My Lord. I had no idea... But I wouldn't fret, honey," he assures me. "I'll bet that document's been long forgotten."

"I just wish you would've told me."

Dad sighs and rubs his hands over his flushed face. "I'm sorry, Nicole."

"Anya's entire case revolves around the fact that hospital was shut down. Her mother died because of it."

"And it's downright terrible that she did. But nobody, and I mean *nobody*, wanted anything like that to happen," Dad answers sincerely. He continues in a sympathetic tone. "Do you think I *wanted* to shut those hospitals down? That war made us all do some crazy things."

"What if they have the document and expose it? I'm dreading not only what it will do to Anya's chances, but also the impact it'll have on my presidential bid and your legacy of excellence."

"I agree. It'll be devastating on all fronts. If you wish, I'll gladly go public with the truth before it comes to that. And distance you from the entire story."

"I can't let you do that. There has to be another option," I say, deep in thought.

"Regrettably, I think it might be our only recourse, honey."

"No, I can't let you do it," I insist. "I'd rather defend your honor in the triangle—if it comes to that."

"Is that your flash-pad buzzing?" Dad asks.

"Yes, it is," I reply as I reach for the device. "Whoa... this is interesting," I say as I check the message.

"Who's it from?" Dad asks.

"Andy Pemberton. He's asking me to meet him at the Last Frontier in an hour."

"Brr. It's a chilly one out there," Andy says as we meet in the lobby of the steakhouse.

"Mr. Pemberton, your table's ready," the hostess says, and leads us through the restaurant.

"My Lord, Andy, this is the very same table we sat at the day the war began," I say, painfully recalling that dreadful afternoon.

Andy smiles and chuckles. "And now it looks like the two of us will soon be fighting our own war in the Judicial Triangle. Unless of course you've come to your senses and have decided to back away from this charade."

"I had a feeling they were going to put you up against me."

"It's actually an honor to be going up against somebody of your caliber. But what I can't believe is that you're willing to risk your entire reputation, not to mention your political future, on a terrorist. Oh, and don't give me this 'she's merely an innocent victim' garbage. The woman's pure evil."

"Did you invite me here to antagonize me? Or is there actually a purpose to this meeting?"

"I don't know about you, but I'm starving. I think a nice juicy rib eye will do the job," Andy says as he regards the menu in front of him.

"You didn't answer my question."

"Nicole, I can't antagonize you no matter how hard I try, and I've learned that from experience. Even in the playground: those sand castles you made—all us other kids used to be so envious. It even reached a point where I was convinced you were using some kind of magic sand. I mean, the imagination and detail you put into those things—true works of art. Then of course at Summit, I remember thinking how well I did on an assignment, and then you'd sit there with that big smile as the professor congratulated you on your perfect score."

"Okay, please tell me where you're going with this, Andy," I insist.

He looks at me with a sly grin as the waiter pours us each a glass of wine. That grin—it's the same grin he's had since he was a kid. It's one of those grins that's sometimes hard to read—it's not clear whether he's being friendly, or he's mocking you. "Please, Nicole, I'm paying tribute to your brilliance."

"I appreciate your kind words... I think. But I've always preferred looking ahead to dwelling on the past."

"Good, because the real reason I invited you here is to make a deal regarding Anya Ahar."

"Oh?"

"The last thing any of us wants, or this country needs, for that matter, is this ridiculous hearing."

I'm caught off guard. "Well then, let's hear what you have to offer."

Andy leans forward and studies me a moment. "We're willing to grant Miss Ahar a permanent stay of execution."

"And, what's the catch?"

"It's very simple. Life in prison with no chance of parole."

"For someone who just finished praising my so-called 'brilliance,' someone who has known me almost my entire life, you really don't have a clue what I'm about," I say, controlling my indignation.

"Take the deal, Nicole, and end this farce. Or else this time, I guarantee you, I finally will build a better castle… and unfortunately, I'll also be bringing your father down in the process."

"My father?"

"Yeah, it'd be so sad to see such an honorable man's reputation be so tarnished," he says as he places a piece of paper in front of me.

The nightmare has come true. There it is: my father's signature. I remain calm on the outside, but in truth, I'm a nervous wreck as I read the document. I slowly look up, and that grin has returned to Andy's face. This time I'm certain it's the mocking kind. "The MAA gives you our word that America will never learn it was your father who ordered the closure of those hospitals, if you accept our proposal."

I scowl at Andy. "You can take your proposal back to your uncle and Gerald Levin and tell them that no matter how hard you try, you'll *never* get the best of me," I say. I get up and stalk out of the steakhouse.

Later that evening, Dad contacts me via his flash-pad. "How did it go with Andy?" he asks.

"Like we feared, he has the document. He proposed a deal."

"Let me guess: he'll give you a chance to save your good ol' dad's reputation if you back down."

"Exactly."

"Well, I just hope to God you didn't give in."

"No way. Giving in just isn't my thing. Someone very special taught me that a long time ago."

CHAPTER 12

"Her playing is outstanding. Technically strong, but she also plays with incredible feeling," Terence Dwyer, director of the Dwyer Academy of Music, says to Shadow and Jessica as Luanda auditions for a teaching job.

"This is one of my original compositions," Luanda says as she continues to play with unbridled passion.

"That was extraordinary. Breathtakingly beautiful," Dwyer exclaims when she finishes. "I'm glad you contacted me, Jessica. I've been attempting to fill this position for quite some time. Welcome aboard, Luanda," he calls out.

On the way back to the apartment, Luanda can't contain her excitement. "Wow, thank you, Jessica. To be able to teach at Dwyer is a dream come true."

"You earned it, Luanda. Terence was very impressed with you," Jessica replies.

"And he wasn't just impressed with your musical ability and knowledge. He also told me he thought you handled the sample class with real professionalism," Shadow adds.

They enter the building and cross its luxurious lobby. "Every time I walk by this fountain, I'm just so taken by its beauty," Luanda says with a smile as she gazes appreciatively at a golden sculpture of seraphim angels flying above a lavender waterfall. She looks back to Jessica and Shadow. "I can't believe this is happening to me. I owe so much to the both of you."

She's invited them to dinner. After enjoying an array of appetizers, they settle down for the entrée. "This is absolutely delicious, Luanda," Jessica says as she takes a bite of spinach mushroom quiche.

"Cooking isn't a real passion of mine, but Kolton, he just loves creating all kinds of new dishes. He actually showed me how to make this quiche," Luanda replies.

"Speaking of your dear husband, is he going to be joining us this evening?" Jessica asks.

Luanda smiles and nods. "Yes. In fact, he's planning to pick up dessert for us," she says, her smile widening. "I'm so happy for him. His rehab counselor told me he's been showing great improvement on a daily basis."

An hour later, Luanda receives a message from Kolton informing her he's on his way. "So, it looks like we'll finally be able to meet the lucky man," Jessica says.

"Once you meet him, I think you'll realize that *I'm* the lucky one," Luanda replies.

"When and where did you meet?" Shadow asks.

"I met him a little more than two years ago. Actually, he came to me for piano lessons. He hoped learning to play the piano would help to relieve his stress. I think it actually worked, somewhat."

"Well, kudos to him for fighting so hard," Jessica says gently.

"The crazy thing is, just when it looks like he's found the light, he reaches for the bottle and descends back into his world of darkness," Luanda replies, her eyes downcast.

"I can only imagine how difficult it must be for you," Jessica says.

"When you care for someone as much as I care for Kolton, you fight the battles with them. I'm really hoping, this time, he'll finally win the war," Luanda says thoughtfully.

Moments later, following a gentle knock on the door, a booming voice calls out, "The guest of honor has arrived!" Luanda quickly rises, beaming, and goes to open the door. "Hello, my darling," Kolton says. Luanda moves forward to give him a kiss. "I hope everyone likes a good old-fashioned chocolate cake," he adds, holding up the box.

Shadow studies him for a moment. He immediately notices the burn scar on his right cheek. Luanda had said it was the result of a workplace accident.

"I've heard so much about both of you," Kolton says when Luanda introduces him to Jessica and Shadow. "Wow, this place is incredible," he adds as his gaze sweeps across the apartment. He looks to Shadow and Jessica. "Thank you for what you've done. When I get back on my feet, I promise to somehow return the favor."

"I received some great news today, Kolton. I got the job at Dwyer Academy," Luanda says joyfully.

"Whoa, that is good news. I knew they wouldn't be able to resist bringing you on board," Kolton responds as he gives her a hug.

"Well, I wish I could take the credit, but Jessica's the one who made it happen," Luanda says, looking at Jessica.

"Oh, that's not true," Jessica protests. "Let me tell you, I know Terence Dwyer, and there's no way he would've hired you if he didn't believe you were the right person for the job."

"I'm sure he must've immediately felt the passion you feel for your music," Kolton says as he begins serving the cake.

"Even as a child, that was always obvious to me," Shadow says.

"And it's always a wonderful thing to be able to follow one's passion in life," Jessica adds.

"It sure is," Kolton replies. "Although for me, following mine didn't work out so well."

"Oh? How so?" Shadow asks.

"Well, at a young age I became fascinated with creating things, and discovering how everything came to be," Kolton says. "Let's just say I was a curious little bugger. By the time I was a teenager I'd become very interested in things like alchemy and modern chemistry. That eventually led to me studying pyrotechnics and explosives. As I was becoming quite advanced in the field, one of my instructors got me a job with the country's leading weapons manufacturer, Direct Aim. It happened not long before the War Within. And after only six months, I was promoted to a senior position."

* * *

"Come on in, Kolton," said Direct Aim's managing director, Van Smithson. "Have a seat, young man." He indicated a chair in front of his desk.

Kolton sat down, nervously wondering why this meeting was taking place.

"So, let me start out by asking you how you've enjoyed your first six months at Direct Aim," Smithson said.

"Very much so, sir," Kolton replied. "I'm grateful for the opportunity."

"I'm glad to hear that," Smithson said in his gravelly voice. "Many of our employees don't last more than six days. We're very demanding around here, and with good reason. Here, read this."

He slid his flash-pad across his desk to Kolton.

"It's only a matter of time before those HKM parasites attempt to bring about our end," he said angrily while Kolton read a First Source News report. "As a country, we must be prepared. And it's us, Kolton, as the backbone of the US military, who must continue to innovate. That's why I called you here today."

"I'll gladly contribute however I can, Mr. Smithson."

"Great, because I want to follow through with the development of the zap-grenade design you've been working on. I see great potential there."

"I don't know, sir; it'll take quite a bit of time and a lot of resources to see that through."

"That's why I'm promoting you to head up your own development team. I'll be giving you nine months and sufficient funding to complete the project. Think of it as your baby," Smithson said with a sinister laugh.

* * *

"Come on, Kolton, don't do this to yourself," Luanda abruptly interjects. "This is supposed to be a joyous evening."

"It's okay, Lu, I've got it under control. Besides, my counselors have told me that sometimes it's cathartic to be open and face my demons straight on," he answers calmly. He continues, "Well, when they promoted me, it was like a dream come true." He pauses and takes a deep breath. "At times I had as many as twenty people working under me. And all that time—"

"Please, Kolton," an anxious Luanda calls out. "I don't want you doing this. We've agreed to leave all that in the past."

"Okay, you win, my darling." Kolton sighs. "You're right. This should be a joyous evening. That's all in the past." With a sudden burst of energy, he exclaims, "Please, play for us, Luanda." He gestures toward the piano.

* * *

"Hey, Nicole, I think you'd better check this out," Beth says as she places her flash-pad on my desk. "Central Park on Saturday. Judging by these messages, they not only want you to attend, they're requesting you lead the rally."

"Whoa, they're expecting thirty thousand."

"And that's not all," Beth adds. "There's at least another ten rallies being scheduled right across the country in the coming days."

"Well, get the rest of the crew together, and let's get ready to do some traveling."

Thankfully, it's a splendid afternoon. A light dusting of snow covers the ground, and the barren trees appear majestic under a large golden sun. The air is cool, but comfortable. As was the case when I viewed the prior gatherings on UCIT, I remain in awe of the diversity of this massive group. What has really captured my attention is the contingent of middle-aged people who have now joined in.

The atmosphere is highly festive, with various styles of music playing. People are dancing and singing, others are mingling around bonfires. I meet with the organizers in a cordoned-off area. There is a large contingent of event security. My own personal security team is also on site. Some surround me, and some are incognito, scattered throughout the park. I spend time greeting and speaking with members of the crowd. Their words of encouragement are very satisfying. The predominant message is clear: please do whatever it takes to fix this current mixed-up state of affairs.

It's early evening, and my time has come. A large crew scrambles to prepare the stage. Several mammoth flash-screens are set up around the park, along with several stacks of specialized lights. One of my senior advisers pulls me aside to wish me good luck. A rush of adrenaline guides me to the podium. The crowd begins to chant in unison, "Free Anya! Free America!" There's certainly no way I'm about to interrupt. After a minute or so, the crowd breaks into a thunderous cheer. The sound is deafening.

I immediately become concerned when I look to my right and notice a group of young men dressed in military-type clothes, just standing there, gazing around the grounds. It's eerie. There has to be at least twenty of them, and they are being met with all kinds of nasty stares from the crowd. I'm dreading where this could lead.

Through my flash-pad, I immediately alert Mitch, the leader of my security team. He informs me that security has been monitoring the group closely for the last fifteen minutes, and they're prepared to take action if need be. I can't help but think back to that tragic day when JD Wren set himself on fire while I was speaking at the Field of Honor. Nevertheless, the show must go on.

"Hello, my fellow Americans. Thank you for allowing me this incredible opportunity to address you this evening," I bellow at the top of my voice. I'm granted their immediate attention. "You have spoken, and I have listened. And together we will lead America into the future." My words are met with more thunderous applause. I keep the group of extremists in the corner of my eye. Nervously, I continue. "They say 'youth is wasted on the young.' Well, the time has come to put that adage to rest.

"Gerald Levin would like to have you believe America is in a state of extreme peril. Believe me when I tell you this is simply not true. The VX drug plan and the Pinian energy deal are without a doubt the two greatest events in this country's recent history. Soon the return of our complete independence and the reinstatement of our sacred Constitution will help us recapture what it truly means to be American."

I notice the extremist group is now in the center of the audience, facing me. The tension is mounting, but I won't relent. Trying to avoid making eye contact with them, I draw a deep breath, but before I can continue, one of them hollers aggressively, "And what about the military? Are you going to continue chopping it to pieces?"

The crowd jeers. Members of both my personal security team and the event's security staff are now on high alert, ready for action.

This outburst puts me on edge, but I calmly reply, "Thank you for that question, sir. It is a very important one." I repeat the question through the sound-blast, then provide my answer. "I won't stand here and deny that the Westgale Administration has been doing exactly what you just said. And I will tell you as the Administration's former executive director, those cutbacks *were* necessary. But through the efficiencies that will be reaped from the VX drug plan and the Pinian energy deal, I'm thrilled to announce that as president, I will have the opportunity to reinvest in our military, and I will."

When I finish my response, the extremists appear satisfied by my answer and peacefully turn away. *Phew, what a relief.*

"In the coming days, I will be entering the Judicial Triangle in an attempt to right a wrong. Maria Ahar should never have died out on that icy street, that cold winter morning. Where she should have been was in the warm confines of Green Light Memorial Hospital, lovingly holding her newborn daughter, Anya, in her arms. Even my own father, the Honorable Lawrence Kratz, was a victim of this broken system. As US Attorney General at the time, it was he who was forced to make the decision to close several New York State hospitals, including Green Light. It is a decision he regrets to this day. It was a decision that stemmed from the madness of war—a war that forced even the most compassionate of our citizens to compromise their deepest beliefs. Through goodwill and proper governance, we must ensure such a tragic event will never happen again. God bless you."

As I turn away from the podium, I'm whisked down a path cleared by my security into a waiting grand-electro. The crowd erupts into a frenzy. As we head off, I hear the resounding chant of "Nicole for Prez!"

When I tune in to UCIT on the electro's flash-screen, I watch Cryptic approach a middle-aged lady.

"Hello, ma'am. What brings you out here this evening?" the robot asks.

"I think Nicole Kratz has hit on something that is long overdue," she replies before sipping from a cup of hot chocolate.

"Are you not concerned that people of your age group and older will think she's pandering to some kind of young persons' revolution?"

"It's that way of thinking that will always keep us divided. We need a president with an open and fresh mind to help this country continue to be the greatest country on earth. Nicole Kratz is that president. I'm also thrilled to know Hunter Talbot will be by her side. I'll always be grateful to that young man. For God's sake, his teal-berry discovery saved my granddaughter's life."

"Do you not think the office of the country's executive director and seats on the Strategic Council should be reserved for those who are more seasoned?"

"I used to think that way, but look where that has got us. We must change with the times. I think it's so very important that our government represents all adult age groups accordingly."

"That's it. This is the kind of thing the campaign needs," Beth says to me in the back of the electro as we watch the interview.

"Hopefully, we'll be able to continue gaining momentum," I reply as we begin preparing our itinerary for the rest of the rallies.

I'm truly humbled by the support I'm receiving right across the country. And fortunately, support is beginning to come from all ages. But will it be enough? When we return home from the final rally, my team meets at our headquarters. Together we wait for the new polling numbers to be announced. "There's no doubt in my mind we're closing the gap," Hunter says as he paces the floor. "Did you see that response in Los Angeles? The amazing thing is, a third of those people had to be over the age of forty."

"We have to be careful, Hunter," I reply. "Just because they attended those rallies doesn't mean they're on board with us. Ah, here we go," I say as UCIT appears on the flash-screen.

The usual dissonant sound effects precede the arrival of Cryptic. "Good evening, America," the robot says in its monotone voice.

"I can't wait until the country can get rid of that damn machine. It's given me the creeps since I was a kid," Beth says, attempting to lessen the tension in the room. It's not working.

"I'm here to announce the results of the most recent national poll in relation to the upcoming federal election," the robot says. "The current leader at forty-four percent is Gerald Levin representing the Militant Alliance of America. Nicole Kratz, representing the Peace Bringers Association of America, is at thirty-seven percent, while nineteen percent of Americans are undecided."

"It's an improvement, but obviously it's not enough," I say to my team. As usual, Hunter begins analyzing the details from UCIT's view-file page.

"If I were Levin I'd be rather concerned. He dropped thirteen percent," Hunter says as he continues studying the screen.

"Yeah, but we only rose five percent," Beth responds.

"Like I thought, the undecided voters are going to be the key to this entire election," Hunter adds.

"Have faith, Hunter, we'll eventually win them over," I respond, attempting to convince myself.

* * *

With concern running deep at the PBA, Thor Hardy calls the president to his office for a meeting. "We had it, William. We had it locked up. With the VX drug and the Pinian deal, there was no way we were going to lose," Hardy says in frustration. "Now because of this bloody obsession Nicole has with that damn extremist, we might as well just hand the keys of the Freedom Home over to Levin."

"I understand your concern, Thor, but at least the most recent numbers are showing an improvement," Westgale replies, trying to bring some calm to the conversation.

"An improvement? As of now, only thirty-seven percent of Americans are on our side. And once that damn hearing begins, that number will probably be cut in half." Hardy takes a deep breath and slowly exhales. "Can't you get through to her, Mr. President? I know how she looks up to you. I fear it's our only hope. She needs to be done with Anya Ahar."

"Have you seen those gatherings? The numbers are growing daily. In essence, Nicole's doing what any good politician is supposed to do: she's listening to the people," Westagle says with conviction.

"Are you telling me you're on board with her? That you're okay with setting free a woman who manufactured helcin, planned to blow up six buildings, and helped to create a venomous doctrine that goes against all this country stands for?"

"A woman who did these things because our messed-up system of governance killed her mother," Westgale answers, his voice rising. "And if the people of this nation see her tragic story as the reason for change, then it's time we listen."

"So, are we just going to give in to every public rallying call from now on?"

"Believe me, Thor, I was every bit as angry as you when I heard what Nicole had in mind, but as I've watched these recent events unfold, I've come to realize how this story has opened the eyes and touched the hearts of so many."

"My Lord, William, for every person Anya Ahar's story has 'touched,' I would say there's five times as many people who are appalled by everything she stands for."

"Give Nicole time, Thor. I have complete faith in her. There's no doubt in my mind she'll turn this around."

"I'm sorry. I know how much you think of her, but this is complete lunacy," Hardy says as he places a piece of paper on his desk. "And what I find the most disturbing is the *reason* she's doing this."

"The reason?"

"Come on, Mr. President, you can't be that naïve. This is all about redeeming herself," Hardy responds, removing a gold pen from its holder. "I saw the look in her eyes when I announced my decision in the triangle, preventing her precious Anya from being allowed to search for that cure," he adds, pulling the paper closer to himself. "Heck, she even resigned from your Administration right afterward."

"So you think she's doing this in vain?" Westgale snaps back. "You don't know a damn thing about Nicole!"

"Maybe I don't. But I do know a thing or two about reality. And the reality is, Nicole Kratz is going to bring down this entire association, and I won't be going down with the ship," Hardy says as he applies his signature to the piece of paper. "And now it's *my* turn to resign, effective immediately." He slides the paper over to Westgale, who studies it.

Westgale lifts his gaze back to Hardy and says quietly, "It's a shame you feel this way, Thor, because I'm confident Nicole Kratz will be the greatest president this country has ever seen."

CHAPTER 13

"This is going to be very damaging to our integrity," Westgale says as he informs me of Thor Hardy's resignation as chairman of the PBA. "Thor's been an integral part of this association since its creation."

I nod as the implications churn through my mind. "I'm sorry to hear he decided to resign," I say. "I knew he was disappointed in my platform, but—"

"Oh, he was a little more than disappointed... He was furious. Thankfully, the perfect replacement is totally on board with your agenda."

This nudges the insecurity out of the mix. "Justice Malone?" I say with a hint of eagerness.

"Yes. I spoke with Phillip a few hours ago, and he's thrilled with the opportunity. Director Perry and I will be recommending him to council in the coming days. I'm certain they'll vote in his favor."

"I want to thank you for continuing to place your trust in me, sir. You don't know how much it means to me," I say with a rush of emotion.

"And for the sake of not only this association, but this entire country, I hope that trust isn't misplaced."

This evening is the one and only occasion where I'll be in a face-to-face debate with Gerald Levin. The setting is the Prestige Hotel's ballroom. The moderator is Cryptic. The in-house audience is composed of American citizens who were randomly selected by

UCIT. They've been ordered to remain completely silent during the event. Outside the ballroom, hundreds are gathered around the property, watching on flash-screens, while millions watch on the World Connect.

After Cryptic formally begins the proceedings, we're both allotted two minutes to present our case for being president. We then spend the next hour or so vigorously debating the usual topics, such as the economy, the military, the environment, technology, and energy.

Now it's time for the fireworks as Cryptic asks us to explain to America why we believe our opponent isn't presidential material. Since the PBA is the current governing power, it's my choice whether or not to speak first. I defer.

Gerald takes a sip of water and looks directly into the camera. "I have great respect for Nicole Kratz," he begins. "I find her extremely intelligent, and I believe she cares deeply for America. Unfortunately, she's been so immersed in the culture of the PBA and the Westgale Administration that I'm afraid her judgment, or lack thereof, when it comes to important political issues is completely laughable. The fact that she is in full support of Westgale's Pinian energy deal tells us everything we need to know. Yes, my friends, she's willing to make deals with dictators. My America doesn't make deals with dictators. In fact, during my first day in office, I will have that deal terminated.

"My America also doesn't embrace and show compassion toward domestic terrorists. Ms. Kratz's obsession with aiding Anya Ahar is extremely disturbing. The worst part of all is that she's using this as a political device. When she witnessed those recent mass gatherings of our disenfranchised youth, and heard their ludicrous rallying call demanding Anya Ahar be set free, she followed the wave, seized the moment, and saw it as a way to gain mass popularity with our country's youth. In my America, a president is a strong and determined leader—not a follower."

"Ms. Kratz, please tell us why you believe Mr. Levin is not presidential material," Cryptic says.

"Hmm... Anya Ahar, a political device? I'm sorry to disappoint you, Mr. Levin, but I actually think of Anya Ahar as a human being. Troubled? Yes, but nonetheless a human being. And a brilliant human being, at that. A young lady whose psychological trauma stemmed from the tragic death of her mother during the very war that *you* and your cohorts created.

"Now, you are correct when you suggest a president must be a strong leader. But in the end, as we've discovered throughout history, a leader can only guide his or her followers to where they *want* to go. And the only way this can be done is by listening, shaping a direction, and then guiding. Is it realistic for Mr. Levin to stand here and tell you how you should feel, as if you're his own personal robots? Of course not. I guess in his America, human emotion should be suppressed, and the country's youth are to be controlled and not heard. In his America, only society's elite matter.

"And yes, even though I was not part of the Westgale Administration when the Pinian energy deal came to fruition, I do fully support it. I'm well aware of the careful thought and analysis that went into the deal, and I plan to continue moving forward with it if I'm privileged enough to lead this country. It's a monumental international deal that will enable us to regain our full independence.

"I find it interesting that Mr. Levin claims his America doesn't make deals with dictators. If I recall correctly, is this not the same person who set up shop in the HKM to manufacture his treasured consumer robots? In *my* America, there's no room for hypocrisy."

"Now it's time for both candidates to answer one question from the audience," Cryptic says as it turns around to face the crowd with its chest displaying a neon map of America. "Is there a Laura Foster in the audience?" the robot asks.

"Yes, over here," a lady in her thirties calls out.

"I believe you have a question for Nicole Kratz," Cryptic says.

"Yes. While I'm on board with your political agenda and feel you'd make an outstanding president, I still remain very uneasy about why you believe a person like Anya Ahar deserves to be free.

If you are successful in accomplishing that goal, how would I then explain this to my children?"

"Thank you for the question, Laura. It's a very important one," I say as I remove the sound-blast from the podium and move closer to the audience. "I hope you and the rest of America will understand that since I'll be representing Anya Ahar in her upcoming Judicial Triangle hearing, I'm somewhat limited in what I can and cannot say at this time. However, I'd like to make it very clear that I would not be making this request if I believed Anya Ahar posed any threat whatsoever to our society, or if I didn't believe she'd end up being a great contributor to our society. If I am successful in having Anya freed, it will happen through our current justice system, and I think that's the most important thing your children need to know."

"Thank you, Ms. Kratz," Cryptic says. It calls on a middle-aged man to question Gerald Levin.

"Mr. Levin. How can you denounce the Pinian energy deal when it now appears to be our only hope of paying off the debt owed to the Outer Commission?"

"Great question, sir," Gerald says, then pauses to gather his thoughts. "I recommend all Americans visit our MAA view-file page. On there you will find the detailed plan we proposed to the Westgale Administration some three years ago. That very plan, if implemented, would easily have paid off that debt without having to resort to doing business with a dictator such as Cobra Pix. Sadly, President Westgale didn't even have the decency to respond. And when they tell you the Pinian deal is the only current hope, they are misleading you. Many of the strategies in the plan we proposed can still be utilized to meet that deadline. Those, in conjunction with our proposed international VX drug program, would easily enable us to pay off the debt. I, along with my business advisers, would gladly sit down with the Westgale Administration and provide assistance, if they so wish."

Cryptic turns to me. "Would you care to respond, Ms. Kratz?"

"Sure," I reply, attempting to remain calm. "As the former executive director to President Westgale, I can tell you why we didn't respond to the MAA's proposal. It was an insult to both the PBA and America. This farce of a plan showed complete disregard for our environmental laws, and of course provided great long-term financial incentives for none other than ERT Power. It also called for an increase in the sale of armaments to foreign interests, the elimination of the World Harmony Program, and a massive depletion of our space program. And as far as their 'international VX drug program' is concerned, it would mean three-quarters of our supply would leave the country. That is completely unacceptable, especially when a solution is already in place."

When the debate ends and I exit the stage, Beth tells me she has some upsetting news. "Lay it on me, Beth. For all I know, Gerald Levin could already be all over this," I say.

"It relates to the hospitals, and the fact your father's the person who ordered them to be closed."

I nod, not surprised. "I was worried how the public would react."

"Actually, the public has accepted the news extremely well."

I stop and look at her. "Then what's the problem?"

"It's Dr. Ahar. He just returned from Europe and he's demanding to meet with you. He's furious."

"Well, I can't blame him. Please set something up."

Hunter rushes into the hotel foyer, immediately getting my attention. "Wow, it's quite a gathering out there," he says, attempting to catch his breath. "Thank God security's out in full force."

"Are most with us or against us?" Beth asks.

"From what I can gather, it's fairly even," Hunter replies. He gestures at a flash-screen on the wall near a seating area, and we move to it to watch.

I catch my breath. Outside the Prestige Hotel, it's clear that tension has been building. Now it threatens to boil over as supporters on either side begin waging a verbal war:

"Get it through your thick skull: Nicole Kratz is supporting a terrorist!" a middle-aged man shouts at a young woman.

"Why's she a terrorist? Because she wrote a doctrine describing her vision of America. That's called free speech," the young woman replies.

"Listen, princess, that demented little extremist you're so fond of tried to blow up government buildings and kill innocent people," the man shouts back getting right in her face.

"Get a life, buddy," she snaps back.

Suddenly, a young man comes between them. "Hey man, the people who work in those buildings treat animals in the most inhumane ways imaginable. AXE would have done us all a favor if they'd blown those buildings to kingdom come," he says matter-of-factly.

Others quickly join the fray. Several small skirmishes break out. Security moves in.

"So, what do you make of all this?" Cryptic asks a man wearing a yellow raincoat, standing away from the ruckus.

"It's so sad," he says, shaking his head. He looks around and raises his voice. "People, we should be rejoicing."

"Rejoicing? For what reason?" Cryptic asks politely.

"We've recently witnessed the coming of a higher power and we're focusing on the stupidity of politics?" he replies.

"I take it you're speaking of the Vexton Gleam?" Cryptic asks.

"Right on, my friend." The man becomes animated. "It'll probably shock the country to hear this, but there were several shimmering turquoise lights seen in forest areas across the country that night."

"How do you know this?" asks Cryptic. "Are you some kind of mystery chaser?"

"Actually, until recently, I worked for the National Space Department, investigating unsolved mysteries."

"Did you quit?"

"Of course; I'm way too honest." The man zips up his raincoat and tightens his rain cap before abruptly walking away.

The UCIT camera pans the unruly crowd, and the picture fades to black.

"What was with *that* guy?" Beth says, perplexed.

"I don't know. But that's the first I've heard of this," I reply with a raised brow.

* * *

At the Freedom Home, Executive Director Dave Perry was watching the same newscast. He reaches for his flash-pad even as the mysterious man in the yellow raincoat walks away from the robot.

"Hey, Red, did you see that guy who just appeared on UCIT?" he asks Major Redford Cunningham, Director of National Space, when he connects. "What in the world was that all about? Please tell me he was just some kook."

"I'm looking into it, sir," the major answers, his voice gruff with concern. "I'll be by with some answers for you in the next half-hour."

"Come on in, Red," Perry says as he waves the major into his office twenty minutes later. "Can I get you a coffee?" he asks as they settle in.

"Thanks, but I think I've already had my fill of coffee for today," replies the lanky grizzled aeronautical engineer.

"So, what were you able to find out about our friend in the raincoat?" Perry asks.

The major groans and runs a hand through his silvery hair. "He's for real," he answers. "His name's Noah Robbins. And yes, he did work as a case analyst in Unsolved Mysteries."

Perry stands and begins pacing. "Was he being truthful?"

"According to our records, he was," Red replies, his tone cautious. "The case file indicates that, including Vexton, there were sightings reported from fourteen different locations across the country that night. And like Robbins said, they were all in forested areas. Most of the flash-messages came from campers and a few were from pilots."

"And you guys did nothing about it!" Perry shouts, glaring at Cunningham.

"The case file concluded that these people were witnessing some kind of astronomical phenomenon. Nothing that would warrant an investigation," Cunningham says, running his hands over his face. "But after the Vexton story came to light, those events should've been revisited. There's no excuse for this kind of oversight, and I'll be addressing it first thing tomorrow with the department's leader. I guarantee you, this won't happen again, sir."

"Well, it definitely won't happen again under his watch, because by tomorrow morning he'll be searching for another line of work."

* * *

"And they just ignored this?" I say when Dave Perry breaks the news to me.

"That's correct. They simply pushed it aside into some file and forgot about it," Perry answers.

"Well, not being a part of the Administration any longer, I'm well aware it's not my place to give advice…"

"Don't be silly, Nicole; your input is always appreciated."

"I think it'd be wise to investigate the areas where those sightings took place. Heck, maybe we'll discover more of that glittering strata." I chuckle.

"Hmm, that just might be worth a shot," Perry replies.

CHAPTER 14

There it is. That damn clanking sound, coming from the hallway.

Moments later the door opens and the guards bring Anya into the room. They begin to remove the shackles. "I'd rather you not," she says to them.

This isn't a good sign for me. But I smile. "It's okay, gentlemen. If that's Miss Ahar's wish, then so be it," I say.

Exchanging confused glances, they exit the room.

"Are you being defiant toward me, Anya? Is that what that was?"

"Please don't take it personally. I just don't want to be treated differently from the other prisoners," she says, looking me in the eyes.

"That's okay. Have it your way. Now, with your hearing getting closer, we're really going to need to bear down." She continues to study me, unblinking. "Is everything okay, Anya?" I pause, waiting for her reply. Nothing. "If there's something you need to tell me, please come out with it. If I'm wasting my time being here, let me know," I say calmly but firmly. Through her thick lenses, I see tears forming in the corners of her eyes. My curiosity is now at an all-time high.

Trembling slightly, she offers a subtle smile. "Thank you… thank you," she says softly. It's as if the words have oozed through blocks of ice. The ice melts and tears begin to stream down her cheeks.

"What are you thanking me for?" I ask, perplexed.

"I heard your speech—the one you gave in Central Park. Thank you."

I hand her a tissue. "Did you hear the entire speech?"

"Yes… and I was extremely moved."

I'm relieved to hear this, but I'm also somewhat puzzled, considering what I revealed. "And you're not angry with me, knowing it was my father who was responsible for that hospital being closed?"

"No. I don't blame your father for what happened. He was simply part of a broken system. And I'm so elated, so grateful that someone like you is finally willing to try to fix it."

"That's my plan, Anya. And I want to begin that journey by helping you. But I'll need your complete honesty and cooperation," I say firmly.

She shrugs and sighs. "I can't let you do it. There's absolutely no way we'll win in that courtroom," she says, her voice a resigned monotone.

"That's not true. All you have to do is be yourself and stop pretending to be the malicious young woman that you're not. And your father—he needs you to give him a chance. This is killing him."

"Please, Ms. Kratz; honor my request. This country needs you far more than it needs me. And my father… he has everything he needs."

"He's not the man he was. He realizes how neglectful he was toward you in the past, and he wants so desperately to be able to change that," I say earnestly. "And America—it needs the both of us, Anya. Are you aware of the impact your story has had on this country? And it's not just the young. The number of people calling for your freedom is growing daily. Your story has made this entire country reexamine itself. Heck, I know how much it has even helped to open *my* eyes to reality."

"Let it go," she snaps. "I will not partake in such a useless endeavor."

"If you do that—"

"All I ask of you is to please let me meet my fate peacefully."

"And all I ask of *you* is to think about this, and let me help you walk out of here," I plead.

Anya bows her head and presses the buzzer to call the guards to take her back to her cell. "Don't waste your time on me, Ms. Kratz. Make America what it should be."

She leaves with the guards, and I'm left feeling engulfed by waves of sorrow.

* * *

"You have to believe me, I had no idea it was my father who ordered the closure of those hospitals," I say to Dr. Ahar as we meet in his office. "And I apologize for not contacting you in Europe before I made the news public."

Dr. Ahar slowly shakes his head. "I can't believe it, Nicole. I know your father. How could such a good, decent man have done something so callous?" He scowls. "I guess when President Snyder publicly referred to the War Within as an event so atrocious it turned even the kindest souls into architects of evil, he was absolutely correct."

He looks at me and draws a deep breath. "I'm sorry, Nicole. I just keep thinking of what should have been. The joys of a family, together..."

"I understand, Doctor," I reply. My eyes are drawn to the photos behind his desk.

"Nicole, are you okay?" he asks. "Nicole."

"Ah! Sorry, Doctor," I answer as my mind snaps back to the moment.

"So, how was your follow-up meeting with Anya? Were you able to make any progress?" he asks.

I shake my head sadly. "She wants no part of that hearing, sir."

"Whoa, wait a second. Are you telling me my daughter has resigned herself to being executed?" Ahar begins to tremble. "Why? What on earth happened? You told me you thought you were getting through to her."

"I know I was getting through to her, but that's where the problem lies."

"I don't understand."

"I know this seems crazy, but Anya's doing this because she knows my situation. She so badly wants me to become president."

"All the more reason for her to want you in her corner—why wouldn't she?"

"She doesn't think we'd stand a chance in the hearing, and that in the end it'll crush my presidential hopes."

"Oh my... We can't let her do this, Nicole," Ahar says, his tone urgent.

I shrug and lift my hands. "It doesn't look good, Doctor. She was very strong in her position. I doubt anything will change her mind."

"I can't let my beautiful daughter die—something must be done!" he cries. He flops into his chair and puts his head in his hands.

I move around his desk and stop behind his chair to rest my hands on his shoulders. "I'm not giving up on this yet. You have my word."

"I believe you, Nicole... Now please, I need to be alone," he says, his voice choked with emotion.

Before exiting the room, I glance back. He is weeping.

CHAPTER 15

With the number of undecided voters now at twenty-two percent, it's become apparent that this election is anybody's game. While I was on my recent whirlwind tour to speak at various rallies, Gerald Levin had been lying low. But today he has surfaced. Brave Land Stadium, home of Levin's Washington Androids, is filled to capacity as he prepares to speak. The event is expected to be one for the ages.

Marching bands open the festivities, followed by a sensational performance by the remarkable Magic Marcus, who for the climax of his show makes lifelike figures of me and Westgale vanish into thin air. *Very creepy, indeed.* Next comes a performance by the Soaring Pretzels, a combination acrobatic act and percussion ensemble whose stunning physical feats and booming jungle drums work the crowd into a frenzy. Then after the crowd is given time to catch its breath, a red, white, and blue robo-copter lands on the rotating stage in the middle of the stadium.

Earl Pemberton exits the copter. "My Lord, it is incredible to see so many friends of the MAA here today," he says, raising his hands in the air, backing away from the podium, cheering with the audience. The look in his eyes takes me back to the first day of the War Within, when at the Last Frontier steakhouse I saw that same scheming glare. It is the look of a hungry jackal preparing for the kill. As the UCIT camera scans the crowd, the chairman of First Source News, Domingo Diaz, is seen high above in a private box, chomping away on a rack of spare ribs. I'm surprised the blood from his fangs isn't dripping down on those below. Once he realizes he's being captured on camera, he immediately attempts to shift out of view.

Pemberton steps back to the podium. "It is a great honor to present the leader of the Militant Alliance of America, and this country's future president, Mr. Gerald Levin!"

Levin appears, strutting from a tunnel toward a waiting black and silver robo-cycle. Dressed in a black designer suit and sporting an American flag tie, he begins shaking hands and flashing his phony smile before he gets on the cycle and is whisked along the front aisle to the stage. The camera flashes back up to Domingo Diaz, who can be seen fervently waving an American flag and chanting "Gerrrrrald" with the rest of the crowd. Again, he attempts to duck out of view.

Anger consumes me. This is a man who brags about running his media empire in the most unbiased manner possible, who claims he never has and never will cater to any political interests. To think *The Source you can rely on for the truth* is this company's slogan. I shake my head.

"The journey is just beginning, folks," Levin exclaims. "What an incredible journey it'll be. And I'm looking forward to being the person to lead you on the path back to prosperity." The crowd hangs on every word. "Kiddy hour with the PBA is over. It's time to get down to the real business of reshaping the greatest country on earth!"

He spends quite some time outlining his political agenda, which features a drastic lowering of taxes, a complete restructuring of the military, the elimination of the World Harmony Program, the abolition of pretty much all of the country's gun laws, and installation of an international VX drug program and an international energy program led by Earl Pemberton and ERT Power. "These programs will easily eliminate the debt owed to the Outer Commission by that looming deadline, without us having to resort to doing business with a dictator like Cobra Pix. I have formally extended an invitation to President Westgale to discuss this matter, but as expected, he has yet to respond." The crowd boos loudly.

"I find it very interesting that the Pinian energy deal was sealed as Jessica Westgale and Shadow Pix were falling in love. How sweet is that?" Levin says with a devious grin. "It's like a modern-day Romeo and Juliet." The crowd roars with laughter. "However, in all sincerity, I do hope the final outcome isn't so tragic."

He pauses and waits for the crowd to settle before he continues. "Nicole Kratz," he says with a smirk, and jeers fill the stadium.

I knew it was only a matter of time until I became his target.

"The PBA's very own queen of the bleeding hearts. What a joke. Isn't it ironic that the same person who helped develop the ridiculous World Harmony Program is now attempting to divide *America*? She keeps insisting that she wants to give a voice to young America, but her narrative, if anything, actually feeds the insecurities of the disenfranchised. As I look around this stadium I'm honored to see thousands of young faces. I spoke with many of you before this event commenced, and I think it's safe to say you have more important things to do with your lives than parade around crying out for a terrorist to be freed from prison." A mad rush of excitement sweeps through the crowd. The chant of "Gerrrrrald" is deafening.

"Now, I'd like to call Earl back to the stage and welcome him as my official running mate."

The chant quickly changes to "Earl! Earl!"

Beside Gerald, Pemberton gives the crowd a military salute.

"I realize most of you are probably thinking Earl and I are just two boring billionaires who stay at home at night counting our money. Well, I have news for you, friends—we also know how to have a good time!"

Several robo-cycles flashing with neon lights come speeding out of the stadium's tunnels and onto the field to perform death-defying stunts. When a spectacular display of fireworks lights up the evening sky above the stage, the crowd is whipped into a frenzy. The finale sees red, white, and blue blasts form the name *GERALD*.

"Leave it to Gerald Levin to put his name up in lights," Hunter quips as my team and I watch the over-the-top presentation in our headquarters.

"I've heard he's quite revered in Vexton. Is that true?" Beth asks Hunter.

"It all depends on who you ask," Hunter answers. "Many see him as arrogant and insecure. But there's no denying he's a great salesman."

"Well, let's just hope the people of America aren't buying what he's selling," I say, watching the spectacle with disdain.

* * *

The next morning, the always friendly and humorous Justice Phillip Malone pays a visit to my campaign headquarters. "Well, this is a pleasant surprise," I say as he walks through the office checking out the photos on the wall.

"Tell me, Nicole—I know this might be a crazy question—but does Lowell ever grow tired of winning?" he says, chuckling as he looks at photos of my husband celebrating recent World Golf Championship victories. "I would assume he might start becoming rather bored, if he just keeps rolling over the competition like he's been doing."

"Oh, even he realizes every king loses his crown at some point. So I guess he appreciates wearing that crown for as long as he can," I reply humbly.

"And there are the little darlings," Malone says, gazing at a photo of my daughters. "Now, what's it going to be for them, golf or politics?" he asks.

"Well, at the moment it looks like they might be heading in entirely different directions," I reply. "Tiffany wants to be a writer, and January's love for animals has her hoping to one day be a vet."

"I'm sure whatever path they choose, they'll make you and Lowell very proud," he responds, settling into the chair across from me.

"Regardless of what they choose to do, we just want them to be happy," I say with a smile. "So, how are you enjoying being the PBA's new chairman?"

"Hopefully I'll at least last a little longer than my predecessor." He laughs.

We discuss several PBA matters before getting to Anya.

"I feared she'd do this," I say when Malone informs me Anya formally revoked her right to the Judicial Triangle hearing.

"I'm sorry, Nicole, but as long as she refuses to be a part of the process, there's nothing that can be done. And now that Dr. Durant and the two other doctors who have diagnosed her don't see her as being insane, I'm afraid she'll have to face the penalty of death."

We say our goodbyes and Justice Malone exits my office.

"I'm sorry to bother you, Nicole," Beth calls to me over the intercom. "There's a lady here in the foyer who says it's vital that she speak with you."

"This is definitely not a good time, Beth. Has she told you her name?"

"She told me she'd like to remain anonymous."

"All right. Once she's been thoroughly checked by security, bring her in."

Minutes later, Beth escorts the mystery lady into my office. I study her a moment. She appears to be in her fifties. Wearing a hood and large sunglasses, it's obvious she's trying to disguise her identity. "That'll be all, Beth," I say.

Beth leaves and closes the door behind her.

"Thank you for seeing me. I'm Carly—Carly Taylor," the woman says. I can tell she's nervous.

"Carly Taylor? As in First Source News, Carly Taylor?"

"That's me," she replies, and removes the hood and glasses. She looks worn out, with dark circles under her eyes—a far cry from the glamorous news reporter who's been so deeply ingrained into American culture. "I apologize for the secrecy, but once you hear what I've come to tell you, I'm sure you'll understand why I'm being so cautious."

What in the world could this be about? "Well, I must say, you've really piqued my curiosity." I pause. "Sorry for being so blunt, but I don't recall seeing you anywhere in the media since you left First Source News."

"And after you hear what I have to tell you, you'll understand why," she says.

"Oh?" I reply. *I'm all ears.*

"While watching that MAA circus last night, it really hit me, how misguided I was to have once been the face of First Source News," Carly says. She grimaces. "It sickens me."

"I remember watching many of your broadcasts, especially around the time of the war, and you sure seemed quite enamored with the Militant Alliance of America," I say firmly.

"That was then. I'm not the same person I was all those years ago. I didn't know any better. You see, both my father and mother were paranoid about the government; they did whatever they could to instill an extreme militant ideology into me and my brothers. By the age of ten I was firing guns on a shooting range—I can still recall being terrified by the damn recoil every time I fired off a shot."

"How did you end up at First Source News?"

"Actually, I went out on my own at sixteen, and lost touch with my family."

"What made you do that?"

"I was pregnant and decided to have an abortion. I felt terrible about it, but at the time I believed it was my only recourse."

As I look into her eyes I can feel her anguish, even after all these years. "That had to have been challenging, to be out on your own at sixteen."

"For the first few years it was a real battle, but with the help of a few of my friends I hit the beauty pageant circuit and started to become recognized. I was offered several modeling and acting jobs, but turned them down to work for Domingo at First Source News."

"And how did that come about?"

"His staff used to scout the pageants for girls who had 'the look,' and I guess I had it. Domingo would refer to us girls as 'eye candy for the masses.'"

"And that was it? You mean to tell me he brought you on without any training or experience?"

"Once he took me under his wing, he had one of his people teach me the basics for a couple of weeks, and that was it."

"I guess it went well for you, since you ended up being his number one news anchor."

Carly sighs. "Ah... the only reason I became First Source's lead anchor was because I became Domingo's mistress."

"With all respect, Miss Taylor, the story of your life is very interesting, but I still have no idea why you're here."

"I'm here because I believe it's imperative that you win the election. Gerald Levin and Earl Pemberton will destroy everything that's great about America."

"So, I see your political views have changed since your days at First Source."

Originally revered for its highly impartial and direct news presentation, First Source News became, by far, the dominant news station of its time. With that popularity, Carly Taylor emerged as a larger-than-life personality. She appeared to be the perfect combination of brains and beauty.

As First Source continued to flourish, something peculiar occurred. Little by little, the network progressively moved further and further toward an extreme right-wing agenda. And when Jackson Snyder became president and began conveying his political vision and plan to America, the network became downright vitriolic, with Carly appearing more than willing to do her part.

"Like I said, back in those days, I didn't know any better. I was desperate. I'm ashamed to have been Domingo's little puppet. I'm ashamed to have had anything to do with First Source. I hated all the glitz... There I'd be, about to relay some awful news story under fancy lights, with the sound of pop music ushering me in." She looks pained.

"Is there something important you need to tell me?"

"Yes. It's so important, in fact, that if it's made public, I'm sure it'll lead you to victory."

I sit up straight. "I'm listening."

"Do you remember the interview I conducted with Kenneth Pahl, the HKM's former chief military commander, just prior to the war? The one where he warned America that the HKM was on the verge of attacking our country?"

"The interview. Of course; it was a moment in history that'll never be forgotten."

"Well, as you may recall, First Source News claimed that Pahl contacted the network unannounced, from a secret location, strictly of his own accord."

"Are you saying that wasn't the case?"

"I'm certain it wasn't the case."

"And how is it you know this?"

"The network had a huge party that very evening."

"Well, I'm not surprised; that was a blockbuster exclusive interview. I'm sure Domingo and his associates must have been on cloud nine after such good fortune."

"Yeah, but you see, that party was planned a couple of days prior to Kenneth Pahl supposedly contacting the station."

"What exactly is it you're trying to tell me?"

"I'm certain Kenneth Pahl was bribed into doing that interview."

"By Domingo?"

"Oh, Domingo was more than willing to do his part, but I'm certain the true orchestrators were Earl Pemberton, Gerald Levin, and their wealthy friends."

I lean forward. "To further the cause of their newly established Militant Alliance?"

"Yes, with the idea of ensuring their personal fortunes weren't going to be affected by Jackson Snyder's political agenda. I know for a fact those guys would have done anything to have had Snyder removed from office. And Pahl was their perfect conduit, a former HKM military leader and the bearer of very important information—falsified information that would send our country into a panic, including our military."

"Wait a second—you're telling me they not only set up the interview, but you believe Pahl was lying."

"There's no doubt. The HKM was making loads of money off America at that time. Why would they want to destroy us? If any country was on the HKM hit list, it was Russia."

"Can you prove what you're telling me?"

"My word should be proof enough. I was the number one news anchor at that damn station. I saw it all. The backroom payoffs, the—"

"But did you see a payoff being made to Kenneth Pahl?"

"No, I didn't. But I did see both Earl and Gerald, among others, pay off Domingo to either create or bury other stories for their own benefit."

"I understand, but do you have any documents or view-files proving these things happened?"

"Unfortunately, Domingo and his staff made certain everything was kept under wraps, but I can recall at least a half dozen situations that greatly aided either Pemberton and ERT Power, or Gerald Levin and *his* business endeavors."

"And I take it it's your wish to go public with this."

"I want nothing more. So many times during those years, I lied to this country. Now it's time for me to make amends and reveal the truth."

"Would you be willing to be interviewed by the attorney general?"

"Just let me know when and where."

"You do understand that if you go public with these claims, these guys are going to fight back like mad dogs, and expose everything they can about *you*?"

She draws herself up. "Let them. I have nothing to hide."

"I hope you also understand Attorney General Sutton's office will have to perform their due diligence on you before he brings you in."

"I wouldn't expect anything less."

As much as I want to believe this story could be impactful, and put a large dent in support for the MAA, I feel uneasy. Carly appeared to be passionate and sincere, but I'm concerned there may be more to her than meets the eye. That being said, I can't just let this go.

When the Outer Commission was formed, the first action it took was to create a comprehensive report on the War Within. The report's main purpose was to attempt to answer the basic, but important question: what was at the root of that ugly war? At the top of the list of answers was political divisiveness created and fuelled by media manipulation. The *messengers* were shaping the *messages* to fit their political and corporate agendas.

Since under the New Order Treaty, the nonpartisan UCIT is entrusted with all matters related to federal politics, the proper channels must be followed. If Attorney General Sutton believes there is merit to Carly's claims, he can then make a request to UCIT to cover the story. If UCIT agrees to interview Carly, she will be protected against all forms of potential legal action. This is highly significant, because she's making claims against three of America's most powerful men.

I send a detailed report to Sutton.

* * *

"I don't know, Champ," Westgale says, in the emergency meeting Sutton has called with the president. "As Domingo Diaz's former mistress, she might simply be out to seek some sort of revenge."

"According to Nicole's report, Miss Taylor emphatically stated this is political and not personal. Nicole believes she was being truthful," Sutton replies. "At least until Gil completes his research into her life, I think we should give her the benefit of the doubt."

"Wow... if we could only substantiate her claim regarding Kenneth Pahl, it would destroy these clowns," Westgale says as he stares intently at the report.

"Hopefully, the American people will take her at her word."

CHAPTER 16

"Come on in, Gil," says Champ Sutton. "I really appreciate hearing back from you so soon."

"I had my entire staff on this for the last two days," Gil replies as he takes a seat across from Sutton.

"So, is there anything we need to be concerned about regarding Miss Taylor?"

"I'm glad to say there isn't. At least with regards to what *we've* been able to determine. Let's see... she did have an abortion at sixteen. The record is clear on that. Married and divorced twice. It doesn't appear she's had any trouble with the law. Since leaving First Source, she's worked at several different jobs in the hospitality industry... Yeah, it looks like the info she provided to Nicole checks out," Gil responds as he submits the report to Sutton's flash-pad.

"And financially?"

"There doesn't appear to be any red flags. However, as expected, since leaving First Source she's definitely been forced to lead a far less excessive lifestyle."

"Great work, Gil. I'll give this a thorough going over, and unless I find something of concern, I'll be making the formal request to UCIT."

Gil takes a deep breath and exhales. "I don't want to speak out of turn."

"Go ahead, Gil. You know how I value your input."

"I just can't get my head around why, after all these years, she suddenly comes running to Nicole with this information."

"Since the moment Nicole told me about this I've been thinking the same thing. And we'd be totally ignorant not to consider all the possibilities here—including the idea we're somehow being set up to look like fools," Sutton says with a raised brow. "But then again, if what she's telling us has merit, the PBA will reap the benefits. It's a risk we need to take."

* * *

The UCIT analysis team is quick to assess the matter, and votes to allow Carly Taylor to be interviewed by Cryptic.

The interview takes place in a remote park somewhere in New York State. Carly's choice. The specific location is undisclosed to the public. She sits on a bench as large snowflakes fall from the evening sky. They look like floating moths, caught in the spotlights surrounding her. As the UCIT camera slowly pans in, the tomb-like silence of the location seems a far cry from the glitz that used to bombard the airwaves when Carly came into American living rooms all those years ago.

Although it's been almost twenty-six years since she's been in front of a camera, she appears poised and as professional as ever. Her former glitzy and perky presence is now replaced by a refined, calm maturity. It's ironic to see this formerly glamorous woman who brought such energy and interest to television news now being interviewed by an unemotional, utilitarian machine.

"Good evening, Miss Taylor," Cryptic says, positioned directly in front of Carly. *"I'm sure most Americans are wondering why you've decided to speak about your time at First Source News, considering it's more than twenty-five years after the fact. Would you kindly explain?"*

"It's about revealing the truth. The truth needs to be told. I believe First Source's former bias, extreme right-wing reporting, was the largest factor contributing to the War Within. Of course, it's also the reason that you exist." She stares pointedly at Cryptic, then resumes, her voice rising.

"Every time I hear Gerald Levin trying to come across as 'a man of the people,' it sickens me. I saw firsthand how he, Earl Pemberton, and many of the country's other leading industrialists used their wealth and power to control the media."

"Would you kindly provide us with a specific example where Gerald Levin did such a thing?" the robot asks.

"The one that comes to mind involved a massive stretch of farmland he owned in Cleveland, Ohio. An environmental group secretly contacted First Source about severe soil pollution in the area. My boss, Domingo Diaz, promised them he'd run the story, but he only did so after alerting Levin, who sold the property before the news was made public for five times what it ended up being worth after the story was aired."

"Can you prove this?"

"No, but I was there for the celebration. Let's just say Gerald Levin was rather appreciative. Domingo ended up receiving a luxury yacht."

"Can you see how you having been Domingo Diaz's mistress could lead people to thinking there is more to this?"

Carly shrugs. "People are entitled to think whatever they want. I'm simply telling the truth."

"Are you aware of any indiscretions in relation to your most well-known interview, which took place with former HKM Military Commander Kenneth Pahl?"

Carly takes a deep breath, then slowly exhales. "To this day, I'm certain Kenneth Pahl was bribed into doing that interview. At the time of Jackson Snyder's presidency, Gerald Levin and Earl Pemberton were among those who controlled the news leading up to the War Within. The day Kenneth Pahl told the American public that the HKM was planning to attack America, the majority of citizens in this country, including our military, needlessly became immersed in fear, much to the delight of the MAA."

"What are you basing this on?" asks Cryptic.

"Being so entrenched in world news at the time, I never saw any signs the HKM was targeting America. Russia, but not us. Of course, *there was a period where First Source News did everything it could to make it appear the HKM wanted to destroy America."*

After Carly provides a few more examples of the corruption that prevailed at First Source News, she concludes the interview with a final statement. *"I solemnly apologize to the American people for having aided the powers that be at First Source News in helping them carry out their agenda of blatant deception. I take full responsibility for my actions."*

Minutes after Carly's interview, Gerald Levin releases an official response, via a view-file to UCIT. He's standing in the front hall of the MAA's headquarters. Dressed in his usual impeccable manner, he appears relaxed as he begins to speak. *"Good evening, my fellow Americans. As was made evident by the flagrant lies told by Carly Taylor to the UCIT Network this evening, the game of politics remains vicious, especially when your opponent realizes you cannot be defeated in a legitimate manner. I'm extremely disappointed, but not surprised, that the Peace Bringers of America have resorted to such an unethical approach. I am even more disappointed that such untruths were permitted to be presented on the UCIT Network. Don't fret, my friends, the true spirit of America will soon be resurrected."*

"Ha, he put this all on us, just like I thought he would," I say, shaking my head as I turn to Hunter.

"Oh... I'm seeing that Domingo Diaz is scheduled to answer to Cryptic in an hour's time," Hunter says, consulting his flash-pad.

"Hmm, that should be interesting. I just hope this doesn't backfire on us, Hunter," I say, revealing my concern.

Hunter looks at me with a grim expression. "Without any tangible proof, this ends up being word against word," he says. "Honestly, do you believe Carly Taylor?"

"I wouldn't have sent the report to Champ Sutton if I didn't," I reply with conviction. "None of what she said surprises me."

"Hey, isn't that Times Square?" Hunter asks as our attention returns to the flash-screen.

"It sure is," I reply as Cryptic appears on the screen, slowly maneuvering through the hustle and bustle.

"Sir, may I have a moment of your time?" the robot asks a burly, casually dressed middle-aged man.

"Sure, what can I do for you?" the man replies.

"Who are you supporting for president?"

"Gerald Levin."

"I'd like to know how you feel about Carly Taylor's claim that Levin and his wealthy associates often bribed the media for their own benefit."

"Meh, who really knows if that's actually true? And even if it is, hey, they're powerful businessmen in a dog-eat-dog world. They do what they need to do. Levin still has my vote, no doubt about it," the man says.

Cryptic then makes its way toward another man and poses the same questions. "Of course Gerald Levin has my vote," the man says as he tightens the belt of his designer leather overcoat. "I'll bet any money Carly Taylor is the person on the take. She's done nothing since First Source News, and it's obvious she's craving attention. I guess she misses the spotlight, and the money." The man laughs. "This is all part of a typical political smear campaign. Believe me, Gerald Levin is the person who will bring this country back to richness."

Suddenly a woman who appears to be in her mid-twenties enters the scene. "I'm sorry, but these people are out of their minds!" she exclaims. "How can they not see Levin is a complete fraud? First there's the Vexton-Tech scandal, and now this news comes out. How could anybody in their right mind want to see this man run our country? Free Anya! Free America!" she adds before heading off to rejoin her friends.

"It's what it is, Hunter," I say, watching Cryptic continue on through the crowd. "I guess those who support Gerald Levin will stand by him no matter what. And those who don't will never trust him."

"Here's the Diaz interview," Hunter says, nodding toward the flash-screen.

Now sixty-eight years of age, Domingo Diaz remains majority owner and chairman of First Source Media, but he is no longer involved in its day-to-day operations.

On this evening, as he makes his way toward a podium in the foyer of First Source's corporate headquarters, Domingo appears to be his usual charming self. He stops to shake hands with a couple of his executives, then leans in and says something to them. They laugh in response, as if they're supposed to. After running a comb through his mane of silver hair, he adjusts his red silk tie and steps up to the podium.

"I'm extremely disappointed by what has transpired this evening. I've always considered Miss Taylor to be an integral part of the First Source family. That she has decided to fabricate such horrendous lies is very disturbing," *he says vehemently, his expression stern.* "From the day I created this company, I've prided myself on its moral integrity. I'd hoped that by now Carly would have received the help she needs. In all honesty, I'm saddened by the fact she remains so troubled.

"I'll now take some questions."

Standing about six feet in front of the podium, Cryptic's bright red, flashing eyes match Domingo's tie. "When you say Miss Taylor 'remains troubled,' what exactly are you implying?" *the robot asks.*

Domingo clears his throat and takes a deep breath. "While she was working at First Source I would often find her sitting alone in the cafeteria, just blankly staring into space. By the time the lunch hour ended, the plate of food in front of her had barely been touched. One day I joined her at her table and gently asked her if something had been troubling her. It took some effort on my behalf, but she finally opened up to me. Before she could utter a word, she began bawling her eyes out."

"Did she tell you why she was so upset?"

"It was guilt. Even though it'd been several years prior, she still felt immense guilt over having aborted her child. I remember her crying out, 'I'm a murderer—I killed my child.'"

"Was this before you had the affair with her?"

"Yes. I did my best to help her deal with her emotions. My marriage was going through a rough period at the time, so I guess in a way, we were there for each other."

"What brought an end to the affair?"

"She was becoming very difficult to be with—very distant, emotionally torn. And then when I insisted she seek professional help, she became quite upset with me. At that point we both agreed to end our relationship."

"Was it amicable?" asks Cryptic.

"I thought it was, but after what she's now resorted to... I guess I was wrong."

"Would you say you are close to Gerald Levin and Earl Pemberton?"

"Those gentlemen are two of the most powerful men in America, and I run the country's most powerful media company. It goes without saying that our paths frequently cross," Domingo replies. "However, for no reason did I, nor would I, ever compromise First Source's integrity. Without integrity, a media company is nothing but phony, an empty shell," he adds with conviction.

* * *

"Listen to that liar," Carly Taylor says as she watches from the back of a grand-electro.

"You did a fantastic job, Miss Taylor," the man sitting beside her replies as he adjusts the high-tech fencing mask he's wearing. He reaches for a black leather bag and hands it to her.

"It wasn't very difficult. I simply told the truth," Carly replies as she opens the bag and gazes at the five million dollars within. She begins to count the money. "Those bastards and their sickening lust for power are to blame for that war, and I won't sit back and watch them do it again."

"I'm just glad we were able to provide you with the proper incentive to come forward. Now that you've been suitably rewarded, you're free to get away from all this hypocrisy and enjoy your life in Germany, as you expressed was your wish. The arrangements have all been taken care of," the man says calmly. He consults his flash-pad, ensuring the presence of the private plane scheduled to transport Carly.

"I hope you don't mind, but there's something I've been wanting to ask you," Carly says hesitantly.

"Yes."

"I know how much telling the truth and bringing these guys down means to me, but why is it so important to you and whoever it is you're working for that I do this?"

Within the mask, the man sighs. "It's simple, Miss Taylor—we too think it's in America's best interest if Gerald Levin fails in his presidential quest."

The grand-electro pulls onto the tarmac and up to a plane idling before an airport hangar. A man waiting at the bottom of the steps comes forward to escort Carly. As she starts climbing the stairs to the plane, the man in the grand-electro removes his mask and again reaches for his flash-pad.

"Hello, Theodore," the man says. "I'm just letting you know everything went according to plan."

"Excellent. Cobra will be very pleased," Theodore replies. "Let's just hope this evening's news will greatly benefit our friends at the PBA."

CHAPTER 17

"It's great news, Nicole!" Hunter shouts as he sees me in the foyer of our headquarters. "We're now at forty-seven percent and Levin's dropped to forty-one percent."

"I guess Carly Taylor's word meant something after all," I say, my preoccupation with Anya tempering my excitement.

His face falls.

"Whoa, I thought you'd be far more enthused."

"Oh, don't get the wrong idea, I'm thrilled to hear the news," I assure him. "But I'm afraid how this whole thing surrounding Anya is going to play out."

* * *

"I want to thank you for the generous donation. I promise we'll put the funds to good use," Dane Conroy, the director of New York's Finley Rehab Center, says to Jessica. "And I must tell you, your speech today was very enlightening."

"It's a pleasure to be able to help out," she replies, walking beside him down the hall from his office.

"I was overjoyed to learn Judge Kratz had set up the foundation, and even more thrilled to learn *you'd* be heading it up for him. I must tell you, I really enjoyed my time working for your father," Dane says, referring to a past study he coordinated for the Westgale Administration on addiction.

"Yes, my father was very pleased with the analysis your team performed," Jessica replies as they enter a common area looking out over the grounds. "The information was of immense value."

Dane warms to the topic. "That's the thing, Jessica. The only way we'll find solutions is to continue studying the problem. I'll always remain committed to helping these people," he says as he looks around the common area, where men and women are relaxing with books or chatting with one another, "but I hope there comes a day when they won't require my help. Now, I understand you personally know one of our subjects: Kolton Rollins."

"Yes," Jessica says as Dane opens a glass door and ushers her outside.

"I'm glad to see he finally found his way out of this place," Dane says. They saunter along a crushed gravel walkway, their shoes crunching over the loose stones. "But due to circumstances I'm not at liberty to disclose, my team has recommended that he continue to see our psychologist on a weekly basis." Dane turns to her just before they reach the street. "I'm disappointed that he hasn't consented to do so. I'd just hate to see him relapse. Perhaps you and Shadow would be wise to address the matter with Luanda, and try to get her to convince Kolton to change his mind."

"I'll do what I can, Mr. Conroy," she assures him as her car pulls up to the curb in front of her.

When Jessica returns home she immediately discusses the matter with Shadow. "I don't want to interfere, but Finley's director is concerned Kolton will relapse if he doesn't continue to receive therapy... And what was all that stuff the other evening about Direct Aim?"

Shadow shrugs. "I don't know, Jessie. I tried to address it with my mother, but just mentioning the subject really stresses her out, so I didn't want to push it. She thinks it's vital to Kolton's well-being that it's left in the past." He exhales heavily. "But I'll try again."

* * *

That evening, Shadow sits down for a heart-to-heart conversation with his mother.

"Actually, Kolton wants to continue receiving therapy, but just not with Finley's psychologist," Luanda says when Shadow expresses his and Jessica's concerns.

"How about if Jessica arranged it so he could see the man considered to be the best psychologist in the country, Dr. Evan Durant?"

Luanda's eyes widen. "That'd be incredible," she exclaims. Then she pats his hand and reveals, "Kolton thinks very highly of you, son. In fact, it's because of him I went to visit you that day in the hospital. *He* was the person who convinced me to do so. I'm so glad I listened to him." She leans forward and kisses him on the cheek.

* * *

Much to everyone's relief, Kolton agrees to see Dr. Durant, and he returns from the initial appointment to announce that he's much more comfortable with Durant than he ever felt with the Finley psychologist; so much so that they've already set up a weekly schedule, and he's eager to get started.

"Please, tell me about your sister, Indiana," Dr. Durant says as he pours Kolton a glass of water during their second appointment.

"Indy… she was incredible." His gaze grows distant as he remembers. "So intelligent. I'll never forget her buying me my first chemistry set as a birthday present," Kolton says with a fond smile. "There's no doubt she could've been anything she wanted to be. The fact she dedicated her life to helping children with special needs proved just what a compassionate person she was."

"And Victoria?"

"Vicky and Indiana were so close. When Vicky saw what a caring person her older sister was growing up to be, it had a major impact on her. It definitely inspired her to pursue nursing."

"And what about you, Kolton? What inspired you to work for Direct Aim and develop weapons?"

"I wanted to do my part to help ensure America was protected. All we kept hearing at the time was that the HKM was on the verge of attacking us. And I would've done anything to stop those bastards from bringing harm to this country," he replies, his tone vehement.

"Instead, our country ended up bringing harm to itself, and your sisters were among the many who paid the price," Durant says gently. "Please, have a drink of water, take a deep breath, and tell me how your sisters died."

Kolton nods and after a moment, complies. "They were killed on the fourth day of the War Within…"

* * *

"Hey, Indy. Is Vicky with you?" Kolton asked as he waited for his sisters at New York's Ruby's Deli.

"Yeah, she's here with me now," Indiana answered.

Vicky grabbed Indiana's flash-pad. "Hey, little brother; can't wait to see ya!"

Kolton smiled. "My, oh my. When did you get in, Vic?"

"About two hours ago."

"How long do you plan to stay?"

"I'm here until after New Year's."

"Fantastic. I'm looking so forward to seeing you."

"Hey, what about me?" Indiana said with a laugh, taking the flash-pad back from her sister.

Kolton chuckled. "Oh, come on, Indy, you know that goes without saying."

"We decided to enjoy this gorgeous winter day and walk to the deli," Indiana said. "We'll be there shortly. I hope you got a window table."

"Of course, I made certain of that," Kolton replied. "And the special is your favorite, Indy."

"Corned beef on a hot cheese bun?" Indy asked.

"With those delicious pickles on the side. Now, you ladies just make sure you get here safe and sound. Thankfully, it looks like things have finally started to calm down out there," Kolton said, looking out the window into the streets.

"Yeah, we're just about to pass Precinct Five and everything seems rather—"

A powerful blast roared over the flash-pad, followed by a series of rapid, loud pops and frantic screams.

"Indy, Vicky—are you there?" Kolton shouted repeatedly. He rushed outside and looked down the street, hoping desperately to see his sisters approaching. "Oh my God!" he screamed as he saw clouds of smoke in the distance.

Fighting panic, he hailed a taxi. "You've gotta take me to Precinct Five," he cried to the driver.

"I'm sorry, but I don't think I can do that, sir. I just received a message over my radio that the MAA has attacked the precinct," the driver told him.

"Please, sir. I beg you," Kolton almost sobbed. "My two sisters were in the area when those explosions went off."

"All right. This could cost me my job... but I'll do it," the cab driver replied.

When they reached the area, Kolton learned that along with nine New York City police officers, Indiana and Vicky were dead.

* * *

"I'm so sorry, Kolton," Dr. Durant says. "I understand how devastating reliving that memory must be for you. But when you developed those grenades, did you ever think they'd be used against fellow Americans, let alone your sisters?"

"Of course not," Kolton snaps. "I had no idea those bastards at Direct Aim were working with the MAA," he adds.

"Right. When you developed those grenades you were doing it with the most sincere intention: to protect America, and that included your sisters. You had absolutely no control over things during that shameful war. Do you understand?" Durant asks.

Kolton nods and takes a deep breath. "It's taken me forever, but yes I do, Doctor."

"When you look at the glass in front of you, are you wishing it was filled with whiskey rather than water?" Durant asks.

"That'd be very selfish of me, considering the support I've received from my wife in overcoming my issues. I love her way too much to go back to the hell I was living in," he replies with conviction.

After seeing Kolton for a third time, Dr. Durant meets with Luanda, Shadow, and Jessica. "After I read his case history, I was somewhat concerned. But I'm thrilled to tell you he's made incredible progress."

"Do you think there's a chance he'll relapse?" Luanda asks nervously.

"I'm sorry, but that's an impossible question to answer, Mrs. Rollins. However, I believe Kolton has finally come to terms with the idea that he wasn't responsible for the deaths of his sisters. And I also believe it's your love that has made him see the light."

CHAPTER 18

"They were incredible, Mother," Shadow says after watching a showcase performance put on by Luanda's music students.

"Well, it's no surprise; they have an amazing teacher," Kolton quips.

"Oh, come on, Kolton. The students deserve the credit, not me," Luanda says, blushing.

"According to Terence Dwyer, you've found a way to really motivate your students like he's never seen before," Jessica adds.

"I've simply done my best to help them express themselves as individuals through their music," Luanda says humbly.

"Kolton, I want to thank you again for agreeing to speak at the foundation's upcoming events," Jessica says, smiling as the topic shifts to the Kratz Foundation. "I just hope it's not going to be too stressful for you."

"Actually, I'm looking forward to the opportunity. And because of this lovely lady beside me here, I'm glad to announce that the word 'stress' is no longer in my vocabulary," Kolton says as he embraces Luanda.

* * *

After a comprehensive meeting of Westgale and his executive committee discussing all aspects relating to the Pinian energy deal, the UCIT crew arrives for a press conference to be given by Energy Secretary Harrison Deacon.

When the pudgy, ruddy-faced Deacon steps in front of the camera he appears extremely relaxed, smiling from cheek to cheek like a jolly uncle. "The most important aspect of this incredible deal is the fact that the fera-bean biofuel and the other natural resources we are bringing in from Pinia will have no negative impact whatsoever on our natural environment, our land use, and our food security," he exclaims. "Also, due to the biofuel's unique composition, we will no longer need to worry about nitrous oxide emissions contributing to global warming."

Meanwhile, in an office down the hall from where Secretary Deacon's speaking to the nation, Professor Kinsley is meeting with Director Perry.

"I still have no idea what it was that actually took over our skies that evening, but this is excellent news, Director Perry," the professor says as he explains that the glittery pebbles found under the surface of a grassy hill in Boise, Idaho, match those that were discovered at Moon Shade Bluff.

"Whoa, that is incredible!" Perry replies. "And the other thirteen locations?"

"Unfortunately, even with all our advanced equipment, only one of those locations is immediately accessible to begin excavating. The other dozen sites are extremely complex and will take quite some time to evaluate, probably months," Kinsley says. "I'll be submitting a plan to Secretary Gibson."

* * *

As Dr. Ahar and his lab director are reviewing Kinsley's findings, he receives a flash-message from the warden of the Federal Justice Center. He starts trembling as he reads the message that Anya has asked to meet with him. *What could this mean?* he wonders. *Hopefully she's changed her mind, and is willing to fight for her freedom.* The visitation is scheduled for 10:00 a.m. the following day.

For Jack Ahar, the night passes as slowly as the minutes on a schoolroom clock. Abandoning the sleep that will not come, he sits in his apartment staring at photos of Maria and Anya, his memories taking him back to a few days before his wife died and Anya was born.

* * *

"I can't believe it, Jack. Soon we'll be able to hold our little baby girl in our arms," Maria said, lightly tapping her belly and then looking at Jack with a sheepish grin.

"Whoa... did I hear you just say 'baby girl'? Maria Ahar, I thought we made a deal," Jack replied with a laugh.

"I couldn't help it. I had to know."

"When did you find out?" Jack asked, still smiling.

"This morning," Maria replied softly. *"Dr. Henderson told me everything is looking great."* She bowed her head to hide a frown.

"Then what's with the long face?" Jack asked.

Maria turned her head to regard the flash-screen in the corner of the room. Her lower lip quivered, and she finally sobbed, *"I'm afraid, Jack. What kind of life will our daughter have, with this country destroying itself?"*

They silently watched a clip showing a series of MAA military vehicles patrolling eerily silent suburban streets in cities throughout the country. Jack shook his head and grabbed the remote to shut off the screen. Then he embraced Maria.

"We'll get through this, Maria," he said to the woman in his arms. *"This country always prevails."*

"Just promise me one thing," Maria said looking into Jack's eyes.

"Sure; you name it," Jack replied.

"Promise me that if something were to ever happen to me, you'll always make certain our daughter's properly cared for."

"Oh come on, Maria," Jack replied, gently brushing the hair from her eyes.

"Just promise me," she pleaded.

"You have my solemn word," Jack answered as he pulled her closer and gently kissed her forehead.

* * *

When Dr. Ahar arrives at the prison, Anya is already waiting for him in the visiting room. "Gentlemen," he says, acknowledging Anya's guards. They move to the exit, glancing back at Anya as they leave.

"Good morning, Anya," the doctor says, trying to keep the anxiety from his voice.

"Father," she replies, her tone and face emotionless. She barely blinks.

"Please tell me you've changed your mind, and you're going to let Nicole fight for your freedom."

"I'm sorry to disappoint you, but that's not why I asked you here," says Anya.

"Then *why* am I here?"

"So I can say goodbye," she replies.

Those words freeze the doctor's movements for a moment. Then he drops into a chair.

"I'm prepared to meet my fate," she adds, remaining emotionless.

Dr. Ahar begins to weep. "What do you expect from me?" he cries. "How many times can I tell you I'm sorry?"

"You have nothing to be sorry about, Father," Anya answers, looking her father in the eyes. "You're simply part of a broken system. I love you. Now, all I ask of you is to let me die in peace, and be with my mother," she adds, remaining stoic. She presses the buzzer to summon the guards.

Her father places his head in his hands and continues weeping.

Forewarned that this meeting would be taking place, I felt it wise to be on the scene. By the time I enter the visiting room, the doctor is alone and listless. "Doctor, would like to talk about it?" I say softly.

He doesn't respond, just stares into space. Then suddenly he lets out a heavy sigh. "It's over, Nicole. She's prepared to die, and there isn't a damn thing you or I or anyone can do about it," he says. "We have no choice but to let this go," he adds, rising abruptly and moving toward the door.

"Doctor, can I—" He's gone before I can finish.

A young man appears in the doorway after Ahar leaves. He has bright orange hair and is dressed in a form-fitting black and white checkered suit. "Hello, I'm Guardian Macdonald," he says in a voice with a British accent.

"What can I do for you?" I reply.

"Ms. Kratz, it's a pleasure to finally meet you. It's not every day I get to meet a hero. I'd ask for an autograph, but I'm much too shy," he says with an annoying laugh.

Westgale told me about this guy, and how annoying he can be. He wasn't kidding. He already reminds me of one of those obnoxious salesmen trying to sell me something that I've no interest in.

"I'm hoping you'll be able to join me and a couple of important guests for lunch today at the Prestige Hotel," he says.

I look at him curiously for several seconds. Despite my annoyance, I accept his invitation. "I'll be there."

When I arrive at the Prestige, one of Macdonald's underlings leads me into the dining room. As he did for his meeting with Westgale, he's reserved the entire dining room. A curtain has been set up in front of the back half of the room to ensure privacy. When the underling leads me around it, I'm surprised to find Westgale and Gerald Levin sitting at the table with Macdonald.

"Great. Everybody's here," Macdonald says as he stands and pulls out a chair for me to be seated. "I hope everyone enjoys Italian. I've ordered the chefs to cook us up some spaghetti and meatballs." He gazes across at the three of us. "Wow, talk about being surrounded by power," he adds sardonically, then begins typing something into his flash-pad.

"Would someone please tell me why the hell I was taken away from my busy schedule?" Gerald Levin demands.

"Yes, it would be nice to know why we're here," Westgale adds.

"You elitists; always so uptight. I know, time is money—and of course there's never enough time in the day. But you people should seriously learn to ease up a little. Enjoy the finer things in life—like this," Macdonald adds, looking up at the servers as they arrive with the food. "Let's enjoy," he says with a wide smile as he tucks his napkin into the front of his lime green cashmere turtleneck.

"Now, as to why we're here," he says, twirling the spaghetti around his fork and then effortlessly shifting it to his spoon. The rest of us stare at him, oblivious to our own plates of food. "I've called you all here to address a very important matter… Anya Ahar," he says just before placing the spoonful of spaghetti into his mouth.

"You mean to tell me you had me dragged down here because of that deranged anarchist?" Gerald shouts, tossing his fork onto his plate.

"Now, now, Mr. Levin, settle down and pay attention. That so-called 'deranged anarchist' happens to be the most talked about person in America—even more talked about than the three of you," Macdonald says, before annoying us all by slurping his spaghetti.

Where the hell did they find this imbecile? "Oh, you'll have to excuse Mr. Levin," I say with a snicker. "It's difficult for him to accept that there's currently someone in America more popular than he is." *I couldn't resist.*

As expected, Levin scowls at me.

"What is it you need to tell us?" Westgale calmly asks, attempting to defuse the tension.

"It's now official. Anya Ahar's execution date has been set," Macdonald answers, plunging a fork into a meatball.

Although I knew this was inevitable, actually hearing it leaves me feeling very sad.

"I'll be darned. There is a God after all," Gerald exclaims. "I hate to be so insensitive, but it's about time she's put out of her misery."

"You cold, heartless bastard!" I shout, unable to control my anger.

"Oh, Nicole, let go of the ridiculous obsession you have with that little demon," Gerald scoffs.

"Do you think this is something to celebrate? This news will cause mayhem right across the country," I say.

Macdonald continues to enjoy his spaghetti, appearing amused by our verbal sparring. He sets down his fork and spoon, and chews and swallows another meatball before saying, "We at the Outer Commission share your concern, Ms. Kratz, and therefore we feel it's wise to allow Anya to address the public via an interview with

UCIT. We believe it'll help calm the waters," Macdonald says before taking a sip of wine.

"I'd be shocked if she agrees to that," I respond, shaking my head.

"She already has. I personally spoke with her, and it's something she's actually looking forward to," Macdonald replies.

"I can't believe this," Gerald says in frustration. "Why in the world should a criminal who's on death row be permitted to address the country? Have you people lost your minds?"

"Well, unfortunately for you, Mr. Levin, you have absolutely no say in the matter," Macdonald answers smugly.

Immediately following the meeting, I go to Dr. Ahar's office to relay the news.

"I guess it was just a matter of time, Nicole," he says, unsuccessfully fighting back his tears. "When is she going to speak?"

"Tomorrow evening," I answer.

"Oh my Lord," he responds, shaking his head in disbelief. "I want to thank you for all the compassion you've shown my daughter. You've done so much."

"I just wish I could've done more," I say softly.

"To think here I am, performing an analysis on a new drug that will enable the average human to live to 120, and soon my daughter will be dead before her twenty-sixth birthday."

"I'm so sorry, Doctor. I wish there were words I could say to ease your pain, but…"

"Like I said, you've done everything you could. We have to find it in our hearts to move on… And you, my dear, have an election to win."

* * *

When Dr. Ahar arrives home he switches on the hallway light and heads aimlessly into his dark living room. Still in his wet winter coat and boots, he sinks into his easy chair. He thinks back to the dreadful day his wife died in the middle of that icy road. He thinks of what could have been… what should have been. Over and over he relives the day in his mind, each time hoping the outcome will be different; it never is. In his mind he sees that yellow blanket lying across his wife's lifeless body. He recalls the sound of baby Anya's cry. It was as if the baby could sense something was wrong. He'll forever remain haunted by the memory of coming home with his newborn, and having to arrange his wife's funeral at the same time.

Suddenly his mind snaps back to the present and he reaches to turn on the lamp on the table beside him. Eventually he's successful, but not before knocking over the remnants of last evening's frozen food dinner and a glass of brandy.

He slowly stumbles to the hallway closet, where he retrieves a file box that is labelled *Anya's Stuff*. With an unsteady hand he reaches into the box and removes several old medical and science books, several of which he himself wrote. There are also several magazines featuring articles on Maria. As Jack peruses the magazines, he discovers a sealed envelope in the middle of one of them. *What could this be?* He takes the envelope out and places it on the table in front of him, staring at it intently. *Should I or should I not open it?* The battle plays out in his mind.

Finally, curiosity gets the best of him and he sits back down in the easy chair and slowly opens the envelope. Inside is what appears to be a poem. It's titled "No-One." Jack begins to read.

NO-ONE
Drifting through a field – The wind tells me I'm real
Phantoms in the trees – Swaying in the breeze
I take up a small space – In such a giant place – Clinging to my faith
When someone is a no-one
I gather forgotten flowers – I make a bouquet
I reach out to the phantoms – But even they turn away
Drawn to a flowing stream – The ripples ignite a dream
A swan taking flight – I control the night
Nomads seize the land – Under my command
But suddenly the dream fades away

> *And I lose my grip on faith*
> *I take up a small space – In such a forsaken place*
> *When someone is a no-one*

The doctor picks up the glass lying on the floor and throws it across the room, smashing it against the wall. He looks at the shards of glass and is instantly reminded of the broken promise he'd made to the woman he so dearly loved.

CHAPTER 19

Great anticipation across the country greets the announcement that Anya Ahar will be interviewed by Cryptic this evening. As the moment draws closer, Hunter and I gather with the president and Dave Perry in the Freedom Home's communications center to view the broadcast.

"I'm really concerned," Westgale says, his face flushed. "We have absolutely no idea what she's going to say tonight, and frankly, that scares the hell out of me."

"I've made sure all our security forces are on high alert, sir," Dave Perry says as he paces the floor. "I can't believe this damn Commission has decided to do this."

"You know, gentlemen, you might be worrying for nothing," I say, trying to ease their anxiety, along with my own.

After Attorney General Champ Sutton relays all the facts pertaining to Anya's situation, the UCIT broadcast shifts to the visiting room of the Federal Justice Center.

Dressed in a lavender prison jumpsuit and sporting her enormous glasses, Anya appears relaxed as she waits for the interview to begin. Suddenly a series of dissonant sound effects can be heard as the camera zooms in on Cryptic. Then silence. Cryptic is now a few feet away from Anya. She appears to be staring directly into the robot's eyes, which are shifting rapidly between baby blue and jet black.

"Good evening, Miss Ahar," the robot says in its monotone voice.

"Hello," Anya replies softly.

"Your refusal to fight for your freedom in the Judicial Triangle comes as a shock. Would you kindly explain why it is you've decided not to fight?" Cryptic asks.

Anya gathers her thoughts for a moment before answering. "I refuse to continue to be judged by a broken system," she responds firmly. "A system that chooses power and greed over love and compassion. A system that suppresses individuality and is rife with hypocrisy."

"So, is this your way of protesting?"

"You may call it that if you like."

"Do you believe you'll be regarded as some kind of martyr?"

"That is not my intention."

"What would you like to say to those who have been behind you, and have demanded you be set free?"

"First of all, my death will be my freedom. To the youth of America, I ask you to please remain strong and continue to fight for the things you believe in. The future is yours. You must hold it close to your heart!" Anya replies, her voice rising with every syllable.

"Do you think a revolution is the answer? Or is it all a matter of proper leadership?"

"To repair a broken system, yes, strong leadership is required. A leader who heeds the concerns of their followers and sets a proper example. A leader who listens and attempts to understand their followers, regardless of age, gender, ethnicity, and social status."

"Do you believe such a person exists?"

"Yes. Nicole Kratz is that person," Anya answers firmly.

I look to my left at Hunter, who's grinning from cheek to cheek.

"This is perfect. Exactly what we need," he crows.

"I don't know, Hunter," Westgale says, scratching his head. "Nicole's just been endorsed by someone on death row."

"Unjustifiably on death row," I chime in.

"It'll be interesting to see the reaction on the World Connect," Hunter says, motioning toward the flash-screen at the front of the room.

"Well, I knew it wouldn't be long before *he* had his say," Dave Perry quips as Gerald Levin appears on the screen.

"*Good evening, my fellow Americans. Election Day is drawing closer,*" he says from the MAA's headquarters. "*I'm very grateful and honored to have a very special guest with me this evening. I'm even more honored by the fact that after all these years he's decided to venture over to the dark side, if you like, and provide me with a much-appreciated endorsement,*" he says with an unscrupulous grin. "*Ladies and gentlemen, a former president of the United States, Jackson Snyder.*"

"What the hell!" Dave Perry shouts.

"God help us," Westgale says, shocked at the thought of his political hero endorsing "the enemy."

"*Thank you, Gerald. I'm thrilled to be here this evening,*" Snyder says from the podium. "*I never thought the day would come when I would be re-entering the political spectrum, let alone providing support to the very men who led the insurgency to overthrow me as president.*" He chuckles. "*I've enjoyed my quiet life of farming for the last twenty-five years. It's such a far cry from the nasty world of politics. However, there is no way I will sit by and watch my country be turned into a giant spectacle,*" he says boldly.

Known for his potent speeches, Snyder doesn't seem to have lost his touch, even after all these years.

"*It's my understanding that I'm President Westgale's political hero. And up until this past year I actually thought he'd been doing a rather fine job. But when I consider what has recently transpired, anger fills my heart.*

"*Over the last several months, corruption and mass confusion have plagued his Administration far beyond the pale. Westgale's insane decision to do business with Cobra Pix is in opposition to everything democracy stands for. To make matters even worse, President Westgale has handed the rapidly dimming PBA torch to Nicole Kratz.*

"*It's difficult for me to be critical of Ms. Kratz, considering the respect I have for her father, who was a highly valued and respected US Attorney General under my Administration. Nonetheless, when it comes to the importance of the president's office, the truth must never be sugar-coated. Nicole Kratz's support of Anya Ahar is downright appalling. By continuously supporting such a criminal extremist, she has made it clear that she has no sense of justice. This is not a person fit to be president. I sense we are seeing the beginning of the end of the Peace Bringers Association of America.*

"If it's your wish to see America rise back up from the perilous depths of complete irrelevance, you must embrace Gerald Levin as your next president. He's a man who has..."

"I've heard enough. Turn the damn thing off, Hunter," Westgale says, his face flushed. "My Lord. Levin is being praised by the greatest president this country has ever known. The man who created this very association," he adds, slamming his fist on the table. "This will crush you, Nicole."

An hour later, I'm thrilled to learn a mass gathering of my supporters have made their way to Central Park. "Check this out," an excited Beth says to me, showing me her flash-pad.

"Down with the old, vote for Nicole!" my supporters shout in unison while holding up signs that read "Nicole for Prez!" The camera scans the grounds. Several young men and women can be seen destroying a police electro. As they smash the car with clubs, they continue the chant, "Down with the old, vote for Nicole!" Others are seen setting off fire-zaps and shouting the same words, thrusting their signs in the air. When the UCIT camera provides a wide angle view of the park, several small fires can be seen spreading across the property.

"It has become absolutely crazy out here," Cryptic says as it observes the area. *"I've been told three police electros have been demolished, and five police robo-cycles have been set ablaze. I'm here with a young lady who is one of the organizers of this event. Can you tell me what has happened here tonight?"*

"I wish I knew," she answers as she glances around. *"The purpose of gathering here tonight was simply to show support for Nicole Kratz, in a peaceful manner."*

"Are you surprised some of her supporters have chosen to behave this way?"

"Most definitely... I really can't tell you why this has happened."

* * *

Earl Pemberton and his nephew Andy watch the chaotic scene over a few drinks in the lounge of the Prestige Hotel. "Great work, Andy," Earl says with a smirk. He chugs down what's left of his beer and slams his glass on the tabletop before adding, "They did a good job of spreading themselves throughout the crowd—everything looks authentic."

Andy laughs. "I must admit that was some of the best acting I've ever seen. It's amazing what some people will do for a little cash."

"Heh, you were right; it was worth every cent. Dirty, but worth every cent."

"I assure you, Uncle Earl, we're on our way."

Pemberton smiles and rubs his hands together. "Yeah, I can feel it. We're going to pull this off. With Snyder on our side, I'm certain our friends at the PBA are reeling."

CHAPTER 20

"If you asked us here because you're planning to ambush Nicole and have her candidacy revoked, you're wasting both your time and ours, Phillip," Westgale says to Chairman Malone as he and Director Perry meet with him in his office.

"I don't see any other choice, Mr. President. With Jackson Snyder now backing Levin, there's no way Nicole can pull this off. We need to put a contingency plan in place," Malone insists, leaning forward in his chair. Westgale looks away, shaking his head.

"Just out of curiosity, what is it exactly you have in mind?" Dave Perry asks.

Malone relaxes slightly, as if drawing that question from Perry signals capitulation. "I think I know the very person who can turn this thing around," he says, his voice conspiratorial, "and get us back to where our focus should be."

"And who might that be?" Westgale asks with a raised brow.

"The very man I replaced as chairman," Malone answers smugly.

"Thor?" Westgale blurts.

"Yes. I spoke with him late last night and he's completely on board. He was actually quite excited about the opportunity," Malone replies. "All we need is for you and David to let this go to council, and I'm sure Nicole's candidacy will be revoked."

"Are you aware that David and I literally begged Nicole to get into this race?" Westgale says, keeping his voice level with difficulty. "We're sure as hell not about to stab her in the back!"

Dave's been peering at something on his flash-pad. "Whoa..." he says. He looks at Malone. "May I?" He indicates the control panel for the flash-screen at the front of the office. Malone nods. Dave activates the flash-screen and calls up what he's been viewing on his flash-pad.

"I'll be darned," Westgale exclaims.

"Hmm, that is something," Malone says uncertainly, studying the most recent polling numbers on the screen.

"Who would've thought!" Westgale crows, jumping up from his seat. "This is unbelievable—sixty-four percent!" He pauses to study the screen again. "Anya Ahar endorses Nicole, Snyder endorses Levin, and it gives us a stranglehold on this damn thing," he adds, his voice cracking with excitement.

* * *

After I'm informed of my incredible surge in popularity in the polls, my security team discreetly escorts me up to Room 823 of the Prestige Hotel. Before I have a chance to knock on the door, Jackson Snyder flings it open. "Nicole! Come in," he says, moving out of the doorway to let me pass.

I turn to the two men who escorted me. "Thank you, gentlemen. I'll message you when I'm done," I say, and step into the room.

"Come on in, come in," Snyder says, still ebullient as he leads me into the room. "I'm so glad you agreed to meet." He indicates a chair, then offers me a coffee as I sit down.

"Thank you, sir," I reply formally as he hands me a mug. Mystified, I regard him with cold eyes. This is the man who declared for my opponent.

"So—I just saw the recent poll numbers," Snyder says happily as he plops down on the sofa across from me. "I'm thrilled to see my plan worked."

About to rebuke him for gloating—for what reason, I have no clue—I clamp my mouth shut and do a double take. "Your plan worked? What in the world does that mean?"

Snyder leans forward and regards me with wide eyes, smiling incredulously. "Did you actually think that was for real?" He studies my astonished face for a moment, then throws back his head and laughs. I gape at him as he chuckles. Then he lowers his head and looks at me with such satisfaction, I'm further mystified. "I knew it'd backfire on them. Serves those bastards right!" he brags, chuckling again.

"You'll have to forgive me, sir, but I'm rather confused," I admit when he stops.

He draws a deep breath and looks at me seriously. "Clarity, Nicole. I've always believed it's the most important aspect of any form of communication," Snyder says. "You see, when that ignoramus brought me up to the podium to praise him and trash you, he clouded his political position, came across as a hypocrite." He pauses to calmly sip his coffee. "Hell, I'm the president he and his cronies toppled. His people thought my support would help him capture the best of both worlds. Foolish. Very foolish."

I inhale sharply as understanding dawns. "Oh my. You mean to tell me this was some sort of strategy you came up with to help *my* cause?"

"Exactly." He nods, chuckling again. "I'm yesterday's news, Nicole; an already exceedingly dim light fading faster and faster into oblivion. Having me endorse him was the worst move Levin could make."

"But—your legacy! You'll never be looked at in the same way again," I almost wail. I pause at a memory, and shake my head before saying, "You should've seen the way the president and Dave Perry reacted when they saw you standing up there with Levin."

"The future of America is far more important than *my* reputation," Snyder says. He looks sheepish. "The only difficult part in all this was saying those nasty things about *you.*"

"Did Levin ask you to come on board with his team in the aftermath?"

"No. The crazy thing is, I got the impression Levin himself wasn't thrilled about the whole idea in the first place. It was his staff and that pompous jackass Earl Pemberton who thought they were being clever." Snyder pauses thoughtfully. "I'm actually still shocked Levin went along with it."

"Well, thankfully, for once in his life, he listened to others," I say sarcastically.

Snyder looks intently at me. "You keep up the good fight, Nicole. Make this country proud. I'll be out on the farm, pulling for you. Heck, I'm even going to have Warren get me one of those flash-screens. And then maybe someday down the road, I'll meet with William Westgale and fill him in on our little secret." He grins devilishly. I grin back.

* * *

The mood at the MAA headquarters is one of anger and trepidation. "How in the world could this have backfired so badly!" Gerald Levin shouts at his two lead advisers.

"We have no idea, sir," one of them replies, shaking her head.

"No idea? Why the hell do you wake up in the morning, get yourself all fancied up, and come down here, if you have no idea what's going on!" Gerald continues, his voice bouncing off the walls of the boardroom. "You people are paid to have your ear to the ground, your eye on the ball—and not fall flat on your ass."

"I guess we underestimated the impact Anya Ahar's interview would have on the—"

"Don't use that as a cop-out, sweetheart," Gerald sneers. "The research report you people provided me told me it'd be wise to accept Jackson Snyder's support, and sure enough, it ended up being a complete failure." He pauses and takes a deep breath. "Termination packages will be sent to each of you tomorrow morning," he concludes, and storms out of the conference room and into Earl Pemberton's office.

"You fired both of them?" Earl asks, frowning. "They're two of the most brilliant political minds in the entire country."

"I went along with what those so-called brilliant minds recommended and it just may have cost me the election. Having Snyder endorse me... what a stupid mistake," Gerald says, staring into space.

"Before they came to you, I was the person who approved it. So I should probably be clearing my desk with them. Or perhaps we really need to take a step back and admit the truth," Earl says calmly.

Gerald looks at him. "The truth?"

"Yeah. As much as we both hate to admit it, this Anya Ahar thing is the catalyst behind all of this."

Gerald loosens his tie and thinks for a moment. "You're correct. I hate to admit it, but you are. I just can't understand how she's attracted the interest she has."

"It's as if she's some kind of evil saint who has this country under a spell. And frankly, I have no idea what we can do about it," Earl admits, shaking his head.

Gerald squares his shoulders. "We keep fighting, Earl, until there's no fight left." He moves to the sideboard. "Once word gets out that America's supposedly greatest golfer is not who the country thinks he is, I'm sure the tide will begin to turn," he says as he pours two glasses of brandy.

"I hear you, Gerald. Andy's been on it nonstop," Earl says, thinking back to the conversation his nephew related to him two weeks ago.

* * *

"Shale, it's been far too long, buddy," Andy Pemberton said to his long-time friend, pro golfer Shale Michaels, when they met in the café at the Pemberton's private golf club in Orlando. "Thanks for agreeing to do the clinic. We're expecting quite the turnout. Heck, judging by my game of late, I know I could use some pointers."

"I don't know, Andy. The last time we played, you gave me a run for my money. Soon I may be the one coming to you for pointers." Shale laughed.

"I highly doubt that'll be happening anytime soon, but if you ever require any legal assistance, you know I'm only a flash-message away," Andy replied. To his surprise, the smile instantly left Shale's face. "Is everything okay, Shale?" Andy asked, concerned.

Shale sighed. "I might be taking you up on that offer sooner than later," he said, staring out the window of the café.

"Are you in some kind of legal trouble?"

Shale released a heavy sigh and looked at Andy. "As much as I hate to face it, it's only a matter of time before all hell breaks loose."

"Talk to me, Shale. What's going on?" Andy asked, leaning closer to his friend.

Shale dropped his voice. "I know you'll probably find this impossible to believe, but up until recently the Eternal had been controlling our entire association."

"The AGA?" Shale nodded. "The crime syndicate was controlling it?" Andy asked in disbelief.

"Yes." Shale's voice turned bitter. "It's a massive cesspool of corruption."

Andy subconsciously dropped his voice. "How so?"

"The tournaments; they've been rigged. When this whole gambling on golf thing became popular a few years back, the Eternal swept in and took control."

"My Lord... Was Lowell Billings involved in this as well?" Andy asked with a raised brow.

"Of course he was. Actually, everything was done to ensure he remained at the top of the heap."

"Oh?" Andy replied, his curiosity boiling over. Hmm, Nicole Kratz's husband, a fraud. This could be exactly what we need, he thought. "I guess we should start off by having you tell me everything you know."

* * *

"Thanks for seeing me, Nicole," Attorney General Sutton says as I enter his office.

"Is something wrong, Champ?" I ask in response to his grave expression.

He sighs. "From a legal standpoint, I shouldn't even be doing this."

"Does this have something to do with Anya?" I ask, his concern putting me on edge.

He looks at me. "It's not Anya. It's Lowell."

"Lowell? As in my husband?" I say in surprise.

"That's correct. I'm sorry, Nicole," Champ responds, and then explains.

"Wait a second—when did your office find out about this?" I think to ask only after my mind has stopped reeling.

"We've been working on this since the day Edgar Fryman was exposed as one of the biggest crooks this country has ever known," Champ answers. "We've been thoroughly investigating the inner workings of both the Fryman Group and the Eternal. Edgar Fryman's nephew has been singing like a bird. He claims it's his wish 'to cleanse himself of sin,'" Champ says sardonically.

My mind is racing, trying to sort through this information. "Are you certain Lowell was involved in this?"

"Your husband's been the premiere golfer in this country for the last fifteen years," Champ says. "Of course he was involved."

I can't just accept this. "Do you have proof?" I ask.

"We're still gathering all the facts. Look, Nicole, like I said, this is not something I should be discussing with you," Champ says calmly. "In fact, the only reason I called you here was because Westgale asked me to. He's really concerned about the impact this will have on the election."

"Please, Champ, give me the details," I say, my body trembling.

Champ looks at me for a few seconds and sighs. "All right. From what we've learned so far, Edgar Fryman had things set up so that both his investment firm and his racketeering outfit, the Eternal, were getting the best of both worlds."

"How the hell was he pulling that off?"

"When betting on golf recently became such a popular trend here in America, the Eternal did what it usually does—it muscled its way in with payoffs and threats, got the executives and players on board, and the next thing you know, the whole system became rigged. But you see, both the executives and the players were taken care of financially, so as hard as it seems to believe, purposely missing a three-inch putt sometimes worked to a player's advantage."

"The association *and* the players were being paid off?"

"Let's just say it was the cost of doing business. Oh, don't worry; through the Eternal, Fryman was making back at least five times his investment."

"And the Fryman Group?"

"This is where Lowell came into play," Champ says gently. "The plan involved fixing it so he won most of the tournaments, or at least was always in the top three."

"Hold on a second," I say, feeling like I'm now entering my worst nightmare. "From what you're telling me, this whole ordeal began after Lowell had already established himself as the country's number one golfer."

"That's correct," Champ says. "And Fryman made sure it stayed that way, even through your husband's battle with injury."

I look at him. "I don't understand."

"He had a deep financial interest in Lowell."

"I still don't understand."

"Think about it, Nicole. Lowell Billings, an elite golfer, the all-American hero, married to the most powerful woman in the country. I don't have to remind you of how many companies your husband became the face of, do I?"

"And let me guess—the Fryman Group was heavily invested in those companies?"

"Exactly. Panther Electros, KT Sports, Starcrest, Jiggs Beverages, to name a few."

"Lowell somehow had to have been threatened into this," I insist.

"We should have that answer soon," Champ says. "Unfortunately, when it came to your husband, even Fryman's nephew wasn't privy to all the details."

"Are you going to be arresting him?" I ask somberly.

"I'm sorry, Nicole, but as of right now, it doesn't look like we'll have a choice. Once due diligence has been performed we'll be doing an entire sweep. I think it'd be in everyone's best interest if Lowell came forward."

"Oh my Lord," I say.

To say I'm preoccupied as I leave Champ Sutton's office a short time later is an understatement. To think my husband may have been threatened into participating in such a sinister scheme is ripping at my heart. Oblivious to my surroundings, I find myself back at the grand-electro that brought me here, so perturbed that I barely acknowledge Edward, my driver.

He immediately notices my anxiety. "Is everything okay, Ms. Kratz?" he asks gently as he opens the back door of the grand-electro for me.

"I'm fine, Edward," I reply, although truthfully, I want to say, *No! I'm a complete wreck.* "Please, just take me home," I add.

Safe in the back of the electro, I can wipe away the tears that I finally let come to my eyes. I think of Lowell. I met him when I was eighteen at one of my mother's charity galas. At the time he was a rising star on the golf circuit, having won every junior championship there was.

What I find most attractive about Lowell is his sense of humility. Even though the world is constantly telling him how great he is, he views himself as just another person, albeit one who happens to be extremely gifted at the sport of golf. Lowell will be the first one to tell you the many things he isn't good at, like, for example, cooking. Although he does claim to be a master at preparing a bowl of cereal. "It's all about perfect proportions," he jokingly intones, displaying his bowl of Raisin Honey Flakes to me and the girls during family breakfasts.

Sadly, those family breakfasts have always been few and far between. Lowell and I have really lost touch with each other; no surprise given the hectic lives we've been leading. I guess the crazy world of high-stakes politics and being the country's premiere golfer don't allow for a lot of overlap in schedules. There even came a point when we almost separated. But we felt we owed it to our daughters to try and work it out.

During the time I was President Westgale's executive director, Lowell was dealing with an awful back injury. Here I was, travelling around the world promoting the World Harmony Program, while my husband could barely get out of bed. Fortunately, with the aid of some of the country's foremost specialists, he recovered well enough to golf again, but I regret not being there for him the way I should have been. I also regret not taking his last name when we married. By that time the name Kratz was highly regarded in American politics, and I deemed keeping it beneficial to my own political career. Though he'd never admit it, I know this hurt Lowell.

As the electro approaches my home, my anxiety is becoming overwhelming. With the girls away on a school trip, this evening is supposed to be the two of us enjoying a very rare romantic Friday night dinner. Instead I'm struggling with a maelstrom of emotions, none of them romantic.

I immediately notice the lack of lighting within the house as the car comes to a stop in the drive and I get out. Knowing Lowell and the effort he puts into these occasions, I'm sure when I enter I'll discover a house lit by candles and a man in a tuxedo, playing a violin. As I open the front door, I feel lost in a haze. *How could this be happening?* My hands are shaking and my heart feels like it weighs a thousand pounds.

I enter and take a few tentative steps down the dark hallway. There's not a candle in sight, and no violin music. I reach for the nearest light switch and flip it on, then head toward the living room. "Lowell," I call out. "Lowell, are you home?" As I pass the bar area leading to the living room, I see a half-empty bottle of whiskey on the counter. *Hmm, that's strange, Lowell never touches alcohol.*

"I'm here... in the living room," Lowell finally answers. His voice sounds scared.

It sure doesn't sound like the usual happy-go-lucky Lowell I know. I grow alarmed. My heart is hammering in my head.

I enter the living room and stumble to a stop. "Oh my God!" I cry out.

He's sitting on the sofa, holding a lit-up styngor to his head. His thumb is trembling an inch away from the trigger. *One push of that button and he'll be dead.* "What are you doing, Lowell?" I ask, my body shaking uncontrollably. I try my best to remain calm, but the more I look at the styngor's glaring red light, the more I fear the worst is about to come.

"I'm sorry, Nicole. I failed you—I failed everybody. I'm a fraud," he moans. Tears flow down his cheeks.

My eyes remain glued to that styngor. "It's okay, Lowell. We'll get through it," I say gently.

"You don't know what I've done," he cries.

"I know all about it, honey. It's going to be okay," I say, trying to keep my voice level, keep it from quavering.

"I wanted to... I wanted to come clean. There's no excuse." Suddenly he moves the styngor right up against his head.

I sway, light-headed with fear. "Put that thing down," I say. "I'm right here with you. I love you, Lowell. Please put the styngor down," I say in sheer desperation. I ever so slowly reach for a photo of Tiffany and January on the table to my right. "Do you remember this, Lowell?" I say, and manage a slight chuckle as I show him the recent Halloween photo of the girls in their zombie costumes. "I'll never forget how you spent days designing those costumes for them. All I can remember is January complaining about how spooked she was by dressing up as a zombie, and of course Tiffany couldn't get enough of it." I look up at him. "These beautiful young girls need their father. *I* need you, and the rest of your family needs you."

Finally, Lowell moves his eyes toward the photo. Oh my God! I see his thumb make a rapid movement. A split second later the styngor's red light vanishes. The weapon is off. He places it on the side table. I quickly reach over, pick it up, and put it on lock mode. Lowell sits with his head buried in his hands. I can hear his sobs.

"What have I done?" he moans.

"It's going to be okay. I'm here with you," I answer, quickly sitting down beside him and holding him in my arms. I pull the blanket normally folded over the back of the couch around his shoulders. "Just lie back and relax." I rise and spread the blanket over him as he lies down. I sag with relief when he calms down and quickly falls asleep. But I remain a nervous wreck.

I call in one of my bodyguards and ask him to sit in the living room with Lowell, then go to my office and make some phone calls, first to Lowell's brother Norm, quickly explaining the situation and asking him to come over, then to Champ Sutton.

"Oh my, we need to address this. Have you called for help?" Champ asks after I explain what transpired.

"Things are under control, Champ," I answer confidently. "He'll be okay."

"You told me he almost killed himself. How can you say that?"

"Trust me. I wouldn't tell you that if I didn't believe it was the case," I reply.

"Let me at least send a doctor of some sort over there."

"I appreciate your concern, Champ, but that won't be necessary."

"I'm sorry, Nicole, but if your husband's in that state of mind, I don't think you should be alone with him."

"I'm not alone with him; Milos is watching over him," I answer. "Plus, Lowell's brother is on his way over as we speak. We'll be all right."

"I wish it were that simple, Nicole. The arrest warrant for your husband is in place, and I'm afraid—"

"I'll make certain he turns himself in first thing tomorrow, so we can get this stupid ordeal over with," I cut in. "I still can't believe those bastards forced my husband into doing something so despicable."

A few minutes after I end the call, Milos notifies me that Lowell's older brother has arrived. Norm rushes into the house. "How is he?" he asks as I intercept him in the bar area.

"He's asleep in the living room," I answer, leading him into my office. "A member of my security team is watching over him."

"What in the world happened?" Norm exclaims.

I take a deep breath and explain.

"Now I get it," Norm says.

"Get what?"

"Why there was a period recently when he had me call in a couple of my men to keep an eye on your daughters," Norm says. He has his own private eye business, here in Washington. "He wouldn't tell me why. I just thought it had to do with one of his obsessed fans. He also gave me strict orders not to worry you."

I stare at him. My daughters were in some sort of danger? My heart starts hammering again. "I can't believe this has happened." I move to sit down.

"I wish he would have just called it a day after that damn back injury," Norm says, taking one of the two other chairs in the room. "He already would have gone down as one of the greats."

I draw a shaky breath. "They're going to be charging him, Norm. This is really serious stuff."

"Once it comes out that he and his family were being threatened, I'm sure he'll be held blameless," Norm says, then adds solemnly, "I just hope it doesn't hinder your run for president."

"It shouldn't," a strained voice says from the office doorway. It's Lowell. I start to rise, but he waves for me to stay put and plops into the other chair. He sighs. "I don't deserve you, Nicole," he says.

"How are you feeling?" I ask gently.

"Like a complete imbecile," he answers, looking directly at us. "I'm so sorry."

"Come on, little brother," Norm says, "I know if my life and the lives of my loved ones were being threatened, I'd probably—"

"Nobody was being threatened, Norm. I was totally complicit in everything." His voice is harsh, as if he's already found himself guilty and is delivering his verdict.

"Yeah, but what about when you came and asked me to have my guys keep an eye on the girls?" Norm counters, sensing, like me, that Lowell's mental state is still fragile.

Lowell impatiently waves that away. "That was because of some deranged fan who'd written some unsettling letters to me."

"If you weren't being coerced, then why in the world did you do it?" I ask calmly.

"When the AGA executives came to me with their scheme, I'd just got back on the circuit after the back injury, and as you'll both recall, I was far from being at the top of my game. I was afraid I never would be again," Lowell answers, subdued. "I guess the one thing I'd always worked so hard to put aside finally got the best of me: my ego."

Norm glances between us as if sensing awkward tension between husband and wife, and slaps his knees, then rises. "Well, it's getting late. I'll leave you folks to yourselves. I'll be in touch, and if there's anything you need, call me."

We murmur our goodbyes.

With Lowell in a very fragile state of mind, I'm still trying to maintain my calm disposition, but it's rapidly crumbling, and I'm growing furious. "Your ego got the best of you! Why? Why in the world did you do this? You have everything you need, including two amazing daughters who adore you. And you have to know how deeply *I* love you."

He lifts his head and looks at me with sad eyes. "Maybe that's the thing, Nicole," he replies solemnly. "Maybe that's why I went to such lengths to stay on top—to fill a void, the void that once was our love… What happened to us?" he blurts, rising from the chair and reaching out to me.

With my emotions reeling, I rise and walk into his arms.

To the outside world, we were the "perfect" couple—accomplished, powerful, and beautiful. We had everything, right? The sad reality is, what we didn't have was each other. Now, here we are, broken souls.

CHAPTER 21

After spending the entire night tossing and turning, catching maybe three hours of sleep, I awake with a sense of doom.

Lowell is up already, preparing to turn himself in. "As difficult as it'll be, I'm resigned to facing whatever comes my way," he says as he pulls a comb through his wavy locks.

"I hope you don't mind, but I took the liberty of calling Arthur Fine on your behalf," I inform him. "He's as good as there is."

"I appreciate that, Nicole, but I'm not intending to fight this. I'm guilty and that's all there is to it. I need to face what's coming to me," Lowell replies as he slicks back his hair with a daub of gel.

"Nonetheless, I still think it'd be wise to retain Arthur," I say.

"Sure," he answers casually. But then the comb pauses and he looks at me. There are tears glittering in the corners of his eyes. "I really messed up," he says. "I'm so sorry, Nicole."

I rise and shower. We have breakfast, abandoning any effort to make it seem normal. Just as we're about to leave, the story breaks on UCIT, and we pause to watch it in silence.

Minutes later, Tiffany and January return home earlier than expected.

"*Already arrested are several executives of the American Golf Association, and two dozen of the country's premiere golfers,*" the report says. "*The country's number one golfer, Lowell Billings, who is also the husband of presidential candidate Nicole Kratz, is expected to turn himself in this morning.*"

"What the hell!" shouts Tiffany, dropping her bags on the floor. January looks at me in horror.

"Th-this isn't true... is it?" January stammers.

Lowell and I can only stare at them. The lack of a response provides her with the answer. The girls exchange a shocked glance, then turn away and leave the room in a huff. I hear the patio door slam.

I start to go after them, but Lowell stops me. "Let me," he says gently, holding me back. "I'm the one who created this mess. I'm the one who needs to deal with it."

I nod. He goes back into the kitchen and opens the patio door. I trail him, then stand near the open window to watch from the kitchen. Outside, the girls are sitting on a bench a few feet from the patio door. Tiffany is holding her younger sister. My heart aches.

Lowell approaches them. They look up. "What's going on, Dad? What are you turning yourself in for?" Tiffany asks.

Lowell answers simply. "There's a scandal in the AGA, and I was involved in it." He sighs and pulls up a chair to sit across from them. "I'm sorry for what I've done. It was wrong," he says, and my heart surges with pride.

"Are you going to go to prison?" January asks.

"Most likely I will," Lowell replies. He's still presenting a calm front for his daughters, but I can tell he's struggling to remain composed.

"What happened, Dad?" January asks.

"Tournaments were rigged," Lowell says. "I wasn't competing fairly. I cheated."

"What made you do something so awful?" Tiffany asks.

As Lowell explains, his daughters listen closely.

"We wouldn't care if you didn't win anymore," January says when he finishes.

"That's right," Tiffany says defiantly. "You're our father and we love you no matter what."

As I watch the three of them share a warm embrace, a rush of emotion comes over me.

"I was going to have Edward take the girls to my sister's house, but I think it's best I stay with them for the rest of the day," I say to Lowell when he reenters the house.

"I think that's wise," Lowell answers quietly.

"I called Arthur's office. He and his driver are going to be here to pick you up within the next half-hour."

Lowell looks at me with empty eyes, resigned to what's about to come his way. "Whatever happens, just know that I love you," he says, and we hold each other tightly.

Later on, with sadness consuming every part of our being, the girls and I sit in the living room in front of our flash-screen. Attorney General Sutton appears on UCIT, announcing details of the scandal to the country. *"This investigation has revealed what is definitely the worst sports scandal this country has ever seen. A web of corruption was woven from the highest ranking executives of the AGA, right down to the players,"* he says solemnly, and continues with the details.

"I can't watch this anymore," Tiffany says.

"I understand, Tiff," I reply gently. "Do you girls want to talk about it?"

"What's there to talk about?" Tiffany answers. "Dad told us everything. We always knew anyway."

"Knew what?" I ask with a raised brow.

"That he became really depressed when he injured his back, and that you guys only stayed together because of us," she replies, her expression dejected.

"I'm so sorry, my sweeties," I say, pulling them close to me. "Yes, because of our busy lives your father and I have grown apart, but the one thing you need to know is that we love both of you more than anything in the world. And once this is all said and done with, we'll all pull it back together. The four of us."

"Can you still be president if Dad goes to jail?" January asks with wide eyes.

"I'm still going to try, honey," I reply with a subtle smile.

Seconds later, Lowell appears on the screen with Arthur Fine. It's just been announced that his bail has been set at three million dollars.

"Come on, Jan. Let's go into the study, and I'll show you the really neat parts in the *Book of ZeZ*," Tiffany says. Before she leaves the room she looks back at the screen, then drops her head, frowning.

Watching them exit, I feel immense pride. Being the daughters of two famous people has not been easy for them. Even at the exclusive private school they attend, the other kids can sometimes be ruthless. When I began supporting Anya Ahar, many of Tiffany's classmates continuously ridiculed her. But she exhibited a high level of resolve and never let it get to her.

Lowell and I are very fortunate that our daughters have developed into the fine young women they are, despite our crazy lives preventing us from giving them the attention every child deserves. In retrospect, I guess this is why Anya's story resonated with me so profoundly.

"*My client would like to make a statement,*" Arthur says on the flash-screen.

The camera shifts to Lowell who, understandably, appears distraught. He takes a deep breath and looks into the UCIT camera. "*I want to take this opportunity to apologize to all those I have let down,*" he says, his voice cracking. "*There is no excuse for my actions. I have failed my family, I have failed myself, and I have failed you, the American public. Regrettably, I have also contributed to tarnishing the sport of golf.*

"*As a professional athlete, I've always believed it is paramount to conduct oneself in an honorable manner, setting an example for those who have chosen to cheer me on and view me as an inspiration. I did not live up to my own set of standards.*

"*I'd like to close with a very important fact. My wife, Nicole Kratz, who also happens to be the person who deserves to be this country's next president, had absolutely no knowledge of my involvement in this scandal. Please do not let my actions cause you to view her in a negative way.*"

Shortly after, Lowell contacts me to inform me his bail has been paid and he is free for the time being. "Great. I'll see you later," I happily reply. "I've been summoned to the Freedom Home. I'm going to have Edward take the girls to my sister's house for the next few days. They asked if they could go and spend time with their cousins."

"I think that'd be wise," Lowell responds.

While preparing to leave for the Freedom Home, I realize UCIT is obtaining public feedback on the news of the day in a new segment on *Pulse of the Nation* from Washington's Brave Land Shopping Center.

Cryptic approaches a tall blonde woman in a tan duffle coat, looking for a comment.

"I think all these PBA scandals are just horrendous," the woman says, her expression angry. "I've always admired Nicole Kratz, but I fear her world is crumbling down around her."

"Would you vote for her for president?" Cryptic asks.

"After hearing this news, I don't think so."

"Even though her husband made it clear she had no knowledge of the crime?"

"Oh, come on," a middle-aged man says, joining the conversation. "That's a bloody joke. He's her husband, for God's sake. Of course she knew."

After a few more people voice their scorn, Cryptic approaches a twenty-something man wearing a hoodie.

"People are always so quick to pass judgment," he says, shaking the hood off his head, his shaggy brown hair falling into his eyes. "I believe him. I found him to be very sincere in his apology. From what I've gathered over the years, with their busy lives, they haven't had a very close marriage, which means they may at times be oblivious to what each other is doing. Besides, look at the alternative—a wolf in designer clothing. Free Anya! Free America!" *the young man cheers. Within seconds, others join in.*

By the time Edward returns from dropping the girls off at my sister's house and we head for the Freedom Home, Gerald Levin is minutes away from speaking. *I'm definitely not looking forward to this.* Nevertheless, I don't turn off the flash-screen in the back of the grand-electro. He'll be speaking from the National Soccer League's

Hall of Fame, where later this evening he's being inducted for his contribution as a builder of the league.

Wearing a Washington Androids leather jacket and ball cap, Levin appears agitated as he takes the podium in the hall's conference room. "This is a bittersweet day for me, folks. On one hand I'm honored and proud to be entering the coveted NSL Hall of Fame, yet at the same time, I'm devastated by today's news," he begins, shaking his head. "In any facet of life, if we don't have integrity, we have nothing. To learn that the American Golf Association and a large number of its players sank to such depths is very disturbing.

"I'm especially saddened to learn that Lowell Billings, one of this country's premiere athletes, is at the core of this scandal. I, like so many people across this country, am a big fan of Mr. Billings. It's heartbreaking when one of our sports heroes lets us down. I hope and pray Mr. Billings will one day find inner peace. He obviously is a troubled man.

"On that note, I'd like to let it be known that on behalf of the Washington Androids, I am donating ten million dollars to the Lawrence Kratz Foundation to help in the fight against these dreadful addictions that plague our society. Thank you, and God bless."

Hmm, interesting, I think as the announcement ends. *He expresses sympathy for my husband, donates a large sum of money to my father's foundation, and doesn't bring me up at all. I must admit, very tactful.*

As I enter the main Freedom Home conference room, I immediately notice the concern on the faces of those who've convened for the meeting. The atmosphere is bleak.

PBA Chairman Justice Phillip Malone begins the proceedings. "Let's get right to it, folks. Rebounding from this latest scandal will be a very difficult task." He looks directly at me.

I'm doing my best to remain composed. Hunter and Beth are on either side of me, while Westgale and Dave Perry are seated across from me, making notes in their flash-pads.

Malone continues. "It is my understanding that a new set of polling numbers will be released tomorrow afternoon. It would be reasonable to speculate that this set of numbers will be nowhere near as favorable to us as the last one." He shifts his gaze across the room. None of us are used to seeing Justice Malone so sullen. Considering what's at stake, who can blame him?

I'm torn, as I sense my dream of becoming president fading. I'm even more torn, thinking of an America being run by the MAA. If we discover Lowell's indiscretions are causing panic among the voting public to the degree that it has crushed my chances of winning, then I'll have no choice but to back out of the race and hand over the reins to Thor Hardy. Gerald Levin must be kept out of the Freedom Home.

* * *

"Hey, I've got a good one, Uncle Earl," a drunken Andy Pemberton calls out during the revelry at the MAA headquarters. "How *Low*-ell can the PBA sink?"

"What time tomorrow are those results supposed to come out?" a smirking Earl Pemberton asks Gerald Levin.

"According to UCIT, two o'clock," Gerald replies, checking his flash-pad.

"Hey, are they going to make good ol' Lowell pay all that illegal money back?" Andy slurs as he pours himself another shot of tequila.

"I imagine they will, Andy," Gerald replies with a satisfied chuckle as he dabs a cracker with caviar.

"They should make him give it all to Santa Claus," Andy murmurs.

"Come on, Andy," Earl says, holding up his drunk nephew. "It's time to get you back to the hotel."

* * *

Watching the flash-screen in their penthouse condo the next day, Jessica and Shadow look at each other when UCIT alerts the country that it'll be airing a view-file from Cobra Pix in the coming minutes.

The view-file begins with a group of Pinian children playing soccer. Their smiling faces fill up the screen as they run exuberantly around the field.

Seconds later, Cobra appears on the screen. *"Good day, I'm Cobra Pix,"* he says, walking around the perimeter of the soccer field with a border collie prancing happily by his side. Wearing a black flat cap, mirrored sunglasses, a red windbreaker, and blue jeans, Cobra doesn't look the part of a tyrant. *"Children are the world's greatest gift,"* he continues in his usual commanding voice. *"Their innocence must be treasured. For me, the joy they bring surpasses that of a sunset, the singing of birds, and even that of a night sky sprinkled with stars."*

Jessica and Shadow watch, mystified. "What in the world is this all about?" Jessica wonders.

"As I've told you, there are many sides to my father, Jessie," Shadow answers. "Regrettably, this is a side he rarely displays."

"I've been wondering, Shadow," Jessica says as she caresses his arm, "do you think the day will come when you'll be able to forgive him?"

"I highly doubt it," Shadow says stiffly.

The scene then shifts to past footage of Jessica and her team teaching the Pinian children how to use their flash-pads, with a voice-over by Cobra: *"I want to take this opportunity to thank Jessica Westgale and her team of incredibly compassionate American aid workers for the work they've performed here in Pinia. You are true champions of the human spirit."*

CHAPTER 22

It's almost 2 p.m., and Westgale and his executive committee have reconvened for a follow-up to yesterday's meeting. I'm feeling uneasy as eyes glance in my direction and then quickly move away. "Hang in there, Nicole," Hunter says, noticing the cold reception. "We need to keep our heads up and battle on."

"I don't know, Hunter; I'm having a tough time remaining confident," I answer as I await the poll results. Since the Quick Flash Poll Program began automatically accessing all registered flash-pads and flash-screens, UCIT's political survey polls have been reaching a frightening level of accuracy. For example, back when Westgale was elected, the poll was off by less than three percent.

Images of the American flag fill the flash-screen. "Here we go," Beth says as she gives me a nudge.

There's a twenty second countdown before Cryptic's image appears on the screen. *"I will now present the up-to-the-minute presidential election poll results,"* it says as it slowly fades out of the picture. The UCIT logo flashes several times before the numbers are displayed. I take a deep breath, fearing the worst. The tension in the room is rising by the second. As if to tease viewers, the annoying undecided voter result is presented first, on its own: *UNDECIDED 5%*. More flashing images of the American flag, then suddenly the numbers appear: *UNDECIDED 5%; NICOLE KRATZ 67%; GERALD LEVIN 28%.*

A loud cheer cascades across the room. Glum expressions are instantly replaced by those of sheer delight. Beth and Hunter jump up and down in an embrace. On the other side of the room, Justice Malone, William Westgale, and Dave Perry are all laughs and smiles.

"Nicole, come on, don't hold back," Hunter says, tugging at my arm. "We're in the clear."

It quickly dawns on me that unless the UCIT computer network has made some kind of egregious error, which is totally unfathomable, or another catastrophe arises, I'm going to be the next president of the United States of America. I should be jumping for joy, smiling from cheek to cheek, but I'm not. All I can think of is what has happened to the most important thing in my life, my family. And then there's Anya.

"Excuse me. Uh, excuse me," Director Perry says, grabbing the sound-blast amidst the excitement. "Please proceed to the presidential lounge. We have some celebrating to do!" he shouts gleefully.

Although I actually feel like heading straight for my sister's house to pick up my daughters and tell them how much I love them, I do what's expected and join the celebration. I remain deep in thought, though, and find a spot by myself in the corner of the vast lounge.

President Westgale sees me and approaches. "Wow, who saw this coming?" he says, taking the seat beside me. I sit aimlessly stirring my lemon tea, staring into space. He studies me a moment. "Are you okay, Nicole?" he asks softly.

"Honestly, I'm not, sir," I respond with a sigh.

"Is it Lowell?"

"I'm sorry, Mr. President, but I'm in no mood to celebrate," I answer as I prepare to leave.

"Nicole… Nicole!" he calls out. I stop and turn around. "You're not thinking of dropping out, are you?" he asks with a raised brow.

"I'll speak with you tomorrow, sir."

* * *

As expected, the mood at the MAA headquarters is far from joyous. "This can't be happening," Earl Pemberton says to Gerald and Andy.

"Oh, it's happening, Earl," Gerald replies, scowling. "We can't even hit thirty percent, damn it!" He pounds a fist on the conference room table.

"We've obviously underestimated Nicole Kratz's staying power," Earl says.

"It's not *her* power we've underestimated. This is all about Anya Ahar," Andy Pemberton says, reading from his flash-pad.

"Just as we feared," Earl mumbles, pacing the floor.

"I've been studying the corresponding data that came with the results, and I'm telling you this has everything to do with Anya," Andy says, looking up at his uncle. "That little bitch has really struck a chord with this country."

"It's obvious, gentlemen," Gerald interjects. "Just consider what has transpired. First we learn Nicole's father was the person who ordered the closure of Green Light hospital, and now we discover her husband's at the core of what is the worst sports scandal in this country's history, yet none of this has even put a dent in her armor."

"So, how do we pull ourselves out of this quagmire?" Earl asks, his scowl growing deeper.

Gerald sighs and laces his hands behind his head. "The day we met at my estate and you asked me to take the helm, I sincerely thought we'd take this," he says solemnly. "I thought we could get this country back on the right track. But as much as I hate to admit it, I was wrong."

"I refuse to believe that," Earl says, his face flushed.

"The very things that led us to start that war all those years ago have come full circle, and frankly, Earl, this time it's clear we're completely outnumbered," Gerald says.

* * *

Lowell and I arrive home within a few minutes of each other. "How are things going with your case?" I ask as he enters the house.

"You amaze me, Nicole," he answers with a smile. "Concerned about *me*, after what I did. Like I've said a million times, I don't deserve you," he adds, shaking his head.

"I understand why you did what you did," I say as we stand in the main hallway. "And I want you to know that I share the blame."

"Oh no, this was all my doing. I just couldn't stand the thought of not being the man I used to be," Lowell says. "If those last several tournaments weren't fixed, I'd have been lucky to even make the top ten."

"And I should have been there for you, to help you through both your physical and mental anguish. Instead, I was preoccupied with too many other, less important things."

"Like trying to create world peace?" Lowell asks rhetorically, and chuckles as we move into the living room. "Come on, Nicole. You were the second most important person in the country. On top of that, when you were thinking about taking that position, you came to me and I gave you my full support, because I knew how badly you wanted it. And I wanted it for you, just as badly. You're not to blame for any of this. By the way, I saw the current polls. That must have come as quite a relief," he says, forcing a smile despite his sadness.

"Yeah, I guess so," I murmur as I plop down on the sofa.

"Is something wrong? Did something happen I should know about?" Lowell asks, concerned.

"I've been doing a lot of thinking, and I'm seriously considering backing out, Lowell."

"Whoa… you just learned that two-thirds of the people in this country want you as their president, and you're thinking of turning away?"

"I spoke with Arthur today and he told me you're probably looking at three to five years in prison. I want to make sure at least one of us is always there for our daughters, and with you behind bars, it's going to have to be me."

"The girls will be fine, Nicole. Teresa's done such a great job with them," he says, referring to their nanny. "And I know for certain that you'll be there for them when they need you."

"I'm their mother; I should be there for them all the time," I respond.

Lowell looks at me with a sheepish grin. "I promised Tif I wouldn't show this to you until it's complete, but I think it'll help ease your mind," he says as he lays his flash-pad on the counter.

"What is this?" I ask as he taps the screen and retrieves a document.

"Tiffany's teacher asked the class to write an essay about who they think should be president," Lowell explains. "Thinking it'd be unfair for Tif to do so, the teacher gave her the option to write about something else, but our loving daughter was adamant about writing the essay."

I begin to read:

There is no doubt in my mind that Nicole Kratz should and must be our country's next president. Okay, of course I'm biased because she's my mother, but that also means that I know her better than most people. Not only is she extremely intelligent and patriotic, she is also very compassionate toward everybody she meets. Our country needs her leadership.

When she was the country's executive director, I was always amazed that even with her busy schedule, she never failed to be there for my sister January and me when we needed her. We are both so grateful to have such...

As I continue reading a rush of adrenaline pours through me.

"Are you sure you still want to back out?" Lowell asks with a smile.

"Back out, and face the wrath of Tiffany? I don't think so," I reply, laughing.

Seconds later, I hear the sound of a violin from down the hall. Lowell takes my hand and leads me to our candlelit dining room.

* * *

"Good morning, Nicole," a fatigued-looking Westgale says to me as I join him for breakfast in the presidential lounge. He studies me as he tops his oatmeal with dashes of cinnamon. "Please tell me that the incredible news we received yesterday isn't all in vain," he says.

"I'd be lying to you if I didn't tell you I was very close to backing out," I respond.

"Past tense?" he says, and grins. "I was certain you were going to call it a day. What changed your mind?"

"I realized I'd be letting too many people down—especially those closest to me," I respond with a wink.

"This is excellent news," Westgale says, waving over the waitress. "Get this young lady the special of the day."

"Thank you, sir. I just want to tell you how much I appreciate your honesty and how you've supported me through all this madness," I say sincerely.

His face slowly turns from smiling to frowning. "Well, to be frank, I haven't always been honest with you, Nicole," he says, dropping his eyes back down to his oatmeal.

"Oh?"

"I've been holding something back from you for way too long," he says with a sigh.

Hmm, what in the world is he talking about?

"It has to do with Anya."

"Anya?"

"More specifically, the Judicial Triangle hearing last summer."

"Huh... I'm listening," I say.

"I'm sure you can recall how disappointed you were in me for remaining neutral during the hearing."

"Come on, sir, that's water under the bridge. I have my sights looking forward, as we all should."

Slowly exhaling, Westgale leans forward. "I get that, my dear, but you need to know the truth."

"The truth?"

"Yeah, you need to know it was always my wish to allow Anya to find that cure."

"Please, Mr. President, you don't owe me any explanation."

"After the court decided to reject letting her continue working on the LRS cure, I couldn't accept it. So with the aid of Dr. Muller and Anya's specially assigned guard, she was given every opportunity to find the cure."

"Is this for real?" I answer in shock.

"Yes, it is. When Hunter and Dr. Ahar announced the teal-berry discovery, Anya was actually on the cusp of creating a medicine to combat the illness."

"Why... why didn't you fill me in?"

"You have to understand, if the Outer Commission discovered what was taking place it would've been curtains for all involved. Dr. Muller and I were willing to sacrifice ourselves, but I just couldn't put your future on the line."

"But I resigned because of that."

"And that ended up being a blessing in disguise. I know for a fact it ended up saving what little was left of your marriage... didn't it?"

"Gee... I don't know what to say," I respond, reeling at the revelation. "What made you divulge this to me now?"

"My conscience. I couldn't keep it from you any longer," Westgale answers.

He's distracted by an incoming flash-message. "Hmm, this is interesting. It's from my office," he says as he reads the message. "Apparently Gerald Levin is requesting you and I meet with him and his associates at the MAA headquarters this afternoon."

"I wonder what kind of scheme he's cooking up now."

CHAPTER 23

When we enter the MAA headquarters, Westgale and I are immediately greeted by Gerald Levin's Director of Communications, Brandy Noble. "They're waiting for you in the conference room," Brandy says, leading us down a hall. The walls on both sides are lined with photos of military weapons from the past and present. Just prior to entering the conference room, I notice a War Within plaque containing the words *Bring the Fire to the Torch*.

The first person I see upon entering the room is Guardian Macdonald. The dark brown suit he's wearing is in severe contrast to his bright orange hair. "What the hell is this imbecile doing here?" Westgale whispers to me.

"Please be seated," Brandy says, directing us to our seats. Andy Pemberton nods at me, grinning stiffly as he whispers something to his Uncle Earl.

Gerald Levin enters the room. "Mr. President, Ms. Kratz, thank you for attending," he says, then gestures toward Macdonald. "And thank you, Guardian Macdonald." As usual, Macdonald has his head buried in his flash-pad. He slowly looks up.

"I'm sure you're all wondering why you're here right now," Gerald continues. "Well, the reason is simple, but yet extremely disturbing. Our Alliance has concluded we are fighting a losing battle. And I take no pride in fighting losing battles. Much to our dismay, the American people have spoken. They've decided to enable the obliteration of this incredible nation by once again supporting the Peace Bringers of America. Therefore, under Section 3.3 of the New Order Treaty, the Militant Alliance of America has decided to forfeit its presidential candidacy." Gerald casts a sullen look first my way, then toward Macdonald, whose nose is once again buried in his flash-pad.

Andy Pemberton then submits a formal flash-message, making the MAA's forfeiture official. Macdonald studies the document. "All appears in order," he states. "Once the Commission's legal secretary reviews and seals the declaration, it'll be final."

"Way to go, Nicole!" Westgale says as he practically lifts me off the ground in a bear hug.

Gerald and Earl abruptly exit the room, while Andy remains, staring into space. "Congratulations, Nicole," he says with a sigh. "You've done it again."

"I'm sure we'll meet again, Andy," I reply as I pass him.

On our way back to the Freedom Home, the president and I are still bewildered. "Boy, I didn't see this coming," I say, gazing out the window of the grand-electro at the street passing by. *I'll soon be in charge of all this,* I say to myself, watching the people and the buildings.

"That's the crazy thing about Gerald Levin—the man is so unpredictable. Nonetheless, by doing what he did, he placed his country above all," Westgale says, looking down at his flash-pad. "Whoa... the Commission is planning to announce the news on UCIT this evening," he adds excitedly.

"I can't believe this," I reply, still shocked. "A few hours ago I almost backed out of the whole ordeal."

When we reach the Freedom Home, in a whirlwind, I begin contacting those closest to me to share the news. As expected, Mom and Dad are ecstatic. "We're so proud of you!" Mom exclaims.

"Just like you told us all those years ago, huh, Nicole?" Dad adds. "And as usual, our daughter ends up doing exactly what she told us she'd do."

When I contact Lowell and the girls, who are spending the day at the Brave Land Shopping Center, they too are overjoyed by the news. "You certainly deserve this, honey," Lowell says, his voice filled with enthusiasm.

"So, when do we get to move into the Freedom Home?" Tiffany asks eagerly.

"Whoa, whoa," I quickly answer. "Let's just take it one day at a time." I chuckle.

"Are Tiffany and I going to have our own personal security guards?" January asks.

"Okay, girls, that's enough," Lowell says, laughing.

* * *

As diligently as I've worked to achieve this goal, and as excited as I am to begin living the dream of becoming president, actually hearing the words "the next president of the United States of America" is like having a locomotive bear down on me. But after Cryptic introduces me as such, I quickly realize that that speeding train will soon be mine to conduct. "I consider it both an honor and a privilege to serve my country," I announce with joy from the foyer of my campaign headquarters. "I want to begin by congratulating Gerald Levin and the Militant Alliance of America on a hard-fought, spirited battle.

"In tandem with you, the American people, I will do whatever it takes to ensure this country reaches a level of prosperity it has never witnessed before. Courtesy of the excellent work performed by the Westgale Administration, I am very fortunate to reap the benefits of the VX drug program and the rich, newly struck energy deal with Pinia. Most importantly, the miracle VX drug will enable Americans to live much healthier and longer lives, and along with its many environmental benefits, the Pinian energy deal will allow us to fully pay the debt owed to the Outer Commission and bring back what we crave so strongly: our complete independence, guided by our sacred Constitution.

"I also want to assure you that I will do everything in my power to make certain America is fully protected from those who wish to do it harm. Sooner than later, I will be proposing a motion to the Strategic Council that will involve a hefty reinvestment in our military. I will also continue working on the very important World Harmony Program which, as the country's executive director, I'm so proud to have established.

"Lastly, as I've stated throughout my political platform, my Administration will be representative of all Americans, including our youth. I am extremely excited about growing this country with your valued input. I promise, you will be heard."

As the UCIT camera shuts off, so do the lights in the foyer. Suddenly I see several flashes appearing from the side entrance. It's Hunter and Beth, rolling out a trolley containing a massive cake, with several red, white, and blue streamers and balloons floating above it. Following, are the rest of my staff. I'm so glad to be able to celebrate this monumental event with the people who were so vital in making it happen. "We did it, Nicole!" Hunter shouts above the background music.

Thinking of Anya, I can't help but feel there's a bittersweet irony to all of this. As I celebrate in preparation of becoming the most powerful person in the country, Anya Ahar is on death row, preparing to die. The crazy thing is; it was clearly *her* endorsement that has brought me here. *Damn! I just wish she'd let me fight for her.*

"Hey, Mom!" a voice calls out, bringing me back to the present. I look to my left and see January running toward me.

"Come here, my sweetie," I say as she runs in for a big hug.

"This is so amazing!" Tiffany adds following behind her sister.

"I hope you don't mind the surprise," Teresa, their nanny, says. "It was all your husband's idea."

"Are you kidding?" I answer with joy. "This would be an empty celebration without them... where's Lowell?"

"Dad decided not to come," Tiffany answers.

"Why don't you girls go with Teresa and get some cake," I say, then I find a quiet space to connect with Lowell on my flash-pad.

"I didn't want to tarnish your evening," he responds when I address the matter with him. "It just wouldn't be fair to you."

"Hold on. I thought we agreed that from now on, we're in this together. No more walls between us," I say sincerely.

"Bars maybe, but not walls." Lowell chuckles ruefully.

"You just get yourself down here, or I'll order Gil Robichaud to have his men come get you," I quip.

"Your wish is my command... Ms. President."

* * *

"This is sensational news, Cobra," President Woi says via his flash-screen. "Now it's simply a matter of time." He pours himself a glass of champagne.

"Isn't it something, how Levin ended up being swept away like yesterday's dust?" Cobra gloats, intent on the mirror in front of him as he meticulously draws in his eyebrows. "And soon Nicole Kratz, William Westgale, and all their cronies will be nothing but *tomorrow's* dust."

"Tiny little particles, drifting in the wind," Woi responds, cackling as he lifts his hands and moves them to one side, fluttering his fingers. "I'll be seeing you soon, my friend."

Woi turns off his flash-screen, leans back, and rests his feet on his desk, indulging in memories. Thirty years ago, he'd been a lieutenant under his country's chief military commander, Kenneth Pahl, at HKM Military Headquarters.

"You see, Lieutenant Woi, hostage negotiation is just like a business deal. One's goal must be to gain the upper hand without the other party realizing it. Always," a grinning Pahl said after officially announcing the release of fourteen US agents who had been held captive for the previous ten months.

"I'm sorry, sir, but I thought you would have received far better compensation for those American agents," Woi said, staring at a shipment of heart-shaped green pills.

"Please close the door," Pahl said. Woi obliged immediately and then took a seat in front of his superior's desk. Pahl was gazing at the pills with a devious smirk. *"These drugs, Lieutenant Woi, are special—very special, indeed."* Pahl handed a bag to Woi, along with a sealed document. *"I'm placing you in charge of them. All you need to know is contained in this document."*

Woi opened the envelope and studied the document intently. He was honored to be placed in charge of something so important.

"Now, I must be off," Pahl said, gathering his things. "My American friends have invited me to Las Vegas, as their guest. Is everything clear?"

"There is one question I'd like to ask," Woi said nervously.

"Go ahead, Lieutenant," Pahl answered.

Woi hesitated and took a deep breath. "We're not planning to attack America, are we?"

"Attack America?" Pahl laughed. "Why would we attack a country that feeds us all that delicious money? Now our Russian friends, that's a whole other story."

Woi frowns, though, when he recalls what happened just five years after that. By then, *he* was the HKM's chief military commander.

"You damn liar!" shouted Woi as he and his lead political adviser listened to Kenneth Pahl warn America of an imminent HKM attack.

"Why do you think he's doing this?" Woi asked his adviser. They were watching Pahl speak with Carly Taylor during what became known as "The Interview."

"There's no doubt in my mind he's being paid to lie," the adviser responded.

"Being paid to lie? By who?" Woi asked.

"By American interests who hope to see their current government crumble," the adviser explained. "You see, Commander Woi, America's at war with itself. And by telling this lie, these fools are using paranoia as a weapon."

"But why would Mr. Pahl resort to such a thing when he's already a very wealthy man?"

"Was a wealthy man," the adviser answered. "You of course remember why he was relieved of his duties here."

Yes, Woi remembered—the president had learned that Pahl had become deeply indebted to a group of American gangsters. "The Eternal," he said simply. His adviser nodded.

CHAPTER 24

"I'm glad you could make it, Nicole," Westgale says to me as I enter the Freedom Home's main conference room. "From the brief conversation I had with Colonel Peters, this sounds extremely important," he adds, handing me a copy of a report. I begin reading it, noting that Director Perry and the rest of the executive committee are also present.

A moment later, the colonel enters the room with an exhausted-looking, casually dressed, dark-haired man, who appears to be in his early thirties. "Ladies and gentlemen, this is James Vine from the HKM. He's the chief political strategist for the Gold Star Federation," Peters says as an introduction. "As you're all well aware, our government has done whatever it can to not interfere with the tumultuous politics of the HKM. It's not our place. However, as you're about to hear, this may have to change."

"Thank you, Colonel Peters. And thank you, ladies and gentlemen, for allowing me to address you," Vine says. "Since its formation a decade ago, the Gold Star Federation has set out to peacefully rescue the HKM from the depths of injustice, in hopes of enabling our people to live a life of liberty by deconstructing our oppressive political structure." Vine pauses and gazes around the room. "We are proud of the inroads we have made, and we believe we are on the edge of eradicating the clouds of oppression created by President Woi and those before him. Like your country, our people are craving change.

"Now, the reason our federation has secretly reached out to your government is because we strongly believe Woi is on the verge of attacking America."

There is a collective gasp, then the room becomes unnervingly silent.

Westgale abruptly rises from his seat. "On the verge of attacking America?" he says, his voice faint with shock.

"Yes, Mr. President," Vine answers calmly.

"You're certain of this?" Westgale asks.

"Whoa... with all respect, Mr. Vine, we heard this same warning twenty-five years ago," Dave Perry interjects, "and I'm sure you're well aware of the problems that caused."

"I understand your reluctance to believe me, but this is different," Vine says with conviction.

"With all due respect, Mr. Vine, do you expect us to just accept what you're telling us without any proof?" Westgale says.

"He has proof, Mr. President," Colonel Peters interjects. "Please, everyone, direct your attention toward the flash-screen."

The flash-screen at the front of the room comes to life as everyone turns to watch it.

"These men are two of President Woi's top officials," Vine says of two neatly groomed men sitting in a diner. "This diner is close to his central military office, and is covertly owned by our federation. Knowing how often Woi's men frequent the establishment, we have recording devices throughout the building. I know for a fact they've been ordered to never talk shop outside of their place of operation, but fortunately, as you're about to hear, these guys had loose lips."

The view-file begins.

"Were you able to convince your brother in Jersey to accept your gift?" one of the men asks.

"Both he and his wife were very receptive," replies the other man, who is wearing gray-tinted glasses.

"A first-class trip around Europe—how could they refuse that?" The two men laugh.

"I'm sure they must've wondered why I was so gracious."

"*I just hope you didn't tell them why.*"

"Seriously, do you actually think I was going to tell them that they should leave America because it'll soon be turned into a giant hellhole?" the man wearing the glasses replies.

The view-file suddenly ends.

Oh my God! How could this be happening? I look around me and see faces etched in dread, as mine must be.

Westgale abruptly rises from his seat, his eyes wide, his face haggard. "What else do you know about this?" he asks Vine.

"I wish I could tell you more, sir," Vine replies. "But I'm actually amazed we got what we did."

"Is it possible these men may have known they were being recorded, and staged this whole thing to deceive us, for whatever reason?" Dave Perry asks.

Vine shrugs. "I guess it's possible, but I seriously doubt it."

"Did this just come out of the blue, Mr. Vine, or has your federation had any prior knowledge that Woi may be up to something?" I ask.

"No. This is the first time something of this nature has come up. Woi runs his operation in a most careful manner," Vine replies. "That being said, none of us at the federation are surprised, since he's a megalomaniac whose goal in life is to one day take over the entire world."

"If he *were* to attack America, how do *you* believe he would do it?" Westgale asks.

"Well, since the World Coalition brought an end to his nuclear weapons program a few years ago, I really have no idea how he could launch such an attack."

"Are you aware of how often the World Coalition inspects his weapons facilities?" Perry asks.

"To my understanding, it's every two months."

"Thank you for coming forward with this information, Mr. Vine," Westgale says as he runs his hands through his hair. "Agent Herta will escort you to the Prestige Hotel, where he'll have a couple of his men watch over you until we are able to figure out where it is we're going with this."

As Vine is escorted from the conference room, Westgale again peruses the report. "Could this be some kind of setup?" he asks Colonel Peters. "I mean, what do we *really* know about the Gold Star Federation, and why should we trust them?"

"All our research indicates they're as pure as fresh snow. It appears that for the last several years, they've been doing their part to bring social equality to the country. And with substantial financial backing. They seem to have made enormous inroads," Peters replies. "In all honesty, I don't think it'd be wise to just sweep this away."

"Director Perry... Nicole. What are your thoughts?" Westgale asks.

"I have to agree with the colonel, sir," Perry answers. "It'd be way too risky to ignore this."

"Nicole?"

"Have we confirmed these are the guys Mr. Vine says they are?" I ask.

"Yes, we have," the colonel answers with certainty.

"Well, then, I agree. This definitely must be addressed," I respond.

Westgale reaches for his flash-pad and contacts Guardian Macdonald's assistant to request an emergency meeting. Twenty minutes later, they meet one-on-one in the president's office.

* * *

"Wow, this must've cost a pretty penny!" Macdonald exclaims around a mouthful of steak sandwich as he gazes around the exquisite office setting. "My assistant informed me that this is some kind of emergency. Is this about the deadline?" Macdonald asks before taking a giant bite of the sandwich.

"As I've told you before, we'll meet your deadline and pay back every cent," Westgale says through clenched teeth.

"I'll take your word for it, Mr. President," Macdonald says with a smirk. "So then, tell me why I'm here."

Westgale plays the view-file and hands him the report. He then recounts what Vine said.

"Hmm... so let me get this straight: you and your people are concerned these guys are going to destroy your country?" he asks as he takes out a toothpick and begins picking away at his teeth.

By this point, Westgale is seething. "These *guys*, as you refer to them, happen to be two of Woi's top military officials."

"I'm well aware of who they are, and I'm also well aware that two days before this view-file was made, the World Coalition completed a full HKM weapons inspection, and all was well. Here, see the report for yourself." Macdonald pulls up the report on his flash-pad and hands it to Westgale, who studies it intently.

"This is all very well, but you know as well as I do that the validity of these inspections totally depends on how transparent Woi and his people are being."

"Are you suggesting that maybe Woi is secretly storing a few nuclear missiles under his bed?" Macdonald cackles. "Come on, Mr. President, I suggest you get over the paranoia. As history has proven, it can be very harmful to America's well-being. I think it'd be best for everyone if you'd shift your focus back to paying off your country's debt."

Far from content with Macdonald's response, Westgale and Colonel Peters have James Vine brought back to the Freedom Home.

"Do your people still have eyes on these guys?" Westgale asks Vine.

"Let me put it this way: if they so much as sneeze, we know about it," Vine replies with a nod.

"Keep us posted, Mr. Vine. In the meantime, I'm going to have our Intelligence department liaise with your federation," Peters says.

CHAPTER 25

"Nicole, Nicole—come on in and have a seat," says Secretary Deacon, as he directs me to a chair before his desk. "Wow, *President Kratz*—sounds good to me," he adds in his usual jovial manner. He smiles, his red cheeks swelling like apples with the movement. Reaching for a plate of brownies on his desk, he holds it out to me. "My wife made these this morning. Here, try one."

"Mmm, delicious!" I exclaim after taking a bite.

"I guess you could say they give this energy minister some much-needed energy," he says, laughing as he reaches for another one.

"Good, because I'm going to need you at your best," I say.

"I hope that's your way of telling me you're planning to keep me on board within your Administration."

"Let's just say those brownies are pretty hard to pass up," I say, and we share a chuckle.

"Now, shall we address the matter at hand?" he says, growing serious. "With Gerald Levin and Earl Pemberton officially out of the political picture, it's time to bear down and bring the Pinian energy deal to life. Did you receive my report?"

"Yes, I did, and I'm astounded by the progress. The fact we're so close to receiving the first shipment is very exciting."

"There's never been anything like this," he says, his enthusiasm animating his voice. "Besides the discovery of the VX drug, I think this is the greatest thing to happen to this country in decades. As you can see from the report, the incredible thing about the fera-bean biofuel is that it is in no way temperature sensitive, and the tanks can be shipped by air without a single concern. My people have been working on the logistics and I'm thrilled to say it's all going as smooth as silk. Once we receive the first shipment and everything is deemed okay, the remaining shipments will follow on schedule."

"And from what I got from the report, there also doesn't appear to be any concerns when it comes to storage," I say.

"That's correct." He pauses and his apple-red cheeks bulge again. "This is absolutely incredible, Nicole."

* * *

"Is everything okay, Jessica?" a concerned Kolton asks Jessica backstage as he prepares to address a group of recovering alcoholics in support of the Kratz Foundation.

"Yeah," she says, running her hand back through her hair. She hesitates, then adds, "It's just my father. He's upset that I refuse to have my security around me twenty-four hours a day. As usual, he's just being overprotective." She shrugs.

"That's a parent's job," Kolton answers with a chuckle.

"I know he means well, but I've never been comfortable having a security detail follow my every move. I feel it puts me up on some unwarranted pedestal. Besides, this hall is a two-minute walk from the apartment." She moves to the curtain, and Kolton follows her.

"Wow, this is quite the turnout," he says as they look out at the stage and the auditorium beyond.

"Yeah, I'm glad to see the foundation is gaining momentum."

The announcer is introducing him now. "Knock 'em dead, Kolton," Jessica says, patting him on the back. She leaves the backstage area as he steps out onto the stage.

"Hello," he begins, looking out at the audience. He takes a moment to remove his jacket and roll up his sleeves—the stage lights are putting out a lot of heat. He drapes his jacket over the stool positioned next to the mic stand. "It's a true honor and privilege to be standing here in front of you today. Let me begin by telling you what led me on my downward spiral."

After he describes the events surrounding the tragic deaths of his sisters, there isn't a dry eye in the house. "To think that the very thing I was so proud to have created killed my own flesh and blood left me completely devastated," he finishes, and pauses to take a deep breath and exhale. "It came to the point where I would try to drown my anguish in alcohol. Every day, I sank deeper and deeper into a black hole. For years, I received help from many caring professionals, but no matter how hard they tried to help me, it seemed there was no hope. Every time I believed I was seeing a light at the end of the tunnel, I would sink deeper into that hole of misery.

"Time is the healer, I was constantly being told. Well, let me tell you, more than twenty years later I was still battling my demons, and believe me, they had no mercy. But for the last couple of years I've been fighting back with all my might, guided by the most powerful thing of all: love. And now those demons don't stand a chance. I've learned how to find the goodness in others."

Kolton addresses the audience with passion. "We need to realize that there'll always be challenges in life. And we must face those challenges head on. Through my own personal trials and tribulations, I've come to learn that the alcoholic sinks into a bottle to shelter himself or herself from reality. The problem is, it's far more difficult to get out than it is to get in. Sure, at times we'll fail, hurt, and feel sad, but the truth is, we can't know success without failure, and we surely can't know joy without sadness. It's life. It's reality."

When Kolton finishes his talk and leaves the stage to thunderous applause, Jessica is again backstage. "Fantastic speech, Kolton," she says. "You really moved these people."

"You know, Jessica, when I look at them I see myself," he says as he pours two glasses of fruit punch from a pitcher on a table. "In their eyes I can actually see the battle between sadness and hope playing out." He hands Jessica a glass.

"Well, here's to hope," she says, tapping glasses with Kolton.

"May I have the pleasure of walking you back to the condo?" Kolton asks as he puts on his coat and toque, preparing to leave.

"Thank you, Kolton, but I'm going to stick around and do a meet and greet with the audience, then I'm planning to join Shadow and a few friends at that new restaurant across the street," Jessica replies. "Hey, how about you and Luanda join us?"

"Oh, thanks, but when I contacted Luanda before my speech she was preparing to turn in for the evening," Kolton says.

* * *

"I wonder what's keeping Jessie," Shadow says to Jessica's friends as they wait for her at the restaurant. "She was supposed to be here a half-hour ago."

"That seems to happen to Jessie. Being who she is, people are always wanting to meet her. She's probably held up signing autographs," Andrea says.

"And that's the thing about Jessie—she never turns anyone away," Andrea's boyfriend, John, adds.

Shadow frowns, looking at his flash-pad. "I don't know, guys. I've tried contacting her, and I'm getting nothing." Her friends, content to wait, drift back into their conversation after a few moments, but Shadow is preoccupied. He excuses himself and finds a quiet location from which to call the Kratz Foundation Event Coordinator, Catalina Sanchez.

"All I can tell you is, I know for a fact Jessie left the auditorium about half an hour ago," Catalina replies when he expresses his concern. "She spent at least an hour meeting and greeting tonight's audience."

"Were you with her when she left?" Shadow asks. "How was she? Was she feeling ill or something?"

"Oh no, she was fine. We left the building at the same time."

"Together?"

"No, we exited through different doors."

"What about her security detail? Did they not escort her out of the building?" Shadow asks, his worry shifting to fear.

"She didn't have them with her tonight, or her driver. She said the auditorium is so close to your building that she didn't need either." Catalina pauses, then asks carefully, "Do you know if your mother or Kolton have heard from her?"

"I'll try them next." Struggling to maintain his composure, Shadow calls his mother's number. Kolton answers.

"Oh my Lord," Kolton says. "I left the auditorium about an hour and a half ago. Jessie said she was going to stick around and meet the audience and then join you at the restaurant."

"That's what she was supposed to do, but she hasn't. What in the world could have happened to her?" Shadow's voice rises with panic. "I'll be there in a few minutes. I'll tell the others to stick around here in case she shows up."

Shadow rushes up to Kolton and Luanda's apartment. Luanda comes running to the door with Kolton behind her. "Shadow, what's going on?" she cries, looking as if she just woke up.

"I have no idea, Mother," Shadow replies, rubbing his eyes. "She's not answering her flash-pad. We can't keep wasting time. We have to do something."

"Do you want me to call the police?" Kolton offers, reaching for his flash-pad.

"No. I'm going to call the president's direct line," Shadow says, pulling out his flash-pad and punching in numbers.

"Shadow, this is a pleasant surprise," Westgale says when he answers. "I really want to thank you for the work you've done with Secretary Deacon regarding the Pinian energy deal."

"I'm thrilled things have worked out as well as they have, sir," Shadow replies. Then he explains to Westgale why he's calling.

"Yeah, I have that file in my office," he says, then a minute later explains, "I didn't want to alarm my wife. Now, tell me what you know."

"She didn't have her security with her, sir," Shadow says.

Westgale sighs. "I'm well aware of that. I just finished giving her hell about that earlier this evening."

"I didn't know... I didn't know whether to call the police, or..."

"You did the right thing by contacting me," Westgale says. "I'm going to put my people on this right away. If you hear from Jessie, or anyone who knows anything about where she is, contact me immediately."

As Westgale ends the call, he feels his chest tightening, and takes several deep breaths before returning to the drawing room to tell April what's going on. He then contacts Gil Robichaud and explains the situation. "Do you think we should announce this to the public?" he asks his chief of security.

"No, not at this point. But I'll immediately get word out to all levels of law enforcement," Gil says.

Westgale allows the crack in his calm façade to widen enough to say, "Gil, please do whatever it takes to find my daughter."

"I'll do everything I can, sir," Gil promises.

Gil quickly assembles a team of agents and they fly out to New York. During the flight, he speaks with Catalina Sanchez. "I'm hoping, as the event coordinator, you'll be able to send me every detail pertaining to this evening's event."

"Of course. All our events are carefully planned," Catalina informs Gil. "I'll send you the list of the 237 people who were in attendance."

Seconds later, Gil receives the list of names. He immediately forwards the list to Agent Herta, who begins running the names through the criminal database.

"Eighty-three of these people have had some sort of documented run-in with the law," Agent Herta reports.

"What types of things are we looking at?" Agent Gallio asks as the plane prepares for landing.

"Uh... it's all minor stuff. It doesn't appear we have any serious criminals in this group," Herta replies. "That being said, I think until Jessica is found, it's wise to start contacting everyone who was at the event."

When they arrive in New York, they begin setting up shop in the New York Justice Center. Minutes later, appearing completely flustered, Shadow arrives. "I take it there's still been no sign of her," Gil says to Shadow.

"Nothing. Not a damn thing," Shadow answers as he sits down and buries his head in his hands. "I can't believe this is happening. I should've been there with her," he moans. "Jessie's an angel; why anyone would want to harm her is beyond me."

"I know it's difficult, Shadow, but it's vital we don't panic and think the worst," Gil says as he offers him a glass of water. He studies him for a few seconds.

"Shouldn't we disclose this to the public? Can we not offer some kind of reward?" Shadow asks. "I'll offer whatever amount of money it takes."

"At this stage, I don't think it's wise to make a public announcement," Gil answers as an agent enters the room with Catalina Sanchez.

"Is there any news?" she asks, brushing strands of dark brown hair from her eyes.

"Unfortunately, we're at a standstill, Miss Sanchez," Gil answers.

"Well, hopefully this'll help," Catalina says, handing Gil a data chip. "This is a view-file of Jessica's meet and greet. My assistant recorded it to use as a marketing tool for the foundation. There's no sound, though," she adds.

Gil instantly scans the chip to the flash-screen positioned at the front of the room. As the view-file plays, the group watches a radiant Jessica smiling, signing autographs, and posing for photos. Shadow watches with tears in his eyes. And Shadow, in turn, is observed by those Gil has ordered to watch him.

"Hmm, check this guy out," Agent Gallio says, asking Gil's assistant, Shamir, to freeze the picture and highlight a man standing off to the side. "He's been standing there the whole time, just staring at Jessica." The man is about thirty, and neatly groomed. He seems annoyed as he watches Jessica.

"Back it up. Back it up to the beginning. And keep him highlighted," Gil calls out to Shamir.

"What's with this guy?" Shadow exclaims, rising.

"Hold on. It looks like he just murmured something to himself," Agent Gallio says.

"Zoom in on that, Shamir," Gil orders.

As the man's thin, triangular face fills the screen, it becomes clear he is mouthing the words "stupid bitch."

"This has to be the guy," Shadow shouts.

As the view-file plays on, the man now appears to mutter something to a lady standing next to him.

"Zoom in on that," Gil says to Shamir. "Can anybody figure out what the hell he's saying?" he then asks the others.

"It beats me," Agent Gallio replies. Agent Herta and the others in the room are also at a loss.

"Give me a minute. I'll get it for you," Shamir says as he taps a few buttons on the keypad. A minute later Shamir raises his head. "I've got it," he says.

"Are you certain?" Gil asks.

"Yes, I am," he replies, confidently. "Okay, he's saying, 'Look at her, thinking she's holier than thou... She's nothing but a damn jezebel.'"

"Whoa, I wanna know every single thing there is to know about this guy," Gil says.

Shadow sits frozen, staring straight ahead. Catalina does her best to console him. "It'll be all right, Shadow," she keeps insisting. She urges him to his feet and leads him out of the operations room. In the doorway, he slowly turns and looks back at Gil and his team.

"Please, find her," he says softly.

The agent who's been watching Shadow alerts a couple of his associates that Shadow is leaving the building. The others begin gathering as much data as possible on the man in the view-file.

"His name is Joshua Thompson," Agent Herta calls out. "He's thirty-one and works as a stock trader with a small New York firm. And... he resides a few blocks from the auditorium."

"Any trouble with the law?" Gallio asks Herta.

"His ex-wife filed for divorce, claiming he became abusive and prone to drunken tirades, but he was never charged with anything," Herta answers.

"Here we go," Shamir says out of the blue. "It looks like Mr. Thompson has been quite busy on the World Connect."

"How so?" asks Gil.

"Expressing his political opinions on a view-file page titled Twilight's Last Gleaming," Shamir replies, handing his flash-pad to Gil.

"The guy's definitely a militant extremist. His writing's filled with all kinds of vitriol against the PBA and particularly Westgale," Gil observes as he peruses the material. "Check this comment out. It's in response to Jessica's work in Pinia. 'Cute little rich bitch with nothing better to do than go and lend a hand to our enemy—disgraceful!' Oh my Lord, listen to this. It was posted right after the Pinian energy deal was officially announced. 'If only Westgale and his bleeding heart daughter would somehow fall off the face of the earth, then maybe this country will finally be what it should be.' We may have our man," Gil says as he reaches for his jacket and signals for Agent Gallio to join him. "We need to pay this guy a visit, Nick—and get us the necessary backup," he adds, looking back at Agent Herta.

CHAPTER 26

En route to Joshua Thompson's residence, Gil calls to brief Westgale.

"Oh my God," he breathes as Gil updates him. "I told Jessie it wasn't wise to do these meet and greets. There's just way too many nut jobs out there. And this guy sounds like one of them. But that's my daughter—when she sets her mind to something there's no—"

"I must caution you, sir. We don't have any hard proof linking this guy to Jessica's disappearance, but when you piece everything together, and consider the facts, it's impossible not to be suspicious of him."

"Why, Gil? Why would anyone harm such a loving person?" Westgale says. "All she's done her entire life is help people."

"I wish I had an answer for you, Mr. President, but I don't."

When Gil and Gallio reach the apartment building where Joshua Thompson is supposedly living, they make sure their backup is fully in place before identifying themselves to the building security guard.

"Here, let me escort you up to Mr. Thompson's unit," he says, and leads them up to the twenty-first floor. Gil knocks gently on the door.

"Hey, who is it? I didn't see my signal light up," a deep male voice says. When Gallio informs him of who they are, the man opens the door. "Well, I guess it sure wouldn't be in my best interest to turn you guys away. Come on in."

"Joshua Thompson?" Gil confirms, though the man before him is the same one they saw in the view-file.

"That's me, in the flesh," Joshua replies matter-of-factly.

"Let me tell you why we're here, Mr. Thompson." Gil then explains.

"And you think *I* had something to do with her disappearance," Joshua says, looking shocked. "That is ludicrous," he adds.

Gallio details their suspicions.

Thompson scowls. "That's right, anything to do with her and her father makes me sick. Watching these people run my country to the ground crushes my heart."

"To the point where you referred to her under your breath tonight as a 'stupid bitch,'" Gil says with a raised brow.

"Is that a crime?"

"And according to your view-file page, your wish is for her and her father to fall off the face of the earth."

"Oh, forgive me for not being one of their sycophants," Joshua sneers. "Do we not still have something called free speech in this country?"

"Very well, Mr. Thompson, but what perplexes me is that you've attended the last four Kratz Foundation events knowing very well that Jessica Westgale oversees the foundation," Gil says, his tone growing sharper.

"The only reason I've been attending these meetings is because I'm trying to better myself, Agent Robichaud," he answers, then takes a deep breath. "My alcohol addiction has had a negative impact on so many aspects of my life—worst of all, it cost me the woman I love. I couldn't care less about Jessica Westgale's involvement. The only reason I stayed for the meet and greet was because the person I attended the event with wanted to get an autograph and a photo for his sister. Here's his name." He moves to a side table in the foyer and writes the man's name and contact information down on a piece of paper. He hands it to Gil, who then steps to one side for a murmured conversation with Gallio.

"I thank you for your time, Mr. Thompson, I'm leaving, but I hope you don't mind if Agent Gallio asks you a few more questions," Gil says.

"He can ask me all the questions he wants, but I don't know a damn thing about any of this," Joshua says as he plops down on his living room sofa. Flash-pad in hand, Gallio sits across from him. Gil leaves.

Back at the Justice Center, he and Agent Herta begin diligently analyzing further information. An hour later, Gallio returns.

"So, what'd you make of the guy, Nick?" Gil asks.

"I think it's wise to keep him under surveillance, but I doubt he's our man," Gallio responds, rubbing his hands over his face in frustration. "It's obvious the guy's a militant extremist, but I think he's all talk. Besides, his buddy corroborated everything he told us."

"The more I think this over, the more I feel we have no choice but to go public with Jessica's disappearance," Gil says. "Time is ticking." Sighing, he leans back in his chair and laces his hands together behind his head.

"What about a reward?" Gallio asks.

"We're going to start it at two million dollars. The president insisted we make it higher, but Martin Stevens and I were able to convince him otherwise," Gil replies.

"Who's going to make the announcement?" Herta asks.

"I know the president wants to, but I don't think that'd be wise. Whoever abducted Jessica may very well have done so because of their feelings toward him," Gil says. "I'll talk to him."

Minutes later, in a video conference call, the president is adamant that he be the one to address the nation. "I appreciate and respect your opinion, Gil, but I *need* to do this. And I will."

Not long after that conversation, Gil and his team watch the president's appeal on the flash-screen on one wall of the operations center.

In the Freedom Home drawing room, Westgale gazes directly into the UCIT camera. He looks weary and pale. *"To whoever may know the whereabouts of my daughter, Jessica, I'm asking you to please enter this code into your flash-pad."* He provides a series of three numbers and three letters, which seconds later are presented on the screen. He also announces the reward information. Then his expression softens, and it's clear he's speaking from the heart.

"Jessica is a kind and caring person who, ever since she was a teenager, has dedicated her life to helping people in less fortunate positions. She usually doesn't disclose this information to the public, but today I feel compelled to." Westgale cites several examples of Jessica's generosity.

"The work her and her team of aid workers have performed at an international level is unparalleled; most recently, she has assisted the children of Pinia."

As Westgale continues to speak, video clips of Jessica and her team, hard at work, appear on the screen.

"Jessica is not a politician or a businesswoman; she's a humanitarian who is guided by an altruistic outlook on life. Prior to leading her team into Pinia, she was offered a lucrative high-level position at Step 1 Health. As much as I tried to encourage her to remain in America and accept the position, she wouldn't even give it a second thought.

"Once again, I plead with you, if you know the whereabouts of Jessica Westgale, please immediately enter the code you see on the screen into your flash-pad." He then repeats the code twice before the screen fades to black.

* * *

Jessica wakes slowly, blinking her eyes open. Hazily, she checks out her surroundings. She's lying in a plush, queen-sized bed in a large and elegantly decorated room she doesn't recognize. *Where the hell am I? What in the world is going on?*

She's still wearing her clothes from the evening before, she notes with relief. Other than feeling highly fatigued, she's unharmed. She sits up and reaches for the curtain drawn over a window in the wall beside the bed. *Maybe I'll find some answers out there,* she decides as she pulls the curtain aside.

Steel panels cover the window. Gasping, heart pounding in fear, she springs out of the bed and looks around for her purse and flash-pad. They're nowhere in sight. She catches her reflection in the mirror over the bureau and clutches at her throat. Her dragon-stone necklace is gone. She runs to the door and twists and yanks on the knob. It's locked. Frantic now, she pulls on the handle with all her might, twisting and turning it, but it won't budge. Abandoning the handle, she hammers on the door with her fists, repeatedly hollering, "Where am I? Somebody help me!"

It's to no avail. She is somebody's prisoner.

She turns, back to the door, and again looks around the room, noting details that might help her escape, or tell her where she is. To her right is a rudimentary kitchenette, with a counter where several packaged sandwiches and other snacks are stacked. A fridge reveals all kinds of fruit, vegetables, and beverages when she opens the door. She crosses the room to a bathroom; there is a large supply of toiletries on the vanity. Fresh towels are stacked inside a cabinet. Back in the bedroom, she opens the bureau drawers to see them filled with clothes. Women's clothes. In her size. She steps back in confusion. *What in the world is going on?* She looks again at the counter, at the fridge, and her fear mounts. *Have I been left alone here? How long do they plan to keep me here? Will someone come back, or... will I die here?*

* * *

"We've been able to contact eighty percent of the people who attended the event, and not a single soul claims to have seen or heard anything suspicious. Neither has anybody in the surrounding area," Agent Gallio reports to Gil, shaking his head in frustration.

"Hopefully that will change when we speak with the remaining twenty percent," Gil replies, trying to remain optimistic. He looks across the room at the agent hunched over his screen. "What about her flash-pad signal; what have you learned, Shamir?" he asks.

"It was shut down the night of the event," Shamir replies. "And according to Shadow, the activity logged in the last few weeks shows nothing peculiar. We're checking it out ourselves, though."

CHAPTER 27

"Come on in," a lady named Eva Gould says to Agent Gallio. "I'm sorry it took me the time it did to meet with you, but the day after that event, I headed straight to Long Island to visit my husband in rehab."

"I understand he's the reason you attended the event," Gallio says as he enters the living room of the quaint home.

"Yes. I'll do whatever it takes to help my husband, and I think the Kratz Foundation is doing some wonderful things. I just hope and pray Jessica Westgale comes back safe and sound. I'm a great admirer," Eva says with a smile.

"I don't want to take up too much of your time, ma'am, but did you notice anything out of the..." Gallio hesitates as a young child runs into the living room.

"Grr—and now you will all face my wrath!" the boy calls out as he jumps onto a sofa, thrusting a plastic sword into the air. He's wearing a peculiar mask.

"Austin, you come down from that sofa right now. And take off that bloody mask," his mother barks. "I'm sorry, Agent Gallio. I think letting him keep that mask and buying him that toy sword was one of the biggest mistakes I've ever made," she adds with a chuckle. "Now say sorry and go to your room," she tells the boy.

As little Austin runs off, Gallio pauses in shock. *My Lord. SOH... the Spirit of Hades.* The mask totally matches the description provided by Morris Johns. "That's an interesting mask," Gallio says with a smile, attempting to hide his concern. "I have a young boy as well, and he too always seems to be fascinated by that sort of thing. Do you mind if I have a look at it, and maybe even take a photo of it? I know my son would love something like that."

"Sure, go ahead," Eva says with a raised brow at Gallio's sudden interest in the mask. "I wish I could tell you where you can buy one, but Austin found this one when we moved in here. I had to adjust it so it would fit his face." She laughs.

"Found it?"

"Yeah, the prior owner left it in a box that was headed for the garbage, until Austin got his grubby little hands in there," Eva explains. "And since that day he's been in love with the thing. I probably see that mask more than I see his actual face."

"Did the prior owner have children of his own?"

"Oh no, at the time he sold the house he was single."

"Ah; maybe he was a fencer."

"You know, it's funny this has come up, because I was intending to ask him about the mask the other evening, but I didn't have a chance."

"You still keep in touch?"

"No, no. The other evening was the first time I'd seen him since I bought the house. Sometimes it amazes me, just how small the world really is."

"Oh? What makes you say that?"

"Well, when I saw that it was Mr. Rollins who was giving that speech the other night, I nearly fell out of my chair."

"Mr. Rollins? Kolton Rollins?"

"Yeah, Kolton Rollins, the man I bought this very house from. He delivered such an enlightening speech—are you okay, Agent Gallio?"

Gallio struggles to relax his expression again. "Uh, yes, ma'am. I was just thinking of all those poor souls like your husband, who wake up every day and face the awful battle they do."

Eva nods, then recalls, "I must apologize. You were in the process of asking me a question when my son so rudely interrupted you."

"Oh yeah," Gallio answers, still deep in thought. "I wanted to know if you noticed anything out of the ordinary during or after the presentation."

"The only thing I noticed, sir, were a lot of tears during Kolton's speech, and then a lot of smiles afterward, when Jessica Westgale was kind enough to greet us."

* * *

"Kolton Rollins?" Gil says in disbelief when Gallio meets with him at his hotel suite. "Did you bring him in?"

"We have no idea where he is, sir," Gallio replies as he sighs in frustration.

"Are you certain the mask is a match?"

"I sent a photo of it to Morris Johns and he verified it's the exact mask that was being worn by the members of SOH," Gallio says.

"Do you realize what this could mean? They could all be playing us. All three of them," Gil says.

"I'm sorry, sir, but you've lost me."

"Kolton Rollins, his wife Luanda, and our dear friend Shadow." Robichaud looks at his time-pin. "Westgale and the Lady of Honor are due to arrive anytime now. I'm supposed to meet them at the Prestige. We'll talk further when I return."

"I don't know anything about this Rollins fellow, but I have nothing but full trust in Shadow," Westgale insists when Gil mentions Rollins and Shadow's mother. "That young man saved my life. On top of that, there's no doubt in my mind that he sincerely loves my daughter."

"Well, as much as I trust your judgment, sir, I still think it's wise to continue tailing him," Gil responds.

"Hold on. You've been tailing Shadow?"

"Yes, sir."

"Please, Gil, that's ridiculous. I'm ordering you to end it now."

"Very well, Mr. President, as you wish," Gil replies, reluctantly pulling his flash-pad from his pocket to relay the order to his agents.

"What about Shadow's mother, Luanda? What do we really know about her?" he asks.

When Westgale tells Gil how Cobra threatened her to make her leave Pinia and abandon Shadow, he's taken aback. "Gee, I had no idea that was the case."

"We didn't find out about that until after the Pinian deal was made, and it's definitely not something I want to be made public. Now, even if this Rollins character was linked to SOH, it doesn't necessarily mean he's the person who abducted Jessica."

"Maybe not, but it surely increases the likelihood," Gil says.

"Have you brought him in yet?"

"There's a problem with that, Mr. President. We have no idea where he is."

"Damn it," Westgale yells. "What do you mean, you don't know where he is? You have men tailing Shadow Pix, but the other two are left to wander off?"

"We never suspected them, sir," Gil replies.

Westgale shakes his head. "In the meantime, set up an emergency meeting," he orders. "Oh, and invite Shadow. I think it's vital we fill him in."

Westgale turns away abruptly and moves to stare out the window. Knowing the pressure the man is under, Gil joins him at the window.

"She's out there somewhere, sir," Gil says softly. "And I plan to keep my promise and find her."

"Thank you, Gil. You're a good man." Westgale lets out a sigh and walks over to the sofa, where the Lady of Honor is examining a picture of their daughter she's holding on her lap. As he gathers her into his arms, Gil leaves.

An hour later, at the New York Justice Center emergency meeting, Gil asks Shadow if he's aware of Kolton's whereabouts. "Mom and I haven't seen him since the day after Jessica went missing," Shadow answers. "We feared maybe he relapsed and fell into some sort of drunken stupor. I guess now we know the reason why he ran off. Damn that son of a bitch!"

A team of agents from National Investigation begins arriving.

"Would you have any insight into why he'd have such hatred toward America that he'd join a group like SOH?" Westgale asks Shadow, who responds by explaining how Kolton's sisters died.

"Whoa... the very same bombs he designed ended up killing his sisters? Now that could really mess a person up," Gil says.

"It seemed like his anger was all focused toward Direct Aim, but obviously it ran a whole lot deeper," Shadow says, frowning.

"I hate to do this, Shadow, but considering you just recently reunited with your mother, I have to ask you how well you really think you know her," says Gil.

"All I know is what I feel and what I've heard and seen, and I don't believe for a second that my mother had any idea what this guy was really about," Shadow replies, rubbing his tired eyes. "If anything, I have to wonder how he ended up in her life."

"I hope you understand we'll need to question her."

"I'm certain she'll cooperate fully."

"People, listen up," Gil calls out. "This is the man we are looking for. His name is Kolton Rollins." A large photo of Rollins appears on the flash-screen. "As you will notice from the photo, Mr. Rollins has one very distinguishable feature, the burn mark on his right cheek. Please note that a detailed report on this case and Mr. Rollins has been flashed over to your National Investigation central database. The report will be updated continually. I must stress the importance of capturing Mr. Rollins alive."

Late that same evening, Gil Robichaud meets with Kolton Rollins's ex-wife, Nadine, at Stacy's Diner.

"When was the last time you spoke with Kolton?" Gil asks.

"When we divorced, seven years ago," Nadine replies, nervously pouring cream into her coffee. "That doesn't surprise me," she responds after Gil reveals Kolton's apparent link to SOH. "He came to despise everything America stood for. That was the main reason I had to get away from him. Well that, and of course the drinking. Frankly, I'm surprised to hear he's still alive."

"Did you ever witness him become violent?"

"No, not physically. But he would go into these diatribes against America, referring to the country as one large poisonous pit of wickedness, or something weird like that. Of course, the death of his sisters was at the root of his anger."

"Can you think of anywhere he might be hiding? Do you recall him having any places where he used to visit in order to find some peace of mind?"

Nadine frowns in thought, then says slowly, "There was one place that he often visited. No matter how difficult things became."

"And where would that be?" Gil asks.

"Not far from here at St. Agnes Cemetery; where his sisters lay in rest."

At the break of dawn, Gallio and Herta visit the cemetery. "The grounds here are so sprawling that it's impossible for us to fully monitor them. So many people come and go every day. But yes, I know this man," the manager says as she studies Kolton's picture. "I can't recall the last time I saw him, but I can tell you that he visits quite often. He once told me how his sisters died. Awful story," she adds as she searches the cemetery's database. "Ah, here we are. His sisters are entombed together in Section F 527... This programmed robo-electro will take you directly there." She nods toward the door.

Gallio and Herta clamber into the electro when it stops outside the admin office door. It carries them through the expansive grounds and stops on the pavement fifteen yards or so from the graves. Gallio and Herta exit the electro and begin scouring the area.

Herta calls Gallio's name and nods toward a figure in the distance. It appears to be a man wearing an overcoat and a winter toque. He's sitting, head bowed, on one of the benches scattered throughout the property.

They return to the electro and move closer. Gallio takes out his laser-view scope. "My Lord. I think we have our man," he says to Herta.

"How can you be sure?" Herta asks.

"That's him. I can see the burn mark on his cheek," Gallio answers, his voice strained. Herta immediately calls for backup, informing the command center that they've spotted Rollins.

"Wow, this is quite bizarre… he's holding onto a white box with a red and blue bow," Gallio says as he continues to observe. "He doesn't appear to be moving. Unless he's in some kind of deep sleep, I think he's dead."

They move the robo-electro a little closer.

"Should we move in on him?" Herta asks.

"It's far too risky," Gallio replies as he continues to observe the man they believe to be Kolton Rollins. He pulls out a miniature sound-blast and says through it, "Sir, we are federal agents. Please place both your hands on your head." Nothing. No movement at all. Gallio repeats the order with more force. Again, nothing. "Wait a second, I just saw him press—"

BOOSH!

A thunderous roar precedes a massive fireball that rolls over the robo-electro, blowing it to pieces.

Gil along with a bevy of federal agents descend on the cemetery a short time later. Agents Gallio and Herta are immediately pronounced dead. Kolton Rollins is nowhere to be found.

"Hey, look over here," one of the agents says to Gil directing his attention to a bench.

"Get the hell out of there," Gil hollers to the agent when he sees a white box with a red and blue bow.

The bomb squad moves in. "It's clear," their commander calls out, and brings the box over to Gil. He unties the bow, reaches in, and removes a dragon-stone necklace.

"That's Jessica Westgale's," he says.

* * *

"Are you certain you don't want me to stay with you?" Shadow asks his mother as he takes her back to her apartment after a rigorous interview with a National Investigation agent. Luanda looks exhausted.

"You're a very special young man. I'm so fortunate to have you in my life," Luanda says with a wan smile that quickly fades. "I must be strong, Shadow, and see my way through this. There's no other way."

"Well, just as long as you know I'm here for you," Shadow says as she unlocks the door. He steps inside with her.

"After what I've done to your life, I don't know why you'd want to be," Luanda says, throwing her arms in the air as she moves farther into the apartment. "I caused you to leave your home, and now my husband…" Her shoulders sag.

Shadow quickly moves to grip her shoulders. "None of this is your fault, Mother. Kolton fooled us. He fooled all of us."

Luanda smiles bravely and kisses Shadow on the cheek. "Now go. I'll be fine. You have enough to worry about."

His flash-pad buzzes with an incoming message as Shadow is leaving Luanda's unit. He pulls it out of his pocket and looks at it. Gil wants to meet him in his electro, currently parked at the back of the building.

As he approaches the vehicle, he notices Shamir is with Robichaud.

"Please give your flash-pad to Shamir," Gil says to Shadow, who gives him a puzzled look. Before he can ask what's going on, Gil signals for Shadow not to speak.

Shamir studies and then quickly disables the flash-pad. "You were correct, sir," he says to Gil. "It was an LS 30."

"What's going on? And what's an LS 30?" Shadow asks.

Gil tells Shadow what took place at the cemetery. "An LS 30 is a listening bug that can be scanned onto a flash-pad," Gil tells him. "You're the only person outside of the command center who knew my agents were planning to visit the cemetery. I figured Rollins must have somehow been listening in when I informed you of the plan." Gil sighs. "And damn it, my carelessness cost two good men their lives."

Shadow buries his face in his hands. "I can't believe what is happening."

"I think it'd be wise if I bring a couple of our men in and sweep both your and your mother's apartments for any other potential bugs," Shamir says. Shadow nods.

"There's one more thing, Shadow," Gil says softly. "I think you should have this." He hands him Jessica's dragon-stone necklace.

Shadow stares at the necklace, blinking back tears. "And to think I told her this would always keep her safe," he murmurs.

The next morning, Shamir and his team discover two listening devices in Shadow's apartment. None are found in Luanda's.

CHAPTER 28

The anger over the calculated murder of Gallio and Herta is evident at today's meeting at the New York Justice Center. Gil hears the muttering as he enters the operations room and moves to the front.

"I'd personally love to get my hands on the guy and tear him to shreds."

"Nick always had everybody's back. We owe it to him and to his family to make sure we bring this son of a bitch to justice."

"That's the goal, ladies and gentlemen," Gil says loudly, ending the chatter and drawing all eyes to him. "First we must focus on actually tracking him down. And remember, the goal is to capture him alive," he warns.

"It looks like it's too late for that," Martin Stevens, head of National Investigation, says. His eyes are on his flash-pad.

"What is it, Martin?" Gil asks.

"Rollins… he's dead. I'm being told he walked into Precinct Five and collapsed."

"Precinct Five. That's the area where his sisters were killed," Gil says.

"This guy certainly has a flare for the dramatic," someone calls out.

Gil holds up his hand, eyes still on Stevens. "Are they saying what caused him to collapse?"

"Apparently he took his own life with a styngor," Stevens answers. "Wait a second… I'm now being told that before he collapsed, he shouted out something really peculiar: 'This is the beginning of the end.'"

"This is the beginning of the end? What on God's earth is that supposed to mean?" Gil says.

In Washington, Westgale joins Robichaud's meeting via the World Connect.

"I ask that everyone except Agent Robichaud and Mr. Stevens please exit the room," Westgale orders calmly. Gil nods; he and Martin wait as the room empties.

"All clear now, Mr. President," Gil informs Westgale.

Westgale takes a deep breath and lets it out. "Gentlemen. Now that Kolton Rollins has taken his life, I need your expert and honest opinion." He pauses and takes another deep breath. "Do you think there's even the slightest chance my daughter's still alive?"

Gil hesitates, then admits, "Very slight at best. I'm sorry, sir."

"Martin?" Westgale says. "As a highly seasoned NI director, your experience is unmatched. I need you to be completely honest with me."

"To be blunt, Mr. President, considering the fact there's been no ransom demand whatsoever, I highly doubt your daughter is still alive," Stevens replies.

As if having expected to hear the worst, Westgale quickly moves to his next question. "I also need to know what you gentlemen make of what Rollins said before he died: 'This is the beginning of the end.'"

"Knowing he made that comment has left me uneasy, assuming he was involved with the Spirit of Hades," Stevens answers, glancing at the National Investigation report on the extremist group.

"It is a rather ominous comment, but then again, it could just be the final words of a mentally unstable person," Gil adds.

"I believe the most important thing here is to determine whether Rollins was working alone when he took Jessica. From what we know of SOH, we're looking at a highly financed and very sophisticated operation that was somehow able to disappear without us being able to figure out what and who the hell they are," Stevens says, eyes on his flash-pad.

"Where do we go from here?" the president asks.

"It's imperative we continue to find out every single thing imaginable about Kolton Rollins, and see where the trail leads us," Stevens replies with conviction.

"Gil?"

"I fully concur, sir."

* * *

After a long, but fruitful session with Harrison Deacon and Pinia's strategic coordinator for the energy deal, I'm contacted by the director of the Federal Justice Center. "As I'm sure you're well aware, Ms. Kratz, tomorrow is the day Clifford Sims will be executed," the director informs me.

"I can hear the gates of hell slowly creaking open as we speak," I quip, feeling absolutely no remorse for a man whose evil ways almost brought this entire country to its knees.

"He's requesting to speak with you."

"Hmm, that's a surprise. Has he said why?"

"I haven't the slightest idea," the director replies.

As much as I despise the man, I oblige, and a few hours later, I'm sitting across from him, separated only by a row of bars.

"Nicole, it sure has been a while," Sims says with a smirk. "You didn't forget about me, did you?"

"Please don't be offended, but yes I did. And to be honest with you, I think I made a big mistake coming here."

"Well, since you accepted my invitation, I guess maybe you still care about me after all." He bursts into shrieking laughter.

"Aw, it's nice to see you haven't lost that dreadful sense of humor, even while waiting for the grim reaper," I reply, and allow a malicious chuckle.

"Now, that's not very presidential of you, Nicole, teasing a man who will be zapped from this earth just hours from now."

"You reap what you sow, General."

"And believe me, Nicole, I'm fully prepared to face the music, even looking forward to it. Heck, I'll probably be laughing as the hellfire chars me up. But before my journey into the afterlife begins, I thought it'd be totally inexcusable of me to not congratulate you on reaching your much coveted goal: Nicole Kratz, president of the United States of America. It's such a natural fit."

"Well, if that's why you requested my presence, then all I can tell you is that your kind words mean absolutely not a damn thing to me. What a waste of time this was," I answer in frustration, looking through the bars directly into his stony eyes.

As I turn away, he calls out, "There is one thing I sincerely need to ask you."

In a huff, I turn back. "Go ahead, but hurry up," I snap.

He leans up against the bars and sneers, "How the hell did that freckle-faced punk Macdonald get you and your PBA friends to go along with it?"

"Go along with what?" I answer, shrugging.

"The cover-up."

"Cover-up? I have no idea what you're talking about."

He stares at me intently, then shakes his head. "My Lord. You don't know, do you?"

"You win, I don't know," I say impatiently.

"Little sweet Anya. My, oh my, and here I thought *I* was the corrupt one."

"Stop playing games with me and tell me what you mean."

"Or else what, you'll have me executed? Ha-ha! All right, let me cut to the chase, but I think you'd better sit back down."

Oh boy, I don't like the sounds of this. I sit down, my expression remaining noncommittal.

"You see, Nicole, right around the time you decided you wanted to become the country's top boss and Anya's tale began to capture the hearts of Americans, I made an offer to disclose some very important information to that idiot Macdonald."

"And in return?"

"He would make certain my brother's medical license was reinstated—I know for certain he didn't over-prescribe those pills to that lying bitch. And I know it was because of *my* crimes that he was never given a fair shake to prove his innocence."

"This information: what was it?"

"It pertained to Anya. Information that I most definitely thought he would've shared with you and the rest of the dullards down at the Freedom Home... unless, of course, you were all purposely left out of the loop—for whatever reason."

"I'm listening," I say, my curiosity now engaged.

"Hmm, where to begin?" he drawls, savoring the power he currently has over me. "All right, let's start with the helcin that Anya provided to AXE. Now, that stuff was beautifully crafted, just the perfect mix of baking powder and food coloring."

"Baking powder and food coloring? What in the—"

"Yeah, and if it weren't for our state-of-the-art equipment, Johnny T and I may actually have fallen for it."

"Hold on a second. You're telling me the helcin Anya created and AXE sold you was fake."

He smiles. "Fake and useless—unless, of course, we were going to bake a cake."

"Hold on," I say, reeling in confusion. "That stuff was used to kill General Gibson?"

"You see, once we discovered the truth, we found another supplier, the Spirit of Hades... And that's not all, Nicole. Through some behind-the-scenes work, Johnny T and I discovered it was your visually challenged gnome who actually tipped us off about the planned bombings of those animal research labs."

"If what you're telling me is true, then Anya was actually doing all she could to *prevent* Dwight Wagner, Morris Johns, and the rest of AXE from carrying out their agenda, yet she pretended to be on board. On top of all that, she's willing to face the death penalty, though she's innocent. Do you realize how insane this all sounds?"

"I didn't write the script, Nicole. I'm just relaying the story. Perhaps, for whatever reason, Anya was somehow prohibited from exposing the truth."

"Now tell me, General: why should I believe a single word coming out of your mouth, and more importantly, why have you decided to stab Macdonald and the Commission in the back and tell me all this?"

"Because that's the very thing he did to me. He promised me, and he reneged. Of course he gave me this garbage about trying his best... two-faced son of a bitch."

"What do you know about SOH?"

"Other than the fact they're a deranged bunch of misfits, not a helluva lot. If I knew at the time their goal was to destroy America, I would have had Johnny T blow their delivery guy's head off right there on the spot, when he brought us the helcin. It was never my goal to destroy this country. I simply did what I did for the betterment of my country."

"You're just such a patriotic man, General. And it's fascinating, hearing you, of all people, speak of others as being deranged. Do you ever look at yourself?"

Sims draws himself up. "I sure do, and what I see is a noble patriot. A man whose mission in life was to protect America from bleeding hearts like you."

Sims laughs as I rise abruptly and leave.

In a wave of fury, I head to the warden's office and demand to speak with Anya. My entire body's trembling. While I sit in the waiting area, I try to gather my thoughts. I'm at a complete loss. If what Sims is telling me is true, then it's as if AXE were some wild beast, and Anya was doing everything in her power to tame it. But why?

"I'm sorry, Ms. Kratz, but as of a week ago, Miss Ahar became property of the Outer Commission. In order to speak with her, you'll require clearance from Guardian Macdonald," the sergeant at the front desk explains. "Actually, your timing is very good; he's here finishing up a meeting with the warden. I'll send him a flash informing him it's your wish to see him."

Minutes later, the desk sergeant leads me to the warden's office. I enter to see Macdonald about to putt a golf ball on the warden's miniature putting green.

"Shh," he whispers as he looks back my way. He then removes his suit jacket and neatly places it atop the warden's desk. Gently swaying the putter back and forth, he prepares for the putt. "Geez!" he blurts after sending the ball a few inches wide of the hole. "Well, maybe the stage just wasn't big enough to bring out the best in me," he says with an annoying chuckle, placing the putter in a corner before retrieving his jacket. "Maybe one day, after your husband pays his debt to society, I'll get him to give me some lessons," he adds. That annoying laugh lingers.

"I urgently need to speak with you," I say, panic edging my voice.

"Yes. I understand you wish to speak with me about Anya Ahar," he answers calmly.

"That's correct, sir."

"Please, have a seat." He directs me to the chair in front of the warden's desk.

"Now, what can I do for you, Ms. Kratz?" he asks with a goofy grin as he sits at the warden's desk.

"Just today I learned from Clifford Sims that Anya Ahar may be totally innocent."

"Well, I'm glad to hear you have the trust of felons. The only thing is, at this point in time, Sims's words hold about as much value as yesterday's trash," Macdonald says, shrugging. "Anya Ahar has admitted her guilt and gone through the proper process, per the New Order Treaty. And now she must prepare to face her penalty—that of death."

"She's an innocent woman!" I shout, my anger taking over. "I'm demanding to speak with her."

"Please settle down, Ms. Kratz," Macdonald orders. "The prisoner is no longer at this facility."

"Where the hell is she?"

"That I can't disclose. Since her case was deemed a Code Three, she is now under the Commission's control. I'm sure you're aware of the rules. So, I think it'd be wise of you to begin focusing on other things, such as paying your country's debt—or America will soon be *No*merica," he says. His snicker now sounds sinister.

"Wait a second. You know it's true! You know Anya's innocent! And you and your wretched Commission are willing to kill an innocent woman!" I shout.

"On top of paying the debt, I think you should also be dedicating your time to tracking down those who were behind this Spirit of Hades gang. Who knows what else they may have in mind?"

"What kind of rotten human being are you!" I yell in a rage.

"Your country created this damn mess, and if not for the Commission, the vultures would've swept in a long time ago and you'd be like sheep, living under some tyrant's influence," he answers with a smirk. "You should be grateful. At least I'm a pleasant shepherd."

"No. What you are is a self-centered, unhinged creep," I say, looking directly into his icy green eyes.

"This meeting is over, Ms. Kratz. Now please, I have far bigger fish to fry, not to mention a golf game that needs an awful lot more work," he says smugly.

"This *meeting* may be over, but *this*—it's far from over," I growl as I storm out of the room.

CHAPTER 29

Feeling it's now become vital to bring this matter to Westgale's attention, I return to the Freedom Home. As I enter the hallway to the drawing room, I'm intercepted by the Lady of Honor. "Nicole, it's been a while," she says, greeting me with what I instantly notice is a forced smile. I can see her pain by looking into her eyes. Normally sparkling blue with an undeniable vibrancy, they now appear haunted and dull.

"I'm so sorry... I'm so sorry," I say softly as I move toward her.

"Thank you, my dear," she replies as we embrace. "He keeps blaming himself," she says as we regard Westgale from the drawing room entrance. "I'm very concerned about him," she adds.

"And what about yourself, ma'am? How are you?" I ask.

"Truthfully, I'm falling to pieces," April replies, her voice tightly controlled. "But just as I'm about to completely crumble, I think of Jessie and how she'd demand that we be strong and 'fight like troopers,' as she used to say."

I smile back at her, blinking back tears. "I hate to be a bother at such a time, but it is rather urgent I speak with him," I say hesitantly.

"By all means, Nicole. He thinks the world of you, and right now he could sure use the support," she responds softly. "Go on in."

When I enter, Westgale's watching a view-file of Jessica at a Washington children's hospital. Her security guards are carrying several bags containing all kinds of toys and stuffed animals. Together with an effervescent Jessica they begin working their way through the hospital, handing out gift after gift. Jessica is seen speaking to and embracing each child, a huge smile permanently etched upon her face.

"That's her, Nicole," Westgale says, his voice cracking as he acknowledges my presence. "A kind, compassionate soul... nonjudgmental. If only she were the daughter of... I don't know, an insurance broker or a plumber, and not a man who—"

"You can't do this to yourself, sir. This is not your fault," I tell him instantly, thinking of my own family issues.

"My God, Nicole. To think she'd just discovered true love, and was doing such terrific work, assisting your father with his foundation," he says wistfully as he turns off the flash-screen. "I just hope to God that Gil and the rest of the good folks assisting him will finally be able to uncover the truth behind the Spirit of Hades. I'm certain this runs far deeper than just Kolton Rollins..." He mentally shakes himself. "Listen to me rambling on," he says in a brisker voice. "Now, I guess you're here about Anya."

"Yes. How did you know?"

"I just received the notice a few minutes before you arrived."

"Notice?"

"Yeah, the notice indicating Anya's been executed. I take it you didn't receive one."

"Oh no!" I cry out in disbelief, sinking into the sofa beside me. "Those damn bastards! How could they do this!"

"I'm sorry, Nicole. I know how much you thought of her."

"They just executed a completely innocent young woman," I say, fighting to find the words.

"Completely innocent? I'd say that's a bit of a stretch, my dear."

"No, no. You don't understand, sir. The truth was concealed." I then explain what Sims had told me along with the details of my visit with Macdonald.

"How can this be?" he says, stunned by my revelation. "And Macdonald claimed Sims was lying?"

"Of course, but I saw through his deception."

"Yeah, but can we trust Sims?"

"In this instance, we'd be foolish not to."

"Hmm. It sounds like Anya was being prevented from telling the truth. But why?"

"I think the Outer Commission has some explaining to do, sir."

"I wouldn't hold your breath, Nicole. Very rarely does a king answer to a servant, and sadly, until we pay that debt in full, that's exactly what we are—servants to a higher power."

"I refuse to just let this go, Mr. President. I'm certain they knew of her innocence, and still decided to kill her."

"You're probably correct, but the way I see it, it's too late; the damage has been done. When you take the helm you can go back and question the Commission all you wish, but for now, this Administration's focus needs to be on the Spirit of Hades, along with paying that debt."

"Oh my God, the doctor! He shouldn't learn this from the World Connect. Do you know if he's in his office?"

"Actually, for the last few days, Jack has been doing some research from his home. Here, I'll contact him," Westgale offers, reaching for his flash-pad.

"No," I say, stopping him. "I need to do this in person. I think it's important that he hears the entire story, and isn't alone when he does."

"Well, you'd better get a move on; UCIT will announce the news any time now," Westgale cautions.

When Edward lets me out in front of Dr. Ahar's condo, I gaze up toward his penthouse, my heart racing and my emotions whirling out of control. I'm oblivious to the noise that surrounds me. All I keep asking myself is how I'm going to tell this man his daughter has ended up a victim of the War Within again.

I enter the building and the concierge offers to discreetly escort me and my security up to Ahar's penthouse. "Why thank you, sir," I say, accepting his offer. "Should we notify him that I'm here?"

"There's no need. Dr. Ahar has personally requested that whenever you, Director Perry, or the president visit, I am to personally escort you up to his unit."

With my security by my side, I enter the VIP elevator with the concierge.

I disembark on the top floor and take a deep breath before pressing the door's flash-signal.

"Nicole, what a pleasant surprise," Dr. Ahar says, beckoning me in.

"I hope I didn't catch you at a bad time," I say as I step inside.

"Oh, no. I could use a break," he answers as he takes my coat. "I've just been so busy, working on the VX drug program," he adds. I notice he appears rather uneasy, looking several times toward a partially closed door to one of the rooms off the living room.

"Make yourself at home," he says, focusing on me. "Would you like some coffee?"

"Sure, that'd be great," I answer. He still seems on edge.

As he leaves to fetch coffee, I turn my attention toward the living room's flash-screen. *Oh no, there it is,* I think as I see the UCIT logo appear on the screen and hear the usual jarring sound effects that accompany Cryptic.

"I come to you today to make an announcement on behalf of the Outer Commission," the robot says in its monotone voice. *"This evening at 7:00 p.m. Eastern Time, Anya Ahar was..."*

Suddenly I hear a female voice call out, "Well, I guess I should probably…"

I quickly look behind me. I'm jolted from my seat in shock. "Anya! Is that… you?" I stammer. My eyes are seeing but not believing. "What in the world?" I gasp, attempting to catch my breath, dazed beyond belief.

"Yes, it's me, Nicole," she answers calmly.

I turn back toward Dr. Ahar, who is standing in the doorway to the kitchen, his eyes shifting nervously back and forth between me and his daughter.

He then enters the living room and settles the cup of coffee on the table beside me. "I think it's best if I allow the two of you some time alone," he says anxiously as he moves to the front door. He pushes his feet into shoes and pulls on a jacket as he exits the apartment.

"Doctor, wait a minute—" I call out, but too late; he's gone. "What in the world is going on?" I say, turning back toward Anya.

"I guess I owe you an explanation," Anya says as she takes a seat across from me but doesn't lean back. Gone are the horn-rimmed glasses, and her hair is neatly styled and now a few shades lighter.

"Yeah, I think at this point an explanation would probably be very helpful," I reply sardonically, wondering if I'm travelling through some very strange dream.

She begins by explaining how she'd come to join AXE. "I'd had numerous conversations with Morris Johns when we were at Summit, regarding politics and the future of America. At first I was very impressed by the fact that he believed America's youth needed to have a voice. I guess you could say, like many young Americans, we'd both become somewhat radical in our way of thinking. The strained relationship with my father left me extremely confused about the meaning of life.

"I truly thought AXE was going to emerge as a massive political entity focusing on youth empowerment, and through forceful but peaceful methods, our message would be heard. But then I began to realize I was terribly mistaken."

"How so?"

"One afternoon while we were conversing on the Summit University lawns, I saw a side of Morris I hadn't seen before. He began speaking about how, for our message to be heard, we'd have to create anarchy... sabotage corporations and government view-files, and even blow up buildings. I was taken aback."

"But yet you agreed to go along with his plan."

"Yes, but it's not what you think."

I settle back on the sofa. "Go ahead, I'm listening."

"When Morris left for class that afternoon I remained out on the lawn, reviewing a paper I'd been working on for the last few days. I tried my best to concentrate, but what Morris had told me had left me feeling very uneasy. Then a young male jogger with fiery orange hair approached me. He said his name was Macdonald."

"As in Guardian Macdonald?"

"Correct. You see, he'd been watching Morris. The Outer Commission was well aware what he and Dwight Wagner were up to. In fact, he knew Morris and I had been having these long conversations almost on a daily basis, so he researched my background."

* * *

"The young man you were speaking with earlier; is he your boyfriend?" Macdonald asked.

"Oh no, he's just a friend I enjoy conversing with... or at least I thought I did," Anya replied, frowning suddenly.

"Is there something you'd like to tell me about Mr. Johns?"

"Yes... there is..."

* * *

My mind begins to form a picture. "I get it—the Commission forced you to infiltrate AXE," I say.

"You're partly correct. But the Outer Commission didn't 'force' me to do a single thing. It was all my idea. I volunteered. With an election on the horizon I believed it was imperative for the PBA to remain in power, and I knew every time my story was told it would have a great impact on the country and serve as a strike against the MAA."

Anya describes her follow-up meeting with Macdonald. "I met with him at a secret location, in a warehouse…"

* * *

"Infiltrate AXE? I can't let you do that, Miss Ahar. It's way too dangerous," Macdonald said. "As long as you're willing to provide testimony, we'll have these guys locked away in no time."

"And do you think locking up Dwight Wagner and Morris Johns will calm this current massive wave of disenfranchised youth?" Anya asked.

"It surely won't, but at least it'll stop these punks and set an example for others who are considering following in their footsteps."

"That's the problem, sir. It's always the same thing over and over, the good guys versus the bad guys. Have you ever thought for a moment why it is young adults feel so marginalized?"

"Please—enlighten me," Macdonald urges.

"It all comes down to having a sense of purpose—feeling like one matters in the world."

"Are you saying youth must be coddled and constantly told how wonderful they are?"

"Not at all. What I'm saying is that we need to be heard; enabled to express ourselves and not just be slaves to the powers that be."

Macdonald looked thoughtful at that. He nodded. "My superiors at the Outer Commission are more than twice my age," he said, and added that he had to fight twice as hard to be listened to and accepted. "So I understand what you're saying and it's all wonderful, but how is your infiltrating AXE going to help accomplish such a lofty goal?"

"You know how my mother died on that cold December day, don't you, Guardian Macdonald?"

"Yes, and I must say it's one of the most tragic stories I've ever heard."

"And that's why you need to let me do this."

"With all respect, Miss Ahar, how does your mother's tragedy relate to bringing down a group of extremists?"

"The tragic story of my mother needs to be told. As a warning sign, it needs to be pounded into the minds of the entire country. And this isn't just about bringing down extremists; this is about fixing a system that has been broken for way too long. A system that chooses power and greed over love and compassion."

"How about I speak with the people at UCIT and have them prepare a view-file of your mother's story?" Macdonald suggested.

"And that would be relaying just another sad story about the War Within. Oh no, for the story to have a real impact, I, as a victim, must do something impactful. I must grab the country's attention."

* * *

While listening to Anya relay this information, I feel as if my brain is about to jump out of my head and shatter into a thousand pieces. "So, Macdonald and the Commission actually went along with your plan?" I ask in disbelief.

"It took some coaxing on Macdonald's part, but his superiors gave in. Macdonald made me aware that the Commission actually dreaded the idea of an MAA government."

"Your behavior? That empty look in your eyes? That cold, unemotional disconnect? Your dedication to that doctrine? Are you telling me it was all an act?"

"Some of it was. Once the plan was in place, the Commission had me under strict twenty-four-hour surveillance. They even knew the president was allowing me to work on the LRS cure while in prison. I'm just sorry I had to act that way toward you, especially considering how strongly you believed in me. And I'm sorry your father's life was placed in harm's way. But it was the only way."

"And *your* father?"

"For years I truly despised everything my father stood for. But after he faked his suicide and worked with Hunter Talbot on the LRS cure, it made me do a lot of soul searching, and I came to realize he was a far better man than I'd given him credit for."

"I have to ask you, Anya. If I didn't find you here today, would you have expected me to go through the rest of my days thinking you'd been executed?"

"Frankly, that was the plan. They didn't even want my father to know about this, but in the end I insisted. Please understand, this isn't about me. It's about the future of America. That being said, I'm truly glad you did find out."

"So are you planning to live in disguise, secluded away in this apartment for the rest of your life?"

"No," she answers with a delicate smile. "The Commission will assist me in beginning a new life far away from America. It'll mean a complete overhaul of my identity, but I'm prepared."

"My Lord, Anya. To think of what you've done and what you're about to do for this country—the sacrifice—it's incredible," I say, shaking my head in disbelief.

"I just hope I've made a difference," she replies softly.

"And what about your father?" I ask.

"Yeah, what about your father?" says Dr. Ahar, standing in the doorway. "Don't you dare tell me this is goodbye."

"Of course not," Anya answers. Beaming, she walks over to Jack and embraces him. "Once my new life has been established, we'll have plenty of opportunities to make up for lost time."

"Well, I guess I should be off," I say as waves of emotion fill the apartment. "But before I go, I'd love for you to have this, Anya," I add, handing her my Liberty Bell pendant. "This was given to me by the Strategic Council the day I was officially named incoming president."

"Wow... it's exquisite," she replies, studying the pendant. "Are you certain you want to give this to *me*?"

"If there's one person in this country who deserves to wear such a badge of honor, it's you, Anya."

Entering the back of my grand-electro, I'm immediately startled by a man hurriedly climbing in behind me. "Don't fret, Nicole. It's only me," says Macdonald as he slides in beside me. "I hope you don't mind, but I took the liberty of giving your driver a few bucks to get himself a bite to eat."

I look at him, confused, my mind still reeling. "I can't believe this. Your Commission fixed this entire election," I say, staring straight ahead.

"Fixed? I think you might be giving us a little too much credit. It was that young lady you just visited who somehow knew how to penetrate the soul of your country," Macdonald responds, chomping away on his gum. "And America clearly decided that *you* were the person to guide the way. Nobody was forced to do a single thing. And as far as our Commission is concerned, one could say we just helped set the stage," he adds. "So now, pay that debt and it'll be clear sailing. But then, you'll no longer have the privilege of seeing my handsome face." He grins. "Best of luck, Nicole." He slithers out of the electro and walks away, mockingly humming the American national anthem.

As a person who prides herself on honesty, to say I'm left feeling conflicted would be a massive understatement, but I ask myself, what would exposing this shocking story do? Possibly start a series of countrywide riots? Or perhaps another War Within?

CHAPTER 30

With every passing second, minute, and day, Jessica Westgale sees her life pass before her. Still completely isolated with absolutely no contact with anyone, she's certain that whoever brought her here isn't coming back. *Perhaps they're dead,* she thinks, not wanting to believe they simply left her here to die. Why leave her everything she needs to be rather comfortable for quite some time, if they intend to let her die? She's lacking in only one very important thing: her freedom.

A strange buzzing sound draws her attention toward the front of the room. She realizes it's coming from the large flash-screen. Within seconds a bright flash appears, and she hears the now hauntingly familiar opening notes to *Starlight Serenade*. Seconds later, a view-file begins to play. There she is on the screen, dancing with Cobra Pix.

"Cobra! Cobra! Cobra!" she screams frantically. "Get me the hell out of here, now!" The view-file continues to play, showing her and Cobra floating across the room in unison. She scurries over to the door. "Open this damn door!" she yells at the top of her lungs, relentlessly pounding on it. Succumbing to dismay, she falls to the floor, weeping uncontrollably.

When the view-file concludes, Cobra's image takes over the screen. "Hello, Jessica," he says calmly. "Now, I owe you an apology, my dear."

Still reeling in shock, Jessica slowly rises and staggers over to the chair in front of the flash-screen.

"I'm sorry to have neglected you all this time, but sometimes there just isn't enough hours in the day," he adds.

"Where the hell am I?" Jessica shouts at the screen.

"Ah... please excuse me. What an awful host I am. Welcome back to Pinia, Jessica," Cobra replies with a smile.

"Pinia? It can't be," she says in disbelief, gazing around the room. "How—wait a second. Oh my God... have I been set up? Please don't tell me Shadow is involved in this."

"Don't be silly, my dear. That young man is completely enamored with you. The love the two of you share is beyond extraordinary."

"Then how and why in the world did I end up here?"

"Now, in due time, I promise to answer your questions," he replies. "Since you've been cooped up in that room for way too long, why don't I have my assistant come and get you out of there and escort you to the courtyard, where we can have a nice chat."

When Victor, Cobra's newly appointed assistant, comes to escort her from the confines of the room—which is on the second floor of Cobra's palace, she notes—she's surprised by his kindness. "He's waiting for you," says Victor as he hands her a wool sweater. "It's a little chilly this afternoon, so you might want to put this on."

As Jessica and the guards reach the courtyard, all she can think of is Shadow and the many lovely dinners the two of them enjoyed in this very enclosure. She recalls how after dinner they'd gaze endlessly into the starry Pinian sky, and relay to each other their innermost thoughts. There's one particular conversation she'll always remember. One which, at this point in time, seems extremely relevant.

* * *

"How do you do it, Shadow?" Jessica asked as they sat gazing at the winking stars.

"Do what, honey?" he asked in reply.

"Not fear for your personal safety, considering the political unrest in this country."

"I know it sounds crazy, but I don't fret over politics or the idea of war. My father, on the other hand, is so paranoid that his assistants are ordered to wear spy-stars twenty-four hours a day."

"Spy-stars?"

"Yeah, they're tiny star-shaped sound- and view-chips that enable Cobra to listen in and watch every move his men make. For me, my only fear is for your safety, especially after Jolio attempted to kill you. If something were to happen to you... I don't know how I would carry on," Shadow said tenderly.

* * *

Now, all Jessica can think of is how Shadow and her family back home probably think she's dead. She sits down directly across from Cobra, takes a deep breath, and glowers at him.

"Please pour a cup of cocoa for the lovely Miss Westgale," Cobra orders Victor. Jessica studies Victor and notices a tiny silver star on his lapel. *That must be a spy-star*. She accepts the beverage, and decides to lose the glower. *There's absolutely no point in being difficult.*

"Now, as promised, let me enlighten you as to how you ended up back in the promised land of Pinia," Cobra says after taking a sip of his cocoa. "And again I do apologize for not addressing you sooner upon your arrival. I realize the situation must have been somewhat traumatic for you, but I at least hope the amenities were to your liking."

"Actually, I was quite comfortable, thank you," Jessica responds, disguising her anger and fear with formality.

"Great, because as I explained to you during our *prior* meetings, I have no intention of bringing harm to you, Jessica. I want you to feel welcomed in Pinia."

"I don't understand, sir. You say you don't want to harm me, yet you had me kidnapped in New York City and brought all the way here. Do you realize how Shadow and my family must be suffering right now? And furthermore, do you realize the suffering you're causing me?"

"That's totally up to you, Jessica. I'm doing my best to make you feel welcomed. There really is no need for you to feel anxious or afraid."

"Please, Cobra, get me on a plane and let me go back home."

"I couldn't do that to you."

Jessica hesitates and looks at him in confusion. "What do you mean?"

"In due time, you'll understand."

"At least tell me how the hell I ended up here. I don't remember a damn thing... Wait a second—Kolton. It had to be. Backstage in the auditorium. The glass of fruit punch he poured for me had to have eventually knocked me out."

"Ah, very good detective work, my dear. One must be careful when accepting drinks from mad chemists."

"My Lord... his relationship with Luanda—you had to have orchestrated it. You had him under your control."

"Tsk-tsk, you're not the detective I thought you were," Cobra says with a smirk. "Believe me, Kolton Rollins was more than willing to do his part. Poor soul. He was a brilliant man who became consumed by misplaced guilt, which eventually led to his demise." Cobra nods to his assistant as Victor refills his cup. "Imagine learning that something *you* created was used to kill your siblings, when all the time you thought your creation was being made to kill your enemy."

"What do you mean his *demise*? Is he dead?"

"Sadly, Kolton decided to take his own life."

"Tell me what the hell is going on!" Jessica demands, losing her patience.

"In due time, Jessica," Cobra says calmly. "That's the thing with you youngsters today; you have absolutely no regard for the process of discovery. You're always in such a rush to know everything right away. Personally, I just don't see any enjoyment in that."

"Why are you holding me captive?" Jessica shouts. "Is it a ransom you're looking for? Or is this your sick way of getting revenge against my father, or Shadow?"

"Whoa, I just hate seeing you worked up like this, my darling. I think it'd be best to pick this up again tomorrow," Cobra says as he waves

Victor toward Jessica. Her glower returns as Victor eases her out of her chair. "Be gentle with her," Cobra says calmly. "Miss Westgale is a very special young lady, and she must be treated as such."

He reaches into the bag slung over his shoulder and pulls out a white box wrapped with a red and blue bow. "This is for you," he says with a smile as he hands Jessica the box. She studies it closely. "No need to worry, Jessica, there's nothing ticking in there," he adds with a chuckle. "It's merely a welcome gift."

On the way back to her room, all kinds of thoughts and questions whirl around in Jessica's mind. She now knows how she got to Pinia, but why is she here? What kind of game is Cobra playing? Despite Cobra's words, she continues to fear for her life.

* * *

In another part of Pinia, Trevor Larsen has been holding a week-long farewell carnival for the children of northern Pinia. "Okay, listen up," Trevor calls out. "I want everyone to go to your stations and gather around your leader, so you can receive your special gift packages. Miss Jessica and Mr. Shadow sent them all the way from America," he says with a lump in his throat. Just a day ago, he had learned that Jessica was missing.

"Mr. Trevor, do you know how come Miss Jessica has stopped sending me flash-messages? And why she doesn't answer mine anymore? Is she angry at me?" little Ulu asks Trevor. Sadness pours out in her voice. "Doesn't she care about me anymore?"

Trevor thinks quickly. "Of course she still does, Ulu. Miss Jessica and everybody else on our team love you and all the other children very much. She's just been really busy back in America. But look at all the gifts she and Mr. Shadow sent over."

The children shout with joy as they open the gift packages, which contain clothing, Laser Flash Frenzy games, toy Sortar dragons, soccer balls and equipment, and a new product from Vexton-Tech called Sky-Scope—a miniature, lightweight yet enormously powerful telescope.

"Wow, this is really neat," exclaims Ulu, running over to Trevor to show him what she received.

"Whoa, that's a Sky-Scope, Ulu. Now you'll be able to see right into space, and look at the moon and the stars," Trevor explains as he playfully lifts her into the air.

"What about spaceships?" she asks with a wide smile.

"Of course," Trevor answers as he gently whirls her through the air.

"And heaven?" she asks, cocking her head in curiosity.

"Sure. You can see whatever you like, Ulu," Trevor replies. His heart races, and tears well up in his eyes as he thinks of Jessica.

* * *

After taking a hot bath, Jessica stares long and hard at the box Cobra presented to her. *What could it be?* she keeps asking herself. *Should I, or shouldn't I?* Finally she removes the bow, then slowly lifts the lid of the box. Reaching inside, her fingers touch a book; she pulls out her father's most recent autobiography. His photo on the front cover generates a rush of sadness that runs through her like ice water. Having been the driving force behind the book's creation, it triggers a lot of memories for Jessica.

* * *

"Come on, Dad, the world should get to know the real William Westgale," Jessica said as they worked on the contents.

"Yeah, but don't you think telling them my favorite show on the World Connect is actually a cartoon might just be a little too much information?" Her father smiled.

"Now, now, who says there's anything wrong with the president of the United States watching weekend marathons of Sandy the Talking Cat?*" Jessica chuckled.*

"And this thing about how I accept ties from strangers. Do you really think it'd be wise to print that?"

"Hmm... seeing as you now have about seven hundred ties, yeah, maybe it'd be a good idea to leave that one out." They both laughed.

* * *

That annoying buzz from the flash-screen abruptly brings Jessica back to the present.

Cobra appears, dressed in his red and black Iron Lotus uniform. "Well now, I'm thrilled to see you're enjoying my gift," he says. "It's surely not on *my* must-read list, but, as they say, 'different strokes for different folks.' Hopefully it'll help to ease your mind."

"Are you enjoying this game?" Jessica snaps at the screen.

"Yes. I'm elated to have you here as my guest, if that's what you're asking," Cobra answers as he moves toward a vast collection of weapons and military equipment. "This is the actual laser-rifle my son Hadar was carrying when he was killed in Oria," he says as he picks up the gun and silently stares at it for about fifteen seconds. "And this helmet, it belonged to my second eldest son, Norro. Do you see this hole?" he says, holding the helmet up in the air for Jessica to see. "This hole is from the laser-blast that was aimed directly at his skull. Killed him instantly. American power at its most deadly. Norro was actually hoping to one day play professional soccer in America. He was by far the best player Pinia had ever produced." Cobra then removes his military cap, rubs his bald head, and sinks into a large easy chair.

"Do you think I'm that naïve, Cobra? I know this is all about avenging the deaths of your sons, and getting revenge by making my father think I'm dead," Jessica says, her voice shrill. "Why don't you just go ahead and kill me? By now the entire world thinks I'm dead anyway!"

"I gave you my word," he shouts, rising from his chair. "You will not be harmed. I will see you tomorrow morning," he calmly adds.

The screen shuts off, leaving her to linger in dread. Deep in her heart, this time around, Jessica's finding it hard to take Cobra at his word.

When she resumes scanning through her father's autobiography and reaches the photo section of the book, she begins to shake in horror. Large red and black *X*s have been stroked through photos of her father, mother, Director Perry, and other Westgale associates. The photos of her are untouched. "Oh my God... what in the world is this!" she cries. Turning the page to the final photo, her horror escalates when she sees a red and black X stroked over an American flag.

CHAPTER 31

After announcing that the initial shipment of fera-bean biofuel is now in Washington, Energy Secretary Harrison Deacon looks over at Westgale and me with a broad smile. "Simply amazing!" he exclaims as his staff let out an enormous cheer. "And the whole process went as smooth as can be," he adds as he walks toward the robo-cargo plane.

"We're gonna do it," Westgale says to me, placing his hand on my shoulder. "There was a time when I highly doubted we'd meet that deadline, but we're gonna do it, Nicole," he repeats excitedly. Then his mood swings. "I only wish Jessica could witness this country regain its full independence. It's not fair, Nicole. It's simply not fair."

"It surely isn't, and it's all because of me, sir. I have to take full responsibility," says Shadow, who has just arrived on site to join in the celebration of this monumental event.

"That's not true, Shadow. Kolton Rollins and whoever the hell he was associated with were on a mission of vengeance. Personally, I don't think anything was going to stop them," Westgale replies.

"I still can't help but wonder how long Jessica had been targeted," Shadow says with a raised brow.

"Why? Do you think this was in the works prior to Kolton meeting her?" I ask.

"I don't know, Nicole, but I agree with President Westgale: I think this entire thing runs deeper than just Kolton Rollins," Shadow replies.

"And that's exactly why I have all the top law enforcement people from across the country on this," Westgale chimes in. "We'll get to the bottom of it. I promise you, Shadow."

* * *

"Let me get this straight, Miss Taylor. Are you telling me you were paid off for disclosing that information?" Gil Robichaud says to a jet-lagged Carly Taylor, who had just flown in from Germany after watching recent events pertaining to Kolton Rollins unfold on UCIT.

"Yes. However, it's not what you think. I was telling the truth. That money simply enabled me to get out of America and begin a new life," Carly replies, nervously twisting her fingers together.

"To get out of America?"

"That's correct, Agent Robichaud. After coming forward with such damning information against such powerful people, I believed my safety would be compromised if I were to remain here in America."

"Although I don't think it was very wise of you to do such a thing, I understand," Gil says.

"When I saw that mask being shown at your press conference, I remembered it right away. The man who paid me the money was wearing the exact same type of mask. By accident the driver turned a light on, and that's when I really got a good look at it."

"But you said the man was much heavier than Mr. Rollins, correct?"

"Oh yes. From the photos I've seen, I know for certain it wasn't him."

"Did you ever think to ask why they so badly wanted you to divulge the information?"

"I have no idea why, but there's no doubt in my mind they desperately wanted the PBA to retain leadership of the country."

"I don't know if we should trust *anything* this woman tells us," a frustrated Champ Sutton says as he reviews the details of Gil's interview a short time later.

"Well, at least she handed over the money, which says something for her credibility," Gil says, pacing Sutton's office floor.

"Okay, let's suppose she's being completely honest with us," Sutton says. "The first question we need to ask is: who would've paid her to come forward with such condemning information on the MAA? And why?"

"Well, when you think about it, we're talking about Levin and Pemberton. Not the most endearing people on the face of the earth."

"I agree. But if we tie this to Jessica's kidnapping, I think we have something extremely large and sinister," Champ responds as he pulls up his file on the Spirit of Hades. "Damn. Other than what Morris Johns has told us, and the fact they were the ones who covertly sold the helcin to Sims, we have so little on these guys. Now, was the lab able to match the helcin with the stuff used against the Pinian government?"

"The tests were inconclusive," Gil says, running his hands through his hair in frustration.

"Hmm... what if whoever paid Carly did so for *political* reasons?" Champ says.

"That makes sense," Gil answers. "I hope I'm not speaking out of turn here, but I know if I were involved with an extremist group intent on attacking America, I'd much rather have the PBA running the country as well."

"And in order to settle things down, you'd probably want to eliminate Blackheart, too," Champ adds.

"Are you thinking Rollins and whoever he was involved with killed Blackheart?" Gil asks.

"Well, once the bomb analysis results come back, we'll have our answer," Champ replies.

As Gil prepares to head back to his office, he receives a flash-message from National Investigation Director Martin Stevens, urgently requesting that they meet. He adjusts his schedule and informs his driver.

When he arrives at the National Investigation headquarters a few blocks from the Freedom Home, Gil is immediately escorted into Stevens's office.

"Thanks for getting here so promptly," says Stevens. He looks distracted, his movements quick, driven by anxiety.

"Of course. You said it was urgent," Gil replies, drawing his eyebrows together.

Stevens directs him to the chair across from him, then taps a few buttons on his flash-pad. "This could be the break we're looking for," he says as his eyes look toward his office doorway. "Ah, come on in, Mr. Verzi," he says as one of his agents appears with a dark-haired, twenty-something man.

The young man takes the other chair in front of Stevens's desk and explains how he recognized Kolton Rollins from the World Connect. "I recall seeing him several times," Verzi says as Rollins's picture is put up on the flash-screen at the front of the room.

"Can you recall *where* you've seen him?" Stevens asks.

"In my homeland of Pinia."

"Pinia. I'll be darned," Gil says, looking at Stevens.

"Where exactly in Pinia did you see him?" Stevens asks.

"I used to work for an electro service at the country's central airport. On a few occasions I offered to drive Mr. Rollins, but he always declined. Instead a large black grand-electro used to pick him up. I'm sure it was an Iron Lotus vehicle."

"Are you certain it's the same man?" Gil asks as he takes out his flash-pad and begins making notes.

"Yes. I'm one hundred percent certain. I recognize the burn mark on his cheek. He usually had a beard covering it, but the last few times I saw him, it was clearly visible."

"Do you recall when you first saw him?" Stevens asks.

"It had to be just over a couple of years ago. Not long after the Battle of Oria."

"And the last time?"

"About six months ago. Right before I moved to America."

"Did he ever say anything to you?" Gil asks.

"Actually, usually he did his best to avoid me. But the last time I saw him, his ride was late so we ended up conversing." Verzi relays the conversation.

* * *

"Hello, sir. How are you today?" Verzi asked Kolton.

"It's just another day, young man," Kolton said gruffly.

"Not for me. I just received my plane ticket, and next week I'll be America-bound."

"Ah, you're visiting America?"

"Oh no. I'm planning to live in America. And I can't wait," Verzi said with excitement.

"Now, what in the world would make you do something like that?" Kolton asked sarcastically.

"It's always been a dream of mine. My cousin owns three restaurants in Baltimore, and he's asked me to help him manage them."

"So, soon you'll be living the American dream," Kolton says, looking Verzi in the eyes. "Oh, good ol' America, she can be rather alluring—much like an extremely attractive woman." He snickers. "Her welcoming smile, radiant eyes, luxuriant hair, and soft voice can really draw you in, making you feel as though heaven is right before your very eyes. But I suggest you be very careful, young man; sometimes underneath all that beauty and sweetness, there's nothing but a cold, heartless bitch."

* * *

"And that was it. By that time his car had arrived and he was off," Verzi finishes.

"Hmm, that is very interesting indeed," Gil says thoughtfully.

"Thank you for coming forward, Mr. Verzi," Stevens says. "I'm going to have the agent who escorted you here ask you a few more questions, if that's okay with you."

"That's fine. I'll gladly do whatever I can to help."

After Mr. Verzi is escorted from the room, Gil notices Martin Stevens deep in thought. "What is it, Martin? Do you believe this guy?" he asks.

"Yes, I believe him," Stevens replies. "What's really got me is the idea that I've been wrong all along."

"Wrong about what?"

"SOH, the Spirit of Hades. I was certain they had nothing to do with Pinia and the Iron Lotus, but now I guess I was completely wrong."

"That makes both of us, Martin. I used to argue with Agent Gallio about that very thing. Nick used to insist Cobra Pix was behind it all, and like a fool I would always shoot him down," Gil says, then notices the NI director is intently studying his flash-pad. "What is it?" he asks.

"It's the interview one of my men conducted with Luanda Rollins. It has me somewhat perplexed," Stevens says, his attention again drawn to his flash-pad.

"How so?" Gil asks. Stevens describes the interview.

* * *

"Was your husband ever abusive toward you?" the agent asked.

"Oh, no. Kolton always treated me with respect," Luanda answered.

"Besides the anger he displayed toward Direct Aim, did you ever see him become angry on other occasions?"

Luanda hesitated. "Well... there was one time."

"Please tell me about it, ma'am."

"It was after Jessica came to see me and asked me to visit Shadow in the hospital. I didn't want to because I knew it would bring a lot of heartache to my son. I felt really strongly about not doing it," she informs the agent.

"Was Kolton angry to hear you decided to visit your son?"

"No, it was the opposite. He insisted I do it. When I kept refusing to do so, he became furious with me. I was really surprised to see him act in such a way."

* * *

"Hmm, why would it have been so important to Rollins for Luanda to reconnect with her son?" Gil ponders aloud.

"After all we've now learned, it's become clear Cobra Pix definitely had some sort of agenda," Stevens replies.

The next morning, Gil and Stevens call an emergency Freedom Home meeting. Shadow Pix is flown in from New York to join us. First comes the news that the bomb analysis has made it clear that Kolton Rollins was responsible for the murder of the extremist Blackheart.

"Although we can't confirm anything at this point, we're strongly considering the idea that the two former SOH members had some kind of a falling-out, leading up to the murder," says Martin Stevens.

When Gil tells the group about Kolton Rollins's visits to Pinia, Westgale appears very agitated. "Do you know anything about this?" he asks Shadow.

"The first time I ever met Kolton Rollins was when my mother introduced us to each other," Shadow responds in disbelief. "If he was meeting with our militia, it's news to me."

"Did your father keep many secrets from you?" I ask.

"From what I've recently learned, it appears he did," Shadow answers solemnly.

"How would you say your father truly feels about America?" I ask.

"Directly following the Battle of Oria, I know my father definitely wanted to avenge the deaths of my brothers, but to my knowledge he never made an actual attempt to seek that revenge. My father is a complex man who can be so many different people," Shadow replies, running his hands over his face.

"This is crazy," Director Perry says loudly. He undoes his tie and walks to the front of the conference room. "It's now become obvious to everyone in this room that it was your father who was behind the Spirit of Hades." His voice rises in anger. "Which, by the way, was an American extremist group with the sole *purpose* of destroying this country. How can you sit in this room and lie to us about your father's contempt toward America!"

"Enough, David!" Westgale interjects forcefully.

"It's okay, sir," Shadow responds. "I fully understand where Director Perry's coming from. After learning how my father treated my mother so terribly all those years ago, it's now become clear to me that he's capable of anything. As far as SOH was concerned, obviously he kept me in the dark because he knew I would never support something like that."

"Everybody just take a deep breath. I think we need to reel this in a little," Westgale says calmly. "We're talking about a man who, although at some point in his life despised America, is now helping to save it with his generosity. I like to think people can change. I won't condemn the man until we have evidence that he's actually involved in this craziness."

"Do you believe your father's a changed man, Shadow? Is that why you left your homeland, because you believe your father has changed for the better?" Perry asks sarcastically.

"I won't accept this, David," Westgale shouts. "This brave young man saved my life and deeply loved my daughter. He doesn't deserve to be treated in such—"

"I sincerely hope my father has changed, Director Perry," Shadow answers over top of Westgale. "But unfortunately, I can't tell you he has."

"I'm sorry to have gotten carried away, Mr. President. And to think *I* was the person trying so hard to convince *you* to make the Pinian deal," Director Perry says as he and Westgale sit in the presidential lounge following the meeting. "After what's transpired around here over the last year, I guess my suspicions are getting the best of me."

"That's totally understandable." Westgale sighs. "And I agree that learning Kolton Rollins and SOH had ties to the Iron Lotus is reason for concern. But as you're well aware, there've been many instances where Cobra's men have gone rogue… Let's just hope this is one of those."

CHAPTER 32

"Good morning, Jessica," Cobra says while sitting in front of a large plate of scrambled eggs and toast. Jessica rubs her tired eyes and looks up at the flash-screen. "I hope you slept well. Your eggs and toast are on the way," he adds, lifting a glass of orange juice to sip. "My father used to always tell me about the importance of a good, hearty breakfast. And you know I tried my best to impart that wisdom to Shadow, but as you're well aware, he much prefers a quinoa fruit salad over a stack of pancakes." Cobra laughs.

Jessica remains silent as she glares at the screen, wishing she could jump through it and take that knife from the table and—but again, as difficult as it is, she realizes she must supress her anger and actually play this lunatic's game.

Seconds later, her breakfast arrives. "Thank you, Cobra," she says, looking at the plate of fluffy golden eggs and crispy toast.

"You eat up. We have a big day today—we're going into the village," Cobra informs her as his image slowly fades from the screen.

"Today's the final day of the carnival," Cobra tells Jessica as they ride in the back of an Iron Lotus electro-van. "Your associates did such a wonderful job, finishing the renovation of the community center. I thought it'd be nice for you to see the final results of your team's hard work."

"Thanks. That's very thoughtful of you," Jessica says, continuing to play along. *He must be wondering why I haven't said anything about the book.*

As the van approaches the community center, Jessica gazes through the tinted window in wonder. The formerly run-down structure is now an appealing building. "Wow," she exclaims, "it came out just as we hoped."

"Pull up toward the front of the building," Cobra orders Victor. "Look, read the sign," he urges Jessica. The sign on the building reads *The Jessica Westgale Community Center.*

"Oh my," Jessica says. "That is such an honor."

"I wouldn't have had it any other way," Cobra says calmly.

The man's even more insane than I thought, Jessica thinks.

As the van continues on along a stretch of sandy roads, Jessica looks up at the sky in the distance. High up, being carried by a strong gust of wind, a remote-controlled, dragon-like kite soars across the Pinian skyline. When she looks downward toward the field, she sees a running man, trailed by a group of children. She can easily tell by his long strides that it's Trevor.

"Aw, the innocence of childhood," Cobra murmurs.

Jessica's eyes immediately grow teary when she notices one of the children running with a limp, having difficulty keeping up with the others. It's frail little Ulu. Jessica remembers how she injured herself only a few days before she returned to America. She then flashes back to the day she said goodbye to the sweet orphan who always found a way to brighten up even the darkest of days.

* * *

"I'm really going to miss you, Miss Jessica!" Ulu cried.

"Hey, I might be leaving Pinia, but you'll always be with me, Ulu. Right here," Jessica said, placing her hand over her heart. "Now, you make sure you battle like a trooper and take care of that leg, okay?"

"Janet's been checking it every day," she answered, referring to one of Jessica's fellow aid workers who was also a paramedic.

"Great. Now that you have a flash-pad we can send each other all kinds of flash-messages and view-files."

"We can be friends forever," Ulu said with a smile as she fell into Jessica's arms.

* * *

When the van suddenly hits a bump in the road, it jolts Jessica back to the present. The kite has now ascended to a point where it appears to be one with the sun. Trevor and the children are standing back, watching in awe. Some of the children have decided to get a closer look with their Sky-Scopes.

"Aw, it's so lovely to see the children, so carefree and full of life," Cobra crows, then he orders Victor to return to the compound. "Why do we have to get old?" he adds, taking one more look back.

"I knew it! I knew it!" Ulu hollers at the top of her voice.

"Whoa, what is it, Ulu?" Trevor asks, turning away from guiding the kite.

Ulu abruptly crumples to the ground and lies there, unmoving.

"What the—Janet!" Trevor shouts.

Janet runs over to check the child's vital signs. "She's breathing," she announces, "but we must get her to the hospital!"

Trevor uses his flash-pad to contact Medical Air Emergency.

"I must admit your team is composed of some of the finest young people I've ever come across. Just like you, they're filled with such compassion," Cobra says to Jessica.

"That's true of most young Americans," Jessica responds.

"Seeing what a terrific young man your friend Trevor is actually brings back memories of my sons," Cobra says as he taps a button on his flash-pad, bringing up a flash-screen in the back of the van. "This is Hadar after saving a mother and her child from a house fire. As you can see, he needed to be hospitalized for smoke inhalation and a number of burns." The view-file continues. "And here's Sye and Norro helping out a disabled farmer whose three sons had recently lost their lives in a farming accident."

Jessica senses Cobra's anger is now overriding his sentimentality. Although she doesn't show it, her fear is growing by the second. She's terrified by the thought of where this is all leading. "I'm sure they were fine young men," she says softly. "I can see why you're so proud of them."

"Oh they were, my dear Jessica," Cobra answers firmly. "And that's why the time has come for your country to pay!" he snarls. "Zap-grenades may have completely singed off my hair and eyebrows in the Battle of Oria, but these incredible young men you're seeing were murdered—murdered by William Westgale and the United States of America! And in honor of the Sortar Dragon, the time has come for their murders to be avenged!"

"Oh, so that's why you placed those Xs throughout the book you gave me. You actually think you can destroy America," Jessica says with a snicker, no longer content to play along. "I'm sure you realize you aren't the first person to make such a threat."

"Oh, I'm well aware I'm not the first—but I guarantee you, I will be the last!" he shouts. His scowl deepens and the veins in his powerful neck appear ready to burst.

The van stops in front of Cobra's palace, saving Jessica from more of Cobra's vitriol—she hopes. Two guards remove her from the van.

"How many times must I tell you to be gentle with her," Cobra scolds them as he also disembarks. "Miss Westgale is not the enemy."

He turns to the guards as they enter the courtyard. "That'll be all, gentlemen."

"If I'm not the enemy, then why are you doing this to me?"

Cobra gives her a cold smile. "It's very simple, Jessica. You're here so I can personally assure your safety while America is once and for all put out of its misery."

"Well let me tell you, Cobra, I'm as American as a person can be, and I'm damn proud of it."

"Showing loyalty to one's homeland is a most admirable trait, even if that homeland happens to be a shameful, dark pit of corruption and hypocrisy," Cobra says smoothly. "But you, Jessica, you're like a ray of ceaseless light."

She ignores the compliment. "I find it interesting that you're more than willing to do business with that 'dark pit of corruption.'"

"Befriending and gaining the trust of one's enemy always eases the course for deception—and destruction, for that matter."

"So tell me: how do you plan to unleash your wrath on America?" she demands. "That militia of yours will be lucky if it can wipe out a small suburban neighborhood before being blown to smithereens." Jessica laughs, attempting to hide her terror.

"Ah, spoken like a proud American. I really do admire that about you. But you see, Jessie, one must never underestimate will and determination, especially when they're accompanied by a well-coordinated plan. And I must tell you President Woi and I have really covered our tracks."

Jessica thinks for a moment. "Woi and the HKM are part of this plan of yours?" she responds in disbelief.

"Why are you so shocked, my dear? For decades your government has told its people the HKM was coming to get them, so President Woi figured it was time to make their wish come true. And I'm more than pleased to join him."

"I don't believe you. I think this is some sick fantasy of yours," Jessica huffs. "You're bluffing."

Cobra looks at her for a moment, then taps a few buttons on his flash-pad. "Come," he says, and leads her back to the front drive, where the electro-van again waits.

Jessica stops dead and crosses her arms. "Where are you taking me now?" she demands.

"There you go again; so impatient." He waits while Victor opens the back door, then sweeps his arm toward it, indicating she should get in. He climbs in after her, and moments later they are driving the length of the expansive compound.

Eventually the van stops in front of a fenced-in, heavily guarded warehouse. "All right, here we are," Cobra says. He sounds excited. At a wave from Cobra, one of the guards enters a code on his flash-pad, and the wide gate in the fence surrounding the warehouse opens. The van drives slowly inside and stops. Cobra, then Jessica climb out.

Cobra looks up at the sky and throws his head back, arms outstretched. "Oh mighty Sortar, may your undying powers soon damn the sinners to hell," he calls out. Jessica gapes at him, petrified. It's as if he's suddenly in a trance. *What could be in that building?*

Lowering his arms and head, he taps his flash-pad a few times, and, presto, the warehouse door opens. Jessica gasps as she sees bag after bag of heart-shaped green pills.

"What—what are *you* doing with those?" she asks, wide-eyed.

"They are special," Cobra says as he picks up a bag and stares at it with reverence. "A miracle. Amazing, how the same mineral that can be utilized to substantially prolong life can also be used to destroy it within minutes."

"Is your plan to get all Americans to overdose on drugs?" Jessica scoffs.

"Ha-ha. Now, that would be interesting," Cobra muses. "But I prefer a much more direct and potent method of annihilation. If you only knew the laughs Woi and I have shared over the fact your inept law enforcement people believed Woi was interested in these pills as drugs. America, outsmarted by the HKM again!" Cobra crows.

"Thirty years ago, when the HKM first purchased these drugs from that fat-faced Edgar Fryman, HKM scientists knew their real value wasn't as narcotics, but rather as an extremely powerful bomb-making agent. And with Kolton Rollins's expertise, we found a way to ensure America's end." With a smirk etched upon his face, Cobra describes how Kolton Rollins came to join him in his quest to destroy America.

* * *

"This Rollins guy is the real deal," said Jolio, who had been sent to America to search for a highly qualified bomb specialist. "He wants to see America turned to ash even more than we do. Trust me,

Cobra, this guy is the man for the job. The funds are in place for him to go forward and lead the Spirit of Hades, and just say the word and I'll get him a load of green hearts so he can start his testing."

"I'm placing my trust in you, Jolio. But the testing, it'll need to be done only here on Pinian soil," Cobra said. "Now, did you also make it clear to him that he must romance Luanda and eventually convince her to reestablish contact with Shadow?"

"It's a done deal. But I have to ask you about Shadow."

"Somewhere along the way, my son forgot what it meant to be a true Pinian warrior, to honor the greatness of Pinia and the spirit of the Sortar Dragon. In order to accomplish my goal, my son must be banished from the Iron Lotus, but for public perception purposes, it must happen of his own accord."

"But if he's in America when we execute our plan there's a good chance he'll be..."

"I will pray for him, Jolio."

* * *

Overwhelmed by what she's just learned, Jessica shunts everything to the back of her mind to process later, and focuses on the bomb. "And do you think my father and his people are just going to stand by and let you attack our country?" Then it dawns on her. "Wait a second, the biofuel shipments—you're going to—"

"Very good, Jessica." Cobra laughs, the sound more a hiss.

He leads her outside to another, much larger warehouse. When Jessica enters she sees rows and rows of large storage tanks. "Welcome to the world of fera-bean biofuel," Cobra says. "In fact, we have several more of these buildings, filled with the stuff. And when mixed with the green hearts and a little bit of this and that... well, let's just say this biofuel gains a whole new function. One that will turn 'the land of the free' into 'the home of the dead.'" He cackles and pats one of the tanks.

"Oh my God!" Jessica gasps. *This is not just a sick fantasy, this is for real.* "You're a madman!" she cries, and lunges at Cobra, only to be grabbed by his guards.

"Easy, gentlemen," he says to the guards as they hold Jessica back. They release her and she falls into a chair and cradles her head in her hands. "Miss Westgale has every right to be filled with anger," Cobra says. "If my father was the idiot that William Westgale is, I'd be outraged as well."

Jessica lifts her head and glares at Cobra. "What's your end game?" she yells. "Do you think the rest of the world is going to let you and Woi get away with this?"

"Do you think the rest of the world any longer gives a damn about your nuisance of a country? They'll be grateful to us," Cobra says with conviction as he motions for the guards to take Jessica back to the van.

Jessica whirls and yells at Cobra, "And what about me? Are you planning to keep me locked up in that bloody room until I die?"

"What a waste that'd be," Cobra says as the guards unceremoniously bundle her into the van. He climbs into the van beside her. "In the coming days, once those cargo planes explode over America and our magic potion does its thing, you'll be free to go wherever you wish. But it is my hope you'll remain by my side. I could really use a formidable goodwill ambassador."

Jessica doesn't respond. Trembling, she stares out the window of the van.

Back in her room, she lifts her father's autobiography and holds it tightly in her hands. Terrified and feeling helpless, she struggles not to panic. Instead, she reaches down into the inner depths of her soul in search of hope, repeatedly telling herself, *American forces are planning to crush Cobra as I sit here in this prison. My father and his people will stop this lunatic, no matter what it takes. Before dawn, Shadow will be bursting right through that damn steel door.*

She remembers her mother's words of advice in times of peril: fear exists if we let it, but so can courage.

CHAPTER 33

"Do you have any idea what Ulu was talking about when she yelled, 'I knew it'?" Janet asks Trevor as they wait in the hospital to be updated on the child's condition.

Trevor sighs and shrugs. "I have no idea. At the time, the children were all admiring the kite."

"She's such a little sweetheart. I really hope she's going to be okay," Janet murmurs.

"Ah, here we go," Trevor says as the attending doctor approaches. "How is she, Doctor?" Trevor asks anxiously, rising. Noticing the somber expression on the doctor's face, Trevor fears the worst.

"She's resting comfortably, but there is cause for concern," the doctor responds.

"Do you know what caused her to pass out?" Janet asks.

"Yes. The child is suffering from a very severe and complex case of pneumonia," the doctor replies. "I've reviewed her medical history and noted that she has a history of respiratory problems, along with prior concerns over malnutrition."

"Have you been able to reach her sponsor?" asks Trevor.

"My nurse has left several messages, but they're not responding," the doctor answers.

"Is her life in jeopardy, Doctor?" Janet asks.

"I'd be lying to you if I said it wasn't," he answers with a sigh. "Due to the complexity of Ulu's condition, I've contacted World Medical, and they're arranging to send us a specialist."

"Are we going to be okay to wait for the specialist?" Janet asks, her brow puckered in concern.

"We'll be able to adequately treat her for the time being."

"Can we see her?" Trevor asks.

"By all means. One at a time though, please."

"Go ahead, Trevor," Janet says. "I'll see her when you're done."

Trevor enters the room, trying his best to hold back his tears. "Hey, Ulu, it's me, Trevor... Let me help you with that," he says as he notices her tiny arms reaching for a cup of water by her bed.

"Thank you, Mr. Trevor," she says with a whimper as he hands her the cup. She slowly sips the water from a straw.

"The doctors and nurses are going to get you feeling all better, okay, Ulu?"

"Where's... where's Miss... Jessica?" she asks, struggling for each breath.

"Miss Jessica?" Trevor hesitates.

"Yes... I saw her."

"You saw her? Were you dreaming, Ulu?"

"No, I saw her."

"You saw her? When? Where?"

"When we were... watching the kite. I saw her... with my Sky-Scope."

"*Where* did you see her?"

"In a truck... a red and black... truck. Will you bring..." Ulu's frail voice fades away, and she falls into sleep.

Trevor exits the room, shocked. "Janet," he calls in a loud whisper.

She scurries over from the waiting area. "Can I see her now?" His expression makes her pause. "What's wrong, Trevor? You look like you've just seen a ghost."

"Come with me," he says, and leads her to an area where they can speak in private. Trevor then relays what Ulu said.

"Whoa, that's incredible." Janet looks as stunned as he feels. "Do you think it's for real? Or do you think she's been hallucinating?"

"I don't know, but she sounded certain, and she did describe the truck as being red and black."

"Oh my God... the Iron Lotus. Do you think maybe *they've* had her all this time?"

"If what the child's saying is true, then it sure as hell looks that way," Trevor says, his tone urgent. "I'm going to contact Shadow."

* * *

"My office received incredible news just a few hours ago," an even jollier than usual Harrison Deacon informs Westgale and his associates. "Pix's people have been able to expedite the process and I'm thrilled to inform you that very soon, those robo-cargo-planes will be reaching every state in the country. And remember, they'll be arriving simultaneously," he concludes with a glowing smile.

"Damn good work, Harrison," Westgale says as the room erupts in applause.

"Phew... thank God. It looks like we're going to meet that deadline after all," Director Perry says.

As he and Sutton are about to exit with the rest of the group, Westgale waves them back. When they approach him, he's staring at his flash-pad. He looks up, his expression a mixture of fear and relief.

Before he has a chance to address them, Gil comes storming into the room, pausing only to close the double doors behind him. "How can we be certain the child isn't making it up?" he immediately asks Westgale.

"She could be, Gil, but we're going to take the position she isn't," Westgale answers as he taps the flash-pad, alerting National Investigation Director Martin Stevens.

"What's going on?" Perry and Sutton ask simultaneously. Westgale tells them of Ulu's revelation.

"My Lord. What if Pix has been behind Jessica's abduction all along?" says a stunned Dave Perry.

"That just wouldn't make sense," Gil interjects. "Why would he do such a thing when he's on the verge of helping to save our country from extinction?"

"Revenge," Perry answers, gazing at Westgale.

"Oh, come on, David; if Pix wanted to kill Jessie, he would have had it done months ago, when she was living in Pinia," Westgale replies, waving a hand in dismissal. "As I told you before, this has to be the work of a few of his men gone rogue."

"If that's the case, Mr. President, then why did they abduct your daughter? If this is about some kind of ransom, then why haven't any demands been made?" Perry fires back.

It's the father, not the president, who answers. "I don't know, David. I just pray to God Jessica comes home alive."

"And the energy deal?" Perry says.

"What about it?" Westgale shoots back.

"Are you telling me we're still going to let Pix send robotic cargo planes into American skies, knowing what we know?" Perry responds, his voice rising.

"There's nothing proving Cobra's been behind any of this, David. Can't you get that through your thick skull?" Westgale shouts back.

"I can't believe this," Perry mutters, shaking his head in frustration. "As your executive director, one of my duties is to ensure the safety of American citizens, and that's not what we'd be doing by letting those planes enter the country."

"So you're telling me, based on pure speculation, you're willing to bring a halt to a deal that will save this country from becoming nothing more than a memory? Our inspection teams have spent weeks in Pinia performing due diligence on those biofuel tanks, and everything has checked out perfectly," Westgale says emphatically.

"Well, I demand we send our inspectors back to Pinia and thoroughly inspect every inch of those tanks prior to letting them within a thousand miles of our airspace."

"There's no time for that, my friend. And there is absolutely no way I will even give a second of thought to terminating that deal!"

"I'm sorry, sir, but I won't idly sit back and risk the lives of our people. I'll be taking this matter to Chairman Malone," Perry answers. Turning abruptly, he stalks from the room.

* * *

Chairman Malone frowns. He and Perry are meeting in Malone's office, and they've invited me. "Normally, a decision such as this would be the president's domain, but with his daughter being involved..."

"So I guess it's up to the Strategic Council," I suggest.

Malone looks at me. "Typically that would be the case, but with you officially being the president-elect, your power supersedes everyone else's. It's in your hands, Nicole."

"Whoa, talk about baptism by fire," I respond as Malone instructs his secretary to schedule a meeting.

* * *

After Gil relays to Shadow that Jessica may have been seen in Pinia, Shadow insists on returning there in hopes of bringing her home. They meet at the US Central Military Base.

"I don't know, Shadow," Gil says, rubbing his chin. "Do you not think your returning to Pinia will raise suspicion and place Jessica in further danger?"

"Well, I think it'd be far less dangerous than launching an attack on the Lotus," Shadow replies indignantly.

"You do realize there's a chance your father is behind all of this."

"Yes, sir. And that won't stop me from doing whatever it takes to bring Jessica home."

Gil lifts an eyebrow. "Even if it means bringing him down?"

Shadow takes a deep breath and slowly exhales. "Whatever it takes, Agent Robichaud."

"Well, if I'm going to let you do this, you won't be doing it alone. I'll be coming along with a team of our top agents."

"With all respect, sir, that's the very thing that *will* create suspicion."

"There's no need for concern, Shadow. These men are the best in the business."

Shadow thinks for a moment. "Well, let's get to it."

* * *

"Is there no other alternative to meeting that deadline?" Hunter asks me.

"I've been going over it repeatedly with our finance and economics committees, and there's absolutely no other solution," I reply in frustration.

"What about the VX drug? I mean, there has to be enormous value in that."

"That's true, but it's way too late in the game to revisit that option."

"And you mean to tell me the Commission will not budge whatsoever on that deadline?"

"We've contacted Macdonald, and he made it very clear they won't. We're going to keep trying, though. But in fairness to the Commission, the final section of the New Order Treaty stresses that that deadline is firm."

"So, either we take the chance and let Cobra Pix send those planes into our skies, or America goes up for sale like auctioned-off cattle," Hunter says bitterly.

"Yeah, and lucky for me, I'm the person who'll be making that decision," I say sardonically.

CHAPTER 34

When Shadow arrives at the airport in Pinia he rents an electro and heads off for the Iron Lotus compound. On his way, a feeling of emptiness consumes him. He feels like a stranger in his own homeland. Familiar signs, buildings, and the lush Pinian landscape now seem like markings on a path to hell, leading to the devil himself, his father.

Deeply touched when Cobra had welcomed Jessica so graciously, and by the fact that he had appeared to put aside his hatred for America, Shadow had believed Pinia was on a course to greatness, and that Cobra had made the tyrannical approach of his grandfather a distant memory. Now he fears he was wrong. Dead wrong.

When Shadow pulls up to the front gate of the compound, he's greeted by one of the guards. "Shadow… this is quite a surprise," he says, eyes shifting nervously. "Is your father expecting you?"

"I thought I'd surprise him," Shadow answers with a forced smile.

"Just give me a second, please," the guard says as he reaches for his flash-pad and walks a short distance away. A minute later he returns. "Okay, he'll see you in the courtyard," the guard says. Following protocol, Shadow parks his electro and is taken by an Iron Lotus van to the courtyard.

"There he is," Cobra crows, approaching his son with open arms. "Now, this is a pleasant surprise."

"Hello, Father, how are you?" Shadow asks, sticking his hand out to avoid the embrace. Cobra looks at it, then shakes it.

"Well, I'm doing a lot better, now that you're here. What brings you back, son?"

"The American aid workers are wrapping things up this week, and I thought I'd make a surprise visit."

Cobra frowns in concern. "I'm so sorry about Jessica, Shadow. Who on earth would do such a thing to such a wonderful person? I hope you received the messages I sent."

"Yes, I did. Thank you." Shadow looks into Cobra's eyes. Having to act amicable in the face of his father's duplicity horrifies him. *Is Jessica being held captive somewhere on this compound? Did the man sitting before me have her killed—or kill her himself?*

"She was a fine young lady, a shining light in a dark world. I'm sure your mother must be devastated, learning that it appears her husband killed her," Cobra says.

Shadow grits his teeth; rather than play dumb regarding Kolton Rollins and his links to the Iron Lotus, he decides to disregard the comment.

His father is signaling a man over. "Victor, please get us a couple of glasses of hot apple cider."

Shadow studies the tall, clean-shaven, dark-skinned man with spiky black hair. *Hmm, I've never seen* him *before. He must be new.*

"So, Father, with the American energy deal in full swing, I'm sure it must be extremely busy around here," Shadow says, surreptitiously scanning his surroundings, looking for anything out of the ordinary.

"Actually, all the work's pretty well been done. Now it's just a matter of fine tuning."

"It's hard to believe—America and Pinia, working together."

"Like I've always told you, Shadow, one must never let personal feelings get in the way of a solid business deal."

"It's funny you say that, because most people believe you're getting the short end of that deal," Shadow says.

"For the time being, from a financial perspective, yes, we are. But let me tell you, son, in the long run this deal will end up being very beneficial in more ways than you can imagine. Now, will you be staying for dinner?"

"Thanks for the offer, but I must be off to the village."

"Oh; why the rush?" Cobra asks with a raised brow.

"I apologize, Father, but I'm really starting to feel the jet lag. I really should be on my way."

"Yeah, you do look a little worse for wear," Cobra says. "How about you leave your electro here and I'll have Victor bring you into the village?" he suggests. "That way you can get some rest on the way there."

"No, no, I'm fine."

"Well, I hope you realize you're always welcome here, son."

Having deceived Cobra, Shadow makes his way to a nearby hotel, where Gil is staked out. "Are you certain I'm not being followed?" he asks Gil, calling from the electro.

"We've got eyes in every direction, and the coast is clear," Gil responds.

Minutes later, Shadow arrives at the hotel and makes his way up to the fifteenth floor.

"Were you able to find out how Ulu's doing?" Shadow asks Gil upon his arrival.

"Trevor Larsen informed me that there's been no change in her condition, but thankfully the specialist from World Medical will soon be arriving," Gil replies.

"That's good to hear. Let's hope they can give that sweet child the help she requires," Shadow says as he removes his coat and rubs his tired eyes.

"How did it go with your father?" Gil asks.

"If he's up to no good, he's sure doing a heck of a job hiding it, which in fact doesn't surprise me," Shadow replies. "He's a master of deception."

"Well, let's see what the camera picked up."

"Here you go," Shadow says, handing Gil his time-pin, in which is concealed a high-tech camera.

Gil scans it across his flash-screen. "Does anything look out of the ordinary to you?" he asks Shadow, who's staring closely at the screen.

"Nah... I can't say anything does," Shadow responds, still focused on the screen.

"Okay, let's move to the next set of images," Gil says, and the screen shifts its display. "What we're looking at here is a series of ground photos from the courtyard. Now, since most of this area is composed of sand, we should be able to—"

"Wait a second," Shadow calls out as he studies the photos. "That footprint right there... please, zoom in a little closer." Gil complies. "Oh my, I recognize that tread... the W pattern... that has to be Jessica's footprint!"

"Hold on, let me enhance it even more... Do you know what size shoe she wears?"

"She wears a size eight and a half. I was with her when she bought those shoes. She bought them in Jersey, a few days after we arrived in New York. Trust me, you won't find those here in Pinia."

"All right, here we go," Gil says as he advances the program on his flash-screen in order to check the shoe size imprinted on the sole. "Okay... I'll be darned. It's a match."

"That bastard!" Shadow shouts.

Gil immediately reaches for his flash-pad and sends off a flash-message to agents who are positioned in other buildings surrounding the compound.

"Are you going to send your men in?" Shadow asks, alarmed.

"I don't think that'd be wise, but I have placed them on high alert. I've also set it up so that they all have a direct link to Washington."

"So, what? Are we just going to do nothing while Jessie's being held prisoner?" Shadow says in disbelief.

"I understand your concern, Shadow, but acting irrationally surely won't be in Jessica's best interest."

Shadow can only gape for a moment. "Irrationally? Her life's in danger!"

Gil holds up placating hands. "I hate being so blunt, but the reality is, we don't even know if she's still alive."

"Okay then, Agent Robichaud, tell me your plan," Shadow responds, throwing his hands in the air.

"We need to be patient and remain vigilant. We've got eyes on the entire compound," Gil assures him.

"Yeah, but we can't see inside. Who knows what they're doing to Jessie!"

"I'm sorry, Shadow, but we're only going to make a move if and when the time is right."

"The damn energy deal. That's what you're worried about, isn't it? I'll bet anything you came here with a mandate ensuring nothing gets in the way of that damn deal."

"That's not true. My orders come directly from the president," Robichaud retorts. "And you know how much that man loves his daughter."

"Oh, I know he loves his daughter, but I also know the pressure he's under to save his country," Shadow says.

* * *

Sitting in the Freedom Home's presidential conference room, listening to Westgale and Dave Perry present their respective cases regarding the Pinian energy deal, I'm torn whether or not to terminate the deal. By far, this is the most conflicted I've ever been.

"Recent events have proven to us that Cobra Pix cannot be trusted," Director Perry argues with conviction. "He could use those planes as weapons capable of doing who knows what? The safety of American citizens must be paramount, regardless of what it means to us as a nation."

Westgale counters with, "The proper inspections have been performed on that biofuel, and I'm confident that Cobra Pix knows better than to mess with America. Besides, we have no actual proof that he was actually involved with the Spirit of Hades or my daughter's abduction. If we back out of this deal, we will be writing the final chapter of America's history, and it'll be the saddest ending of all," he adds, his voice trembling.

And now the decision rests with me. I'm reminded of something my father always told me. He'd say, "Nicole, when I'm unsure of who to side with during a case, I look to the future and the ramifications my decision will have on society as a whole. If I still remain undecided, I dig down deep and follow my heart." *It looks like I'll be going where my heart takes me.*

* * *

Still impatiently watching the watchers, Shadow promptly complies when Gil calls him over to the window. "Look to your left," he says. They watch two black grand-electros disappear into an underground tunnel on the compound. "Would you know what this is about?" Gil asks.

Shadow shakes his head once, eyes remaining on the tunnel entrance. "Whatever it is, you can bet it's important to my father. That's the most top secret area on the entire compound. It leads directly to his war room." Shadow looks away, meeting Gil's gaze with eyes filled with trepidation.

* * *

Wearing a black turtleneck, black slacks, and a black cape with red slashes, Cobra Pix strides to the front of the Iron Lotus war room. Penciled in thicker than usual, his now glowing red eyebrows accentuate the evil in his eyes.

On one side of the room is HKM President Sie Woi, sitting in the middle of his eight leading military commanders. Seated across from them are four of Pix's military leaders, including his chief lieutenant, Theodore. From the lectern, as Cobra gazes at the group, his mind flashes back to the Battle of Oria.

* * *

"This invasion is about taking back what is ours. The greatest man to walk on Pinian soil, my beloved father, Ahmet Pix, is the person who discovered those precious metal ores. How dare the Orian government claim ownership!" Cobra shouted, prepping his militia for battle.

"In honor of the nation of Pinia, we must show no mercy to these selfish mercenaries! We must destroy our enemy!" Cobra's son Hadar added fervently.

"And in the name of diplomacy, I say we call for a truce," a frustrated Shadow called out.

"Through the spirit of the Sortar Dragon we will unleash a relentless attack on these foolish thieves!" added Hadar's brother Dorval, overriding Shadow's unpopular diplomatic suggestion.

As the Iron Lotus prepared to initiate its attack on the Orian government, US President William T. Westgale ordered his American forces to secretly intervene with a surprise attack on the Lotus, leading to massive chaos in the region. American forces began with a direct strike against the Lotus's command post.

"Cobra, can you hear me? This is Theo."

"What in the hell is happening out there?"

"We've been ambushed by American forces, sir."

"Where are you?"

"I'm... I'm in one of our trucks with Alton..." Theo's words were barely decipherable amidst the cacophony of battle. "We just left the command post. We were meeting with your sons and Jolio."

"Are they out of harm's way?"

"I'm sorry, sir... but they..."

"You're breaking up. You'll have to speak louder," Cobra shouted.

"All I know is, I saw Hadar with Jolio—they were engaged in battle with American forces," Theo answered.

"And my other sons?"

"Again, I'm sorry, Cobra, but we have no idea where they are. We'll let you know if we make contact with them."

A few hours later, when the dust had settled, Cobra Pix arrived on the scene to find his six sons lying side by side, dead.

* * *

Shaking off the flash of agony the memory brought with it, Cobra brings himself back to the present and invites President Woi to speak.

Woi stands, buttons his dark gray blazer, and approaches the lectern. His diminutive frame is barely visible behind the stand, but his fury is clear in his voice as he shouts, "We must now proceed with our mutual goal: the destruction of America!" Taking several deep breaths, he begins pacing, eyes on the group. "Vengeance is best delivered cloaked in surprise. And loss is most devastating when one loses what they treasure most. We will turn that gigantic poisonous land this world refers to as the United States of America into a crater of broken dreams buried in ash." He looks toward Cobra, whose eyes are closed, his head tilted back. "May the spirit of your sons be with us as we execute our mission. This destruction will be performed in their honor, as well as the honor of others around the world who have faced great injustice at the hands of this murderous beast!" He slams his fist into his palm. His voice sounds far larger than the man himself. His eyes smolder with rage. The others in the room smile with satisfaction, clinging to every word. "Our alliance is a special union. Together, with our wealth and military power, we will attain a level of domination this world has never seen before!"

* * *

"You need to get your men in there," Shadow urges Gil, who patiently continues to observe the compound. "Or at least let me take my father up on his offer. That way I'll be able to get in there and—"

"What the—oh my God!" Gil shouts at the sound of several consecutive blasts.

Shadow scurries over to join him at the window. They look on in shock as clouds of smoke billow across the sky. Through the haze, they see three robo-copters circling the compound. On the ground, a wave of soldiers with weapons in hand run wildly.

"Gil, can you read me?" an agent says over his flash-pad.

"Loud and clear," Gil responds. "He's in a building facing the east side of the compound," he tells Shadow in an aside.

"Are you seeing this?"

"Barely," Gil responds. "It's hazy from this vantage point."

"Well, I can see perfectly. The entire compound is under siege. I know this seems like a crazy question, but, is this us?"

"It can't be," a stunned Gil replies.

Another agent joins the conversation. "I was wondering the same thing, so I contacted Washington, and it's definitely not us doing this."

"Are you able to make out the uniforms these guys are wearing?" Gil asks.

"Traditional army green, sir," responds the first agent.

"Shadow, do you have any idea what—Shadow? Damn!" Gil shouts.

Shadow is nowhere to be seen. Seconds later, Gil realizes one of his laser-guns is missing.

* * *

Chairman Malone orders me to present my decision. When I enter the chamber in the Freedom Home, Westgale and Perry look at me with piercing eyes. It's ironic; these are the two men who asked me to run for president, and now I will be alienating one of them. After digging into the depths of my heart, I've made my decision.

"Gentlemen, thank you for the passionate arguments you have put before me," I say. Tension grips the room like a noose as I play the part of both executioner and messenger of hope. "Believe me when I tell you this is by far the most difficult decision I've ever had to make." I pause and take a deep breath.

Suddenly, Colonel Peters comes charging into the room. "We've got a major issue on our hands, folks," he says, and quickly fills us in on events in Pinia.

"Does anyone know who's launching the attack?" a dumbfounded Westgale asks. He looks toward Director Perry, who shakes his head.

"We have no idea, Mr. President—none whatsoever," Peters replies.

CHAPTER 35

With most of the mayhem taking place away from the palace area, Shadow's electro enters a secret back passageway that allows him to reach the palatial building undetected. If Jessica is being held hostage, this is where she'll be.

A quick survey of the scene instantly tells him that Cobra's so-called "most trusted men" have gone running for the hills. This comes as no surprise. Although he always kept it to himself, Shadow was very aware that Cobra's men always wished *he* were the Lotus leader, rather than his father. This was made evident by the departure of several of the compound's special guard unit when Shadow left for the US. And with the majority of Cobra's soldiers stationed in other regions of the country, the compound is vulnerable to attack.

Shadow exits the electro, gun drawn. He slowly walks toward the back entrance gate. The coast appears clear. Nonetheless, he knows he must be alert; who knows what may lurk ahead. *Please tell me the code hasn't been changed,* he thinks frantically as he enters a series of numbers into the panel, his heart racing. He lets out a sigh of relief when the gate slowly swings open.

Beyond the gate, he immediately sees one of the large doors is wide open. Eyes shifting from side to side, he enters the palace. All is quiet until he hears a rattling noise coming from around the corner in front of him. It's growing louder by the second. Heart pounding, he backs up against the wall and braces himself. He hears what sounds like heavy breathing, accompanied by a strange pitter-patter.

"Hey, boy, go on now," he whispers as Cobra's dog approaches. He rubs its head and directs it toward the open door. The dog obeys and trots out the door.

Shadow slowly makes his way through the main floor of the palace. He stumbles across a body, that of Cobra's assistant, Victor. The man appears to have been in some sort of struggle that cost him his life.

Two loud thuds from the floor above draw Shadow's attention. With the gun set on kill mode, he scurries up a broad staircase to the second floor. Two steps short of the top, he hears a voice call, "Let her go, Theodore. I'm ordering you, let her go, now!" Shadow knows that voice well. It's Cobra. He leaps the last two steps and ducks around the corner at the top.

"How many times have I told you? She's not to be harmed," Cobra says in a calm but firm voice. "She's what we all should aspire to be," he adds with extra force.

Shadow peers around the corner and sees Theodore holding Jessica with his left forearm tightly around her neck. His right hand is holding a laser-gun to her head.

"All those men lying dead in our war room, and you're worried for the well-being of this little bitch! What's wrong with you, Cobra?" Theodore growls. "Think of your six sons, killed by her butcher of a father," he adds. Veins protrude in his neck and forehead.

"Release her, now!" Cobra demands.

"I'll release her, all right—to the hounds of hell," Theo responds with an evil cackle as he tightens his hold on Jessica.

Jessica sends a forceful elbow to Theodore's ribs and he winces in pain, his grip loosening enough for her to break free and dash down the hall. It's not enough. Theodore takes aim and fires off a blast. Cobra quickly lunges in between the killer and his prey, taking the laser-blast right in the chest. He drops to the floor. Theodore attempts to fire off another blast at Jessica, but in a flash Shadow jumps out and fires a shot at Theodore's skull, instantly killing him.

Unharmed, but reeling in shock, a weeping Jessica crumples to the floor.

"It's okay, honey. I'm right here with you," Shadow says, dropping down beside her. "Everything's going to be fine... everything's going to be fine."

"He's dead, isn't he," Jessica says, looking toward Cobra.

Shadow rises and checks. "Yes, he is," he answers solemnly, rising to stand over his father. Cobra's eyebrows light up the dreary hallway. *Who is this man?* Shadow asks himself as he stares at his father's body. Tyrant, monster, megalomaniac, yet a man who just gave his life for a person he barely knew. A person whose father he blamed for the deaths of his six sons. A person who somehow touched his blackened heart in a most profound manner.

Jessica rises and joins him. "You were correct, Shadow," she says, gently rubbing his shoulders.

"Huh?"

"He was without a doubt the most complex person I'll ever meet," Jessica says softly.

"Yes indeed... complex. Except when it came to you. Just like me, I guess he saw something in you that he surely didn't see in others," Shadow says.

They turn away. As they make their way to the staircase, Shadow glances back at his father and wipes the tears from his eyes.

"How did you know I was here?" Jessica asks when they reach the bottom of the stairs.

"It's a long story, Jessie. I'll fill you in later," Shadow whispers, checking his surroundings, his gun at the ready. "First we need to get the hell out of here."

"Why are you still uptight?" Jessica quietly asks. "I'm sure American forces must have this entire compound under control by now."

"It wasn't American forces who converged on the compound, Jessie."

She gasps. "Oh my Lord. Who was it, then?"

"I don't know, and Gil didn't either," Shadow replies as they sidle out the door Shadow had entered earlier.

Just as they exit, a voice yells, "Drop the weapon and get on your knees!"

Shadow immediately complies. Jessica grabs his arm and drags him down with her.

"Hands on top of your heads!" Trembling with fear, they comply.

Several men dressed in green military uniforms emerge from cover and stand before them with their laser-rifles aimed at them. A white grand-electro drives up behind the soldiers. A man in a black designer suit with an American flag tie climbs from the electro. Jessica gasps.

"It's okay, gentlemen. Put your weapons down and please safely escort Miss Westgale and Mr. Pix from the premises," Gerald Levin says calmly. Then he reenters the vehicle and is off.

Two MAA soldiers move forward to escort Jessica and Shadow back to his electro, while the others disperse.

As Shadow drives the electro back to the hotel and Gil, Jessica tells Shadow what had happened to her. As he updates Gil via a flash-message, Jessica contacts her mother and father. "I'm so sorry, Jessie," Westgale says. "I'm to blame for all of this."

"That's not true," Jessica replies gently. "Cobra did what he did because he was a troubled soul. A highly troubled soul who was searching for something... something he never found."

Shadow hears most of the call. When she ends it, they start exploring the details surrounding the chaotic course of events. "I sincerely believe he never intended to harm me," Jessica tells Shadow about his father.

"To think he had you kidnapped in order to keep you *safe* while he was preparing to destroy America. The man was beyond complex," Shadow says, shaking his head in disbelief.

"I still don't understand how you and my father determined where I was."

Shadow then tells her about Kolton Rollins and Ulu.

"Your father actually gave me the dirt on Kolton, but Ulu... oh my. That sweet little child. Is she going to be okay?" Jessica asks, her voice tight and her eyes glittering.

"It's very serious. They brought in a specialist from World Medical to tend to her, so all we can do right now is hope and pray."

"And what about Levin and the MAA? I wonder how they became aware of the situation," Jessica ponders aloud.

"That's an interesting question," Shadow answers.

"With probably an even more interesting answer."

When they meet with Gil, he immediately wraps Jessica in his arms. "Thank God," he says. "And you," he looks at Shadow, "running off and playing the superhero. Normally, I'd have you arrested, but I think under the circumstances, I'll let it go," he adds with a chuckle.

"I'm sorry, Gil," Shadow replies with a sheepish grin. "I realize it was the wrong thing to do. But thankfully, we got her back," he adds, beaming as he pulls Jessica into a bear hug.

"Hold on. What do we have here?" Gil says, turning up the volume on the flash-screen as the UCIT Network logo appears.

Surrounded by several armed guards at Pinia's central airport, Gerald Levin appears front and center.

"Good day, my fellow Americans. It's with great elation that I'm here to inform you that earlier today, the Militant Alliance of America successfully executed a raid on the Iron Lotus's headquarters here in Pinia, snuffing out a very serious planned attack by Cobra Pix and HKM President Sie Woi on America." He then details how Pix and Woi intended to carry out their plan. *"Arrangements are currently being made by the World Coalition to safely destroy those tanks. I've also been informed that World Coalition forces will be taking control of Pinia within the next six hours.*

"During the raid, Jessica Westgale was rescued by Shadow Pix, and from all accounts they are now both safe and sound," he continues. *"However, one of our MAA agents, Victor Mali, wasn't as fortunate. Victor had been risking his life, infiltrating the Iron Lotus over the last few weeks, and it was his dedication and bravery that led us to this victory... and sadly, to his death. My sincere condolences to his family. He will never be forgotten."*

A picture of the fallen agent appears on the screen for a few seconds prior to UCIT shutting off.

"Oh my... Victor," Gil gasps, looking at the screen in dismay.

"You knew him?" Jessica asks.

"Yes. He was one of my agents until cutbacks last year forced me to release him. A dedicated agent and a family man with a wife and three kids." Gil sighs and shakes his head.

* * *

In the Freedom Home conference room, mixed feelings abound after Gerald Levin addresses the country. Westgale in particular is caught up in an emotional tug-of-war. "Don't get me wrong, Nicole; learning Jessica's alive and well is the greatest news I could ever receive, but to think Pix pulled the wool over my eyes like he did… how could I have been so stupid?" he says, pacing the floor.

"You weren't stupid, sir," I say with conviction. "How could you have known what he and Woi were up to?"

"I just hope to God Macdonald answers our plea and grants that extension," Westgale says, straightening his tie.

"He's here," Dave Perry announces to the group. Seconds later, Guardian Macdonald enters, wearing a blue and yellow striped suit. Westgale is immediately offended—*What is he, a clown that the Outer Commission has sent as some kind of joke?* As if the suit weren't bad enough, he enters the room carrying a bag of carrot and celery sticks.

"Good day, everyone," he says with a wave as he takes a seat at the front of the room. "Wow, it's getting crazy around here again," he observes, and chuckles. "I'm pleased to hear your daughter is safe," he says to Westgale. He then removes a carrot from the bag and begins gnawing on it like a high-strung rabbit as he tends to his flash-pad.

"Let's cut to the chase," Perry says, approaching Macdonald. "We asked you here to request an extension on the deadline—no, in fact we're *demanding* an extension."

"Demanding? The last time I checked, Director Perry, I don't think you and your friends were in any position to demand a single damn thing," Macdonald replies, then devours what's left of the carrot with a loud chomp. "Deadlines. You see, they come with a thing called responsibility, and responsibility comes with a thing called accountability, which none of you apparently know anything about."

"How dare you come in here and speak to us in such a condescending manner! I'm tired of this bloody power trip you're on!" Westgale shouts, rising from his seat.

"As your superior, I'll address this room in whatever manner I see fit," Macdonald replies with a snicker. "For more than two and a half decades, America has had a chance to show the world it can finally come together as one, and God knows this Commission has surely done its part to help," he says, looking sharply in my direction. "But as long as you continue to remain so miserably divided, you will never be what you claim to be." His tone turns upbeat as he rises. "Cheer up, folks; we'll make certain the country ends up in good hands." He calmly exits the room.

"Seventy-two hours… in seventy-two hours we'll be nameless, faceless, a self-destructive, failed nation. Once so powerful, soon so powerless," Westgale says somberly. "To future generations the memories of the great things we have accomplished will be destroyed by the reality of greed, corruption, and apathy… I'm so sorry to have failed you." He sits staring into space in disbelief.

Slowly those present rise and file out of the conference room, leaving Westgale, Dave Perry, and me.

"What about the incredible people of this great county?" Perry says with concern. "We owe it to them to be truthful, so they can begin preparing for the worst. Why prolong the inevitable?"

"How in the hell are we going to tell them that in three days they're no longer going to be Americans, and that they will soon be living under the laws and ways of who knows what and who?" Westgale says, his voice utterly hopeless. "The outrage will be so widespread, within hours there'll probably be nothing left of the country."

"Nicole?" Perry addresses me with a raised brow.

"I agree with the president, David. Let's at least know what we're dealing with before we attempt to deal with it."

"Well, I guess this proves that that obnoxious imbecile was spot-on when he said we know nothing about responsibility… and accountability," Perry scoffs as he rises and exits the room.

CHAPTER 36

As if this day hasn't had enough challenges, Beth informs me that Andy Pemberton has requested a meeting with him at his ERT Power office here in Washington. *Oh well, how much worse can things get?* I think as I summon my driver.

"Actually, Mr. Pemberton called, saying he'll be here shortly," his secretary informs me when she escorts me into his office waiting area.

Taking a moment to reflect, I look out the window of this enormous high-rise, down at the hustle and bustle below. Westgale's words of despair pound in my mind like the wrecking ball I see across the street: *"Once so powerful. Soon so powerless."* I think of recent events, and in particular, of Anya Ahar, a young woman who gave up everything to rejuvenate this country and help me win the presidency. A presidency it appears is only hypothetical now. I just hope that whenever Anya looks at the Liberty Bell pendant I gave her, she'll realize that her sacrifices were not made in vain.

"Hello, Nicole," Andy says. His greeting serves as an instant stop button in my mind. "Come on in," he adds, leading me into his luxurious office. He seems different. More serious than usual.

"So tell me, Andy, did you invite me here to gloat over your recent MAA triumph?" I say, plopping down into the leather chair before his desk. He looks at me, his face expressionless. *His mischievous grin must be trapped somewhere behind that empty stare.* "Aren't you going to brag about finally making a better castle?" Again, he blankly looks into my eyes. "Talk to me, Andy. What's going on?"

"I've had enough of this place, Nicole," he says, throwing his hands up in the air. "I just found out that behind my back, for the last few months, my uncle's had his staff working on an ERT business plan titled 'A Broken America.' It's taken me long enough, but I've come to learn that money and power are all that matter to that man, and he couldn't care less about the well-being of this country. Now, I know you probably think that's me as well, but let me assure you, it's not."

"So, are you planning to leave all this behind?" I quip, looking around at the office.

"Yeah, it's time. I've come to realize that I've been chasing something that's not real. This lust for power people like my uncle and Gerald Levin share is just an illusion. An illusion that slowly tears away at our heart and soul, leaving us empty," he explains solemnly. "I need to live my life and stop searching for something that doesn't exist."

I'm left speechless, instantly realizing Andy's speaking from the heart.

"But before I do, I need to complete one final project."

"Does this somehow involve me?" I ask with trepidation.

"It most certainly does. That matter we spoke about a few weeks back—well, it wasn't easy, but with the help of some associates in Australia I found the solution we're looking for," he replies. His expression quickly changes from sullen to cheerful as he turns on his flash-screen and explains.

* * *

At the headquarters of the former Pinian government, Shadow is meeting with delegates from the World Coalition. Gathered outside, thousands of everyday citizens fervently chant his name. "Judging by the overall reaction of the Pinian people, it's very clear you're the man they want in command," one of the delegates says to Shadow.

"And I'd be elated to take on such a prestigious position, provided it is acquired under a democratic process," Shadow says as he leans out a window and salutes the crowd. The crowd roars back with applause.

Leaving the building through a back exit, Shadow and Jessica make their way to the hospital to visit Ulu.

"I really can't wait to see her," Jessica exclaims.

"I tried to get an update from the hospital, but their communication system has been down all day," Shadow says, frustrated. "I realize it's best to remain optimistic, Jessie, but the child is—"

"I know, Shadow. That's why I haven't let go of this from the second you gave it back to me," she says as she opens her hand to display her dragon-stone necklace.

"Yeah, little good it did you back in New York," Shadow sighs.

"Well, in the end I'm still in one piece and here with you, right?" Jessica smiles.

When they arrive at the hospital, the attending doctor greets them with a pleasant smile. "Come into my office," he says, leading the way. "Please, have a seat."

"How is she, Doctor?" Jessica asks, tightly squeezing Shadow's hand.

"I must tell you it was touch and go for a while there, but thanks to the specialist from World Medical, I'm pleased to tell you the child is going to be fine."

"That is incredible news," Jessica says, her voice light with joy. "Can we see her?"

"Of course, by all means," the doctor replies.

As Jessica and Shadow are about to exit his office, he signals them back. "There is one thing, however," he says, looking concerned. "Although the hospital has contacted Ulu's sponsor on several occasions, we've yet to hear from them. And with the child being released from our care in a few days, this really complicates things."

"Well, we'll make things a lot easier for everybody," Shadow says, giving Jessica a smile. She smiles back. "We'll make the necessary arrangements so the hospital can release her into *our* care," he adds.

Jessica gasps, and her face lights up. "Are you sure, Shadow?" she asks excitedly. "I mean, would it be fair to your mother, now that she'll be returning to Pinia to live with us?"

"I know for certain my mother will be thrilled. She's always wanted another chance to raise a child," Shadow says.

Her eyes shining with happiness, Jessica takes Shadow's hand and they go to Ulu's hospital room together.

"Miss Jessica! Mr. Shadow!" Ulu shouts with joy, sitting up in her hospital bed.

"Hello, Ulu," Jessica says, approaching the smiling child. Shadow blows a kiss to Ulu and quietly exits the room. "I missed you so much," Jessica adds as she squeezes her tightly.

"I missed you too, but I knew you were always with me," Ulu says, placing her hand over her heart.

"I'm so glad to hear you're feeling all better now," Jessica says as she gently brushes the child's hair away from her face.

"Yeah, Dr. Bridgette made me feel better," Ulu says happily, referring to the World Medical specialist. "She was really nice to me—look what she gave me," she adds as she hands Jessica a pendant.

"Do you know what this is, Ulu?" Jessica asks as she studies it.

"Dr. Bridgette said it's called the Liberty Bell."

"Yes, it is." Jessica smiles. "And one day I'll tell you all about it."

Peering through the window of the hospital room door, dressed in her World Medical uniform, Dr. Bridgette, formerly known as Anya Ahar, smiles with absolute delight.

* * *

Today's the day. The dreaded deadline. America's Judgment Day. We always knew this day could come, but as with all things we hope to avoid in life, we prayed it wouldn't. Besides, why should we worry? We're the mighty America: compassionate and tender as a loving mother, and as tough as nails when the need arises. I guess we can sometimes also be overly assuming.

"I call this meeting to order. Would everyone please take their seats," says a grinning Macdonald as the key members of both the PBA and MAA assemble in the Freedom Home's main conference room. "My oh my, the world just keeps getting stranger day by day," he adds, looking down at his flash-pad. "Pinia appears finally ready to live in a real democracy, the people of the HKM are opening their hearts to the Gold Star Federation, and, well... here *you* are." He pauses and slowly gazes around the room as he rolls up the sleeves of his maroon cardigan, which looks at least a size and a half too big. "Endings: they're inevitable, and yes, most of the time they are sad."

I sigh. *Look out, he's in lecture mode.*

"Every beautiful sunset eventually fades to nothingness, and every glittering star at some point succumbs to the darkness of night. It's a fact of life, folks. And now we've learned that even the United States of America is not immune to mortality.

"I realize how difficult it is for all of you to accept this, but you must embrace the idea of a new beginning. Please take solace in the fact that the Outer Commission will do its best to ensure that many of your former country's laws and customs will be considered by your new overseers.

"Now, before I end these proceedings and officially declare the termination of the United States of America, I will be glad to answer any questions from the floor."

I raise my hand.

"Ah yes, Ms. Kratz."

"Having spent quite some time here in America during the last few years, would you agree that Americans for the most part have a fighting spirit?"

"Well, though I don't see what this has to do with the matter at hand, I'm glad to answer your question," he replies with a smirk. "Fighting spirit? Hmm. I'd say your people have a very *overzealous* fighting spirit. I would say it's the very thing that has led to your country's demise—and actually, it's the very thing that has brought us here today."

"That may be true, Mr. Macdonald, but there's a reason we tend to be 'overzealous.' We may not always agree about what's best for America, but at least we sincerely care. This man to my right, Andy Pemberton—we've known each other since we were children, and truth be told, up until just the other day, due mostly to our political differences, we were disgusted at the very sight of each other."

"I don't know where you're going with this, Ms. Kratz, but I suggest you please get to the point," Macdonald warns.

"As I was about to say, there is one thing Andy and I have always shared, and that's a deep love and appreciation for our country."

"Bravo," Macdonald responds, clapping his hands like a trained seal. "Now, since there will no longer be an America, I guess you and Mr. Pemberton will have to search within yourselves and find something else in common."

"Interesting that you say that, because we have. What we've found is a *united* fighting spirit, which in getting to my point, has led us to a miracle. Do you believe in those, Mr. Macdonald?"

"I've had enough of this insanity," Macdonald mumbles. "I now declare the United Sates of—"

"Andy," I say above Macdonald's infuriating squeal. I turn on the flash-screen at the front of the room, and Andy approaches.

"Thank you, Nicole. Today, Mr. Macdonald, we are not Militants, we are not Peace-Bringers... proudly, we are Americans!" he says passionately as he walks toward the screen with his mischievous grin intact. "What you're about to see are several forest areas across the country. Thanks to a benevolent mysterious power lurking above, and our friends from the land down under, who allowed us to test a series of newly developed machines, within a period of three days we were able to uncover load after load of these glittery pebbles." The view-file shows a close-up of the strata. "These are the very same minerals that compose the VX drug."

With a mad rush of adrenaline, I rise and take hold of the sound-blast. "And here, Mr. Macdonald, is a detailed list of advance payments made by countries around the world," I announce with elation. "So now, with one press of a button, America's debt will be paid, and even more importantly, generations of our friends around the globe will reap the benefits of our miracle—heck, there'll even be enough funds left over to help get you a plane ticket back to wherever the hell it is you came from."

"What... what is this?" Macdonald cries, squirming in his chair.

"We call it the Preservation Plan," I say with pride as I gaze around at the smiling faces of my fellow Americans.

= END =

CPSIA information can be obtained
at www.ICGtesting.com
Printed in the USA
LVOW10s1042140217
524207LV00001B/1/P